ICEQUAKE

When it hits it will release a world-shattering storm of energy. It will tear the polar cap apart and set 13 million cubic kilometers of ice sheet into motion.

As it spreads outward, it will start to melt, with disastrous consequences. What—or who—will save the world then?

ICEQUAKE
A Bantam Book

PRINTING HISTORY
Originally published in Canada by
Douglas E. McIntyre Ltd.
tam export edition / November 1979
Bantam edition / February 1980

ISBN 0-553-13114-1

ICE

~~~~~~~~~~

CRAW

B

C
Cover
This book
mimeogr
For

Bantam Books
mark, consisti
trayal of a ba
Office and in
Books, Inc., C

PRINTE

To all the Kilians,
and to the memory of
James De Mille (1833-1880),
Canada's first explorer of
the fabled Antarctic

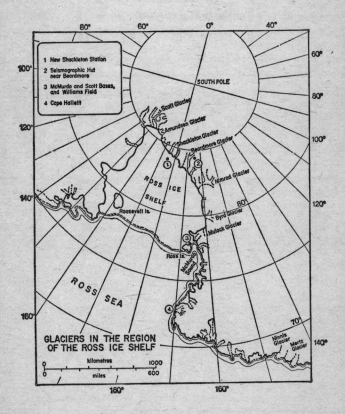

GLACIERS IN THE REGION
OF THE ROSS ICE SHELF

CONTENTS

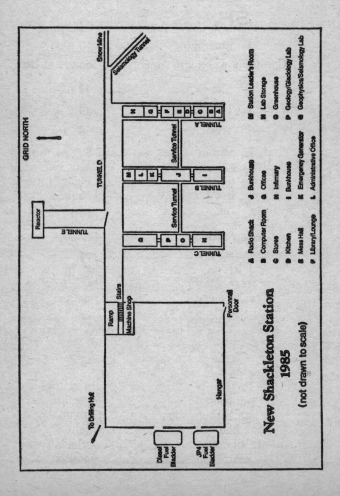

New Shackleton Station
1985
(not drawn to scale)

GRID NORTH

Snow Mine

Seismology Tunnel

TUNNEL D

TUNNEL A

Service Tunnel

Reactor

TUNNEL E

Service Tunnel

TUNNEL B

TUNNEL C

Service Tunnel

Ramp
Stairs
Machine Shop

Personnel Door

To Drilling Hut

Hangar

Diesel Fuel Bladder

JP4 Fuel Bladder

A Radio Shack
B Computer Room
C Stores
D Kitchen
E Mess Hall
F Library/Lounge

J Bunkhouse
G Offices
H Infirmary
I Bunkhouse
K Emergency Generator
L Administrative Office

M Station Leader's Room
N Lab Storage
O Greenhouse
P Geology/Glaciology Lab
Q Geophysical/Seismology Lab

1

SHACKTOWN

Penny Constable woke up suddenly and looked at her wristwatch. The glowing orange light-emitting diodes told her it was 0503 hours, Thursday, February 7, 1985. With any luck, it would be her last day in Shacktown.

The cubicle was dark. In the bunk below, Jeanne Taylor moved restlessly in her sleep. The hut's humidifier was whining away in the corridor outside, but the air was still too dry for comfort; Penny's nose was stuffy, and her tongue felt thick. She reached up to touch the cold, rough plywood ceiling. A few meters above the roof of the hut were the curved steel plates that covered Tunnel B, and above that was the empty whiteness of the Ross Ice Shelf. To the right and left of Tunnel B, separated by meters of solid ice, were the other tunnels of New Shackleton Station; to walk the full length of the station, from the end of the snow mine to the doors of the hangar, took only five minutes. After thirty-seven days here, she knew every square centimeter of the place, and she hated it all. Having a case of "Big Eye"—sleep-lessness—made her hate it even more.

Insomnia in the Antarctic was usually a problem only for people wintering over. The weather had been so bad, though, throughout this austral summer, that almost no one had been able to get outside. Over half of Shacktown's normal summer population hadn't even arrived this year: bad weather and impossible radio conditions had forced many scientists to postpone their projects, and many of those who had managed to reach the station were stymied by the lack of equipment or support personnel. Penny and Jeanne, a student glaciologist, had waited in Christchurch for over a week last December before a break in the radio blackout had enabled their Air New Zealand DC-10 to leave for McMurdo Station; thanks to the same break, Shacktown had sent its Twin Otter to McMurdo to pick up the two women and some supplies.

Since New Year's Day, however, the radio blackout had continued almost without a pause, and "katabatic" winds, raging down the glacier valleys from the polar plateau, had brought day after day of Condition One: blizzards, bitter cold, and whiteouts. Only Gerry Roche and Carter Benson, the geophysicists, had been happy to observe the massive solar flares and resulting magnetic storms that had caused the radio blackout and even knocked out polar-orbit communications satellites.

—Blackouts, whiteouts. And a handful of gray-faced troglodytes trapped under the ice.

She could still savor a sour enjoyment of the irony of her predicament. As a little girl in Connecticut she'd loved being snowbound, safe inside the artificial worlds of her home and a book, knowing that outside was a cold anarchy held at bay. So when the Ottawa office of the Commonwealth Antarctic Research Programme had asked *Science Progress* magazine for a staff writer to visit New Shackleton, she'd asked at once to be sent. Even the bad political climate between the U.S. and the rest of the Western world hadn't discouraged her. CARP was doing important work, after all, work that was almost unreported in the States; she'd be the first American journalist in years to cover the story.

Penny turned in her sleeping bag, trying to find a warm spot. A fat lot of good she'd accomplished. The only really big story had been the Roche Event in early January, when the earth's magnetic field had abruptly vanished and then begun to grow again, reversed in polarity. She still remembered Gerry Roche's expression when his magnetograph had begun to trace straight lines, like the last cardiogram of an old friend. But that story would be ancient history by the time she got home.

There was Steve Kennard's work, of course. The Canadian seismologist had confirmed the fact that East and West Antarctica stood on separate plates of the earth's crust, with the boundary between them running through the Transantarctic Mountains. But he also believed a major earthquake was due somewhere in those mountains (despite the fact that Antarctica was known to be seismically quiet)—and he even thought such a quake might cause a surge of the ice sheet into the Southern Ocean. Good material for the *National Inquirer,* maybe, but not for a serious science magazine. Steve hadn't been very helpful, anyway; he was afraid that someone like Penny would sensationalize his theories before he'd published them in some bastion of orthodoxy like *Nature.*

Even that story wasn't really new. In her already-packed kit bag, Penny had a draft article in which she pointed out that ice-sheet surges had been talked about since the early 1960s by a New Zealand geologist named Wilson and an American named Hollin. People in the U.S. Defense Department had even discussed the idea of starting such a surge with hydrogen bombs. If the theory had appealed to the people who'd given the world Vietnam, Chile, and the Bay of Pigs, it was pretty surely nonsense.

What else? The Shelf Drilling Project? That was just a rerun of what the Americans had done back in the '70s. Will Farquhar, the station's Scottish glaciologist, and Jeanne had learned a lot about the Shelf, and the almost lifeless sea beneath it, but nothing really surprising.

Ben Whitcumb's fossils? Great, if you really cared about therapsid populations in the Permian West Antarctic. She was being unfair, she knew; Ben, the sole American scientist here, was a prick, an all-too-typical modern U.S. careerist right down to his crew-cut hair and right-wing politics. His sermons on President Wood and the official American policy of Dynamic Self-Reliance had been as boring as his lectures on therapsid endothermy. Ben was the kind of scientist she'd come here to escape.

There was Herm Northrop, the Canadian engineer who kept the whole operation going with his CANDU reactor. Sure, it was controversial. The reactor was too powerful for the station's needs; the Canadians had supplied it—and Herm—more for propaganda than in the interests of research. But it was still an elegant, exquisitely automated feat of high technology, and Herm had been glad to explain it to her. She felt good about the article she'd written on him and the CANDU.

After that, though, Shacktown offered only human-interest stories: Terry and Suzy Dolan, the Australian cooks who squabbled all day and screwed all night; Katerina Varenkova, the Russian exchange physician who chainsmoked Rothmans, beat everyone at chess, and was homesick for Vostok, the Soviet base where her husband Ivan was this year's station leader; Al Neal, Shacktown's pilot and chief aircraft mechanic, an ex-U.S. Navy flyer who'd been down here on the ice for over ten years—the Antarctic equivalent of a bush pilot; Don Treadwell, Shacktown's only Black, a Jamaican whose chief purpose was to prove that the Commonwealth still included some nonwhite nations, but who was nonetheless an extremely competent stores clerk and a man who didn't need the crutch of machismo that most of the others hobbled around on. They were good people, interesting people, but *Science Progress* didn't want character sketches.

An objective report on the station itself would sound like anti-Commonwealth propaganda. They didn't call it "Shacktown" for nothing: the place was a mishmash of sophistication and sloppiness. Much of its scientific equipment was the most advanced in the world, but had been supplied as much for publicity purposes as for research. However, most of the station's transport had been scrounged from the Americans' cast-offs at McMurdo, or salvaged from Scott Base, which the Kiwis had closed after joining CARP in '82. Even the design of the station was obsolete; the Americans had tried undersurface installations in the 1960s, and gone on to more efficient designs for surface buildings.

Colin Smith, the station's meteorologist, had predicted clear weather for today. If he was right, Al Neal would fly to McMurdo to ask for a Hercules to evacuate them all. Otherwise they might be stuck here for weeks more—and that might mean months, the whole winter, marooned like old Shackleton's crew on Elephant Island. She'd be glad to leave, but sorry to go home: home was power failures, "security" investigations, fifty percent annual inflation; home was a growing fear as everyone began to realize that there wasn't enough of anything to go around any more, except for the military and the police and the bureaucrats and the corporations and the Ben Whitcumbs . . .

Now she was really awake. It was 0515; breakfast wouldn't be ready until 0600. She decided to get up and go to the dome to see if the weather had cleared up. But Jeanne beat her to it. Penny heard her groan a little, then get up and shuffle down the corridor to the women's latrine.

Unzipping her bag, Penny swung down to the floor and gasped like a sunbather plunging into cold water. She switched on the overhead light and shiveringly pulled wool pants and a heavy shirt over her waffle-weave underwear. (Something else to hate: you couldn't sleep naked.) Fur-lined Wellingtons went over thick socks; in most of the huts the temperature gradient was so steep you could wipe sweat off your face while your feet went numb with the cold.

Women and married couples (this year only the Dolans) were housed at the end of Hut 6; the women's latrine was a buffer between what the men called the Harem and Eunuchsville, the rest of the dormitory huts. The latrine stank, as always. Jeanne was crouched over one of the toilets, throwing up.

"Hey, what's the matter?"

"Nothing," Jeanne mumbled. "Go away. Go back to bed."

"Should I go get Katerina? She's just down the hall—"

"Just leave me bloody well alone, Pen."

"I will, as soon as I pee."

That was about par for the course these days, Penny thought as she sat delicately on a freezing-cold toilet seat. Hugh Adams, the station leader, did a good job in keeping people as busy as possible, but there were still too many empty hours; cliques formed and broke up, everyone snapped at everyone else, people went looking for arguments or retreated into sullenness or sleep.

Feeling sullen herself, she left Jeanne and walked up the corridor. A short, insulated passageway led to Hut 5, another dormitory; from there, service tunnels ran to Tunnels A and C. She turned left and walked to Tunnel C, where most of the labs and offices were housed.

No one was around. Much of the equipment in the glaciology and seismology labs was already crated, ready for shipment home. In the geophysics lab, a few instruments still hummed and clicked. Although the fluorescent lights were on as always, the place looked odd; Penny realized after a moment that genuine sunlight was reflecting down the spiral stairway from the dome. Her boots clanging on the steps, she hurried up toward the light.

The dome was a double-layered plexiglass hemisphere atop a tower three meters across and standing four meters above the surface. The work area was a muddle of electronic equipment, clipboards, coffee cups, technical manuals and cameras. Two wooden folding chairs filled most of the floor space; Penny sat down in one and looked around.

Low in the northeast, the sun blazed. The sky was a

deep, saturated blue, all the stronger for its contrast with the bright red-orange of Shacktown's few surface buildings. Those buildings were heavily drifted over on their lee sides, and the empty oil drums lining the skiway were scarcely visible. Nearby, two radio masts gleamed against the sky; farther away, beyond the smooth curve of the hangar roof, was the smaller tower of the drilling project. Ventilation pipes, crusted with ice, steamed just above the surface. According to some gauges on a workbench in front of her, the temperature outside was -25°C, air pressure was 1240 millibars, and there was no wind at all.

This was the first time since New Year's morning that Penny had seen her surroundings in full sunlight. She felt more cheated than ever. To the north, east, and west, the Shelf extended to the horizon: a vast plain of ice, hundreds of meters thick, as large as France. On the flight from McMurdo she'd seen something of the Shelf's immensity and its varied beauty; even here, from this low vantage point, it revealed much of itself. In one place, shadows clustered blue-black against a low ridge; in another the sun gleamed on a field of sastrugi, wind-carved ice sculptures that sometimes stood taller than a man. Ice crystals glittered, catching the sun for an instant as they condensed somehow from the desert-dry air.

To the south, the horizon crumpled into the pinkish-beige peaks of the Queen Maud Range, part of the Transantarctic Mountains. In the clear air they seemed much closer than forty kilometers; the sun was so bright on their glaciers and snowfields that it hurt to look at them. Due south of the station was Shackletown Glacier; a little to the west, but invisible from here, was Axel Heiberg, the steep glacier up which Amundsen had driven his dog teams to the pole. And off to the east, two hundred kilometers or more, was the great Beardmore, which Scott had struggled up and down on his doomed journey. Beyond the mountains, she knew, was the polar plateau, the greatest desolation in the world.

But she had seen no more than a glimpse of all this, through the scratched windscreen of the Twin Otter or the blurred plexiglass of the dome. What she would really remember would be blowing snow, gray and dense, racing past the dome in a screaming wind. This clear, sunlit stillness was lovely but transient; the real Antarctic was fluid, chaotic, and meaninglessly violent.

On her way to the mess hall, she made a detour to the greenhouse, down at the end of Tunnel C. The hut that housed it had originally been intended for storage, but the first station crew were plant lovers. They had smuggled in sacks of potting soil and packets of seeds, and had later added kitchen compost, discarded soil samples from geological surveys, and sawdust. After four years the greenhouse was dense and lush, the envy of other polar stations. Under fluorescent lamps, flowers, houseplants and vegetables grew in flats on tiered shelves, or in pots made from soup cans.

Unlike most of the huts, the greenhouse was so well insulated that there was little temperature difference between floor and ceiling, and it was the only place in Shacktown—except for the kitchen—that was reasonably humid. As the pleasantest part of the station, it normally had plenty of visitors at all hours, but this morning it was deserted.

Penny was glad to be away from the smells of urine, sweat, and tobacco that filled the rest of the station. She read a neatly printed sign that said: "Leave the fucking tomatoes fucking well alone!" and then rubbed a tomato leaf to luxuriate in its pungency and the memories it evoked of hot summers. She sighed, and continued on her way.

The mess hall was a long, narrow room that took up almost half of Hut 2. Its pale green walls were filmed with grease; the only decorations were two big photomurals of rural New Zealand, and a bad oil portrait of Sir Ernest Shackleton. The place was crowded with battered chairs and tables; the ceiling was low and stained by countless leaks. A steam table separated the room from the kitchen, where Terry and Suzy Dolan were noisily preparing breakfast. Today's housemouse was Sean McNally, but he wasn't around; probably he was down in the snow mine, feeding the melter. At the other end of the mess hall, a door led to the library-lounge, which was dominated by the big screen of a videotape projector and by a map of the Antarctic on which Shacktown's location was indicated by the words ANUS MUNDI, done in a fine italic hand.

Penny walked into the mess hall, got a cup of coffee, and sat down with Hugh Adams, Carter Benson, and Al Neal, who were the only ones there. After a few mumbled greetings, Penny asked Al when he was leaving for McMurdo.

"Not till noon." He scratched at the white beard that made him look a little like Santa Claus, and a lot older than forty-four. "The Otter's got fuel-pump trouble. Howie's working on it."

Hugh Adams looked at her. As always, the directness of his gaze made her feel both wary and exhilarated. He didn't attract her physically, but she could sense why men liked and respected him—and obeyed him. It was certainly more than his strong resemblance to Shackleton—the solid build, square jaw, and hard mouth—that made him the leader of twenty-seven very different men and women.

"I'm not letting this lazy sod sit about all morning," Hugh said; his voice still had more of Ulster in it than New Zealand. "He can take Steve and Tim, and Will and Jeanne, out to the remote stations. They can run some tests, collect the tapes, and be back for lunch. Would you like to go along with them?"

"Yes, of course. I'd be delighted." She knew that Hugh was very aware of her dislike for Shacktown; this little surprise was meant to sweeten her mood, and the tone of whatever she published about this place. But at least she'd see something, and set foot on the mainland.

"So this is it," she observed. "Supper at McMurdo, breakfast in Christchurch."

"Don't bet on it," Hugh said. "We could be stuck at McMurdo for weeks. But I hope you're right. We'll annoy the Yanks enough by asking for one of their precious Hercs. They'll really sulk if they have to put us up for awhile."

"Will the Americans really give you a hard time?" she asked.

Hugh looked at Al, who nodded. "It's a lot different these days," Al said. "When I was flying for the Navy in VXE-6, ten, twelve years ago, we were one big happy family down here. We'd run errands for the Russians, they'd do things for us. The Kiwis and Aussies and Brits were all over the place—McMurdo, Eights, Amundsen-Scott. But nowadays it's all super-political."

"Dynamic Self-Reliance may be a good policy in America, but it's not too suitable for Antarctica," Hugh murmured. "Ah well, Al and I are just a couple of old fogies, moaning about the days of our youth. Don't mind us—and here they are," he interrupted himself as Will Farquhar and Steve Kennard came in. Steve was only thirty-four, though his graying hair and beard made him look older. Long months in the Antarctic had weathered and roughened his strong features, yet his eyes still had the clarity and direct-ness of a boy's. He spoke with deliberation but no hesitancy, and moved in the same way; his tall, spare frame had a slow grace suggesting great reserves of power.

"Morning, everyone," said Steve. "When can we leave, Al?"

"Any time. The Huey's all gassed up."

"Good. If we've only got till noon, I want to leave at once. Terry? Can you put some breakfast in a box for us?"

"Right, Steve."

"Thanks." Steve sat down at the next table and said to Penny, "Coming with us?" She nodded. "Good;

wear your regular cold-weather outfit, and don't forget sunglasses and sunburn cream. The ultraviolet's getting worse."

Penny nodded again, but without conviction. She knew that the ozone layer had been seriously damaged by the continuing solar flares, but it was still hard to imagine being sunburned while wearing ten kilos of clothing.

"Where do you want to go?" Al asked. Steve glanced at the others.

"It's already almost 0630. We can't go across the mountains and be back by noon. So how about remotes 10, 11, and 12?" Those, Penny knew, were near Shackleton, Ramsey, and Beardmore glaciers.

"Good enough," Will agreed. "Tell you what, let's hit remote 10 on our way back. If we're running short of time we can skip it, but I don't want to miss Ramsey and Beardmore."

"Is that all right with everyone?" Steve asked. "Good. Let's get our stuff. I'll come back here to pick up our breakfast; the rest of you meet at the helo."

In their room again, Penny felt a bit breathless as she and Jeanne pulled on their anoraks and windpants and struggled with their mukluks. "Steve really moves fast, doesn't he?"

"He and Tim have been itching for this," Jeanne said. "So have Will and I. It wouldn't be so bad if the telemetry from the remotes were reliable. But when you know you've got almost two months' worth of data out there on tape, and you can't get at it—God!"

"Are you feeling all right now?"

Jeanne gave her a cold blue stare. "I wouldn't go if I weren't up to it."

Fully dressed, their faces smeared with sunburn cream, they went down the service corridor to Tunnel C—to avoid the men in Eunuchsville who were just getting up—and through the labs to the cold porch that led to Tunnel D.

This was Shacktown's main thoroughfare, from which everything else branched off. Tunnels A, B, and C, and the hangar, were north of it. South was Tunnel E, sealed off by heavy doors and over five hundred meters long; at its end was the reactor facility. Smaller tunnels led to the snow mine, seismograph arrays, and climatologist Sean McNally's "oubliette"— a narrow shaft almost seventy meters deep, down to the ice that had been fresh snow during the climatic optimum of the early middle ages.

Tunnel D was garishly lighted by fluorescent lamps. The floor was duckboards, glittering with frost but safer than bare ice. Along both sides of the wide tunnel, the walls were piled with supplies: crates of food, spare mechanical parts, surplus wiring and furniture and insulation. At its western end the tunnel led up a broad ramp to the hangar itself. Alongside the ramp, a flight of stairs gave access to a big hut just inside the hangar: this was the machine shop. Jeanne and Penny bypassed it and went up the ramp.

Temperatures in the tunnels usually stayed between -10° and -15°C. The hangar, now that its outer doors were open, was probably close to -25°. Its floor was ice, discolored by spilled gas and diesel fuel; the place stank. Crowded under its high, curved roof was a collection of Sno-Cats, snowmobiles, a big D8 bulldozer and a smaller D4, and an ancient green Nodwell tractor that looked like a truck with caterpillar treads. The Twin Otter and the Huey took up a good deal of space. The women said hello to Howie O'-Rourke, a big, taciturn Canadian mechanic who was working on the Otter; he paused long enough to nod shyly at them.

They reached the Huey as it was being winched outside. Will and Tim Underwood, a student seismologist, were walking along beside it, throwing gear inside: explosives, geophones, bamboo and aluminum marker poles, survival packs, and an insulated box containing the breakfast Terry had prepared for them. As the cold bit at her face, Penny felt a twinge of envy: if you wore a beard and moustache, as most of the men here did, they frosted up rather prettily. If you had a hairless upper lip, it soon acquired a lump of frozen mucus from your runny nose.

"Where's Steve?" Jeanne asked.

"He's already inside. Up you go," Will smiled, helping her into the door. Penny followed, and found the rest of the party in the passenger compartment. Steve and Al were discussing the flight plan; then they went forward to the flight compartment while the others buckled themselves in and pulled on light helmets, which were plugged into the helo's intercom. As she fumbled with her camera, Penny heard Al's voice in her headphones, a parody-drawl:

"Ah tole 'um, Ah said, 'Orville an' Wilber, you all will nevuh git that thang off of the ground.' Ah did. An Ah *still* thank those boys shoulda stuck to bah-sicles. Ah do. Ain't nobody evuh crashed in thuh Annoctic on a bah-sicle. Idnat right? Nevuh!"

The helo lifted off in a cloud of dust-fine snow, gained altitude, and tilted away toward the mountains.

2

BEARDMORE

In the upside-down world of the Antarctic, where the sun shone all day in December and winter was in July, it made a kind of sense to Penny that directions should be reversed as well. Here you travelled by "the Grid," an arbitrary act of cartography. On the Grid, the North Pole was in mid-Atlantic, the South Pole in the Pacific, and the equator ran through the true South Pole. To fly from Shacktown to the mainland, they would be going Grid North; this afternoon, Al would fly Grid South to Ross Island, where McMurdo Station and its airstrip, Williams Field, were located. Penny reminded herself of this change in bearings as Shacktown fell away below them and swung out of the field of vision.

The mountains ahead stood out with unnatural sharpness in the clear air. But, from an altitude of almost a kilometer, Penny could see that the weather was already changing. The sky was still cloudless, but patches of ice fog had begun to form over the Shelf and around the glacier mouths.

—God, if the weather breaks before we can evacuate, I'll go nuts. She pushed the thought out of her mind and squinted through the window. With each moment, the view changed: shadows on the Shelf and the mountains went from deep blue to black to purple; snow was an impossibly pure white one instant and a rich cream the next. The glaciers were densely textured, their surfaces patterned with countless crevasses, and tinted blue, green, amber, mauve, and black. Penny took a few pictures, though it was hard to handle the camera while wearing heavy mittens.

The flight to the first remote was brief. They landed on a shelf of bare, pinkish-beige rock near the mouth of Ramsey Glacier. The remote was a small prefab hut, bolted to the rock. A small windmill, its blades scarcely turning, rose from the roof of the hut, and there was also an antenna array made useless by the radio blackout.

They stepped out into silence. The helicopter's rotors murmured into stillness; mukluks scuffed on the smooth rock. Otherwise there was a quiet such as few people ever experience. It seemed much colder here than at the station; Penny's eyes began to water at once, and a tear froze halfway down her cheek. Her nose began to run again, and she appreciated the absorbent backs of her bearpaw mitts. Her nostrils hurt, and when she tried breathing through her mouth the air made her fillings ache.

"Welcome to the Dufek Coast," Steve said to Penny. "Let's get inside."

Will and Jeanne, however, would have to stay outside for a while. They collected their gear and set out down the slope to the glacier's edge less than a hundred meters away. This close, it looked dingy and gray, almost like old city snow. The surface was rough, with many sastrugi and ice thrusts taller than a man. It was impossible, as Will and Jeanne were demonstrating, to take more than four steps without clambering over a hummock or striding across a crevasse.

After watching them for a minute, Penny turned and followed the rest of the party into the hut. Steve had already turned on the lights and heater.

"There are over three dozen of these huts all over West Antarctica, and they let us gather a hell of a lot of data," Steve told her. Most of the hut was taken up with seismographs, tilt- and creepmeter equipment, a small radio, and the windmill-charged batteries that powered everything. A double bunk and some shelving gave the hut value as an emergency shelter as well. Penny slid into the bottom bunk to keep out of the way, while Al climbed into the top one. Steve and Tim studied the equipment.

"They're taking forever to set up that damned shot," Tim growled. He pressed the video outlet of the seismograph, and on its screen watched the tracks made by the glaciologists' footsteps.

"As soon as they fire the shot, I'll collect the tape reel," Steve said to Tim. "You get the other tapes."

"Right." Tim pulled out the reels that held two months' worth of seismic and meteorological data. Played back through a computer, they would provide an exquisitely precise account of the movements of earth, ice, and air around the hut.

The video screen erupted into jagged multicolored lines as the hut shook from the thump of the shot. Steve pressed a button and the seismograph spat out a strip of paper, the hard-copy record of the shock waves' path through the ice to the bed of the glacier and back again. He shoved the paper in his anorak pocket, removed the tape reel, and replaced it with a new one.

"At least that'll record the next three months before it runs out. Let's go."

They all helped Will and Jeanne carry their gear back to the helo. After her few minutes of relative warmth inside the hut, Penny felt the cold more than ever.

"Ice is *full* of bloody great crevasses," Will panted as they walked up the slope from the glacier. "We nearly went in a couple of times. The glacier's moving fast near the bottom, and that breaks up the surface."

"How can you tell it's moving?" Penny asked.

Will turned and pointed to a fluorescent orange pennant hanging from a bamboo pole some distance down the glacier. "I planted that marker three months ago—beginning of December. It's moved over a hundred meters downstream. Normally, the Queen Maud glaciers travel less than half that distance in three months

—they're doing well to cover three hundred meters in a bloody year." He laughed as they threw the geophones into the helo. "Maybe that's your famous surge right there, Steve."

"Maybe." Steve didn't look amused. "But I doubt it."

He really did have a bee in his bonnet about surges, Penny thought. Up to a point, she could buy his arguments. He had recorded "seismic swarms" in the Queen Maud Range for two years running now—microearthquakes that often foreshadowed a major quake. As far back as the late '50s, the Kiwis and others had recorded similar tremors around Ross Island; they'd called them "icequakes" on the assumption that they were caused by big tabular icebergs calving off the edge of the Shelf. Will and Jeanne had found unusual amounts of radon gas dissolved in the sea water under the Shelf—another sign, though not a reliable one, that a quake was imminent. The freshness of the water under the Shelf also indicated that more ice than usual was melting under the ice sheet, and leaking down under the glaciers into the sea. But that ice sheet was up to three kilometers thick; as Tim had said in one argument with Steve, expecting a quake to move that immense mass was like expecting a gnat to push the meringue off a pie with one shove. Steve had laughed at that, but he hadn't changed his mind.

They followed the mountains Grid East for two hundred kilometers, past bare brown mountain slopes and blinding glaciers. The ice fog was thickening, obscuring much of the Shelf off to their right, but the peaks of the Queen Maud Range stood out sharply against the deep, empty blue of the sky. The helo curved around Mount Kyffin, an ice-drowned island, and then they were over the Beardmore.

"My God," Penny said.

Will, sitting beside her, smiled as if he owned it. "Bloody gorgeous, isn't it?"

In its length and breadth, it dwarfed the mountains. From the polar plateau to the Shelf, the Beardmore was two hundred kilometers long and thirty wide; when the helo was halfway across it, the mountains on either side seemed like children's sand castles, about to be swept away by the tide. The surface of the glacier was a multicolored jumble, streaked by long bands of darkness: crushed rock, ground away from mountainsides and carried down by tributaries. Crevasses yawned up at the sky, wide and deep enough to swallow a supertanker without a trace. Across the monstrous labyrinth of that cracked and mottled surface, an endless wind screamed down from the pole, carrying ground drift that made the whole glacier seem to be moving.

The sheer scale of it made Penny feel shrunken. If mountains could be overwhelmed and ground to dust by such a torrent of ice, of what significance were human beings? Scott and Shackleton, and their men and ponies, had somehow fought their way up and down that glacier; Scott had been grateful for such a highway to the pole. Penny thought they must have been mad. Against such blind mass and inertia, courage and intelligence and resolve were no more than the buzzing of a mosquito as it flew to meet an avalanche.

The helo crossed the glacier. On the far side, a nunatak—a mountain peak half-buried in ice—rose near the mouth of Garrard Glacier, a tributary of the Beardmore. They landed on a lonely outcrop of black rock on the shoulder of the nunatak, and fifty meters from a small yellow hut identical to the one at Ramsey. Al and Steve came into the passenger compartment.

"Here we are," Al bellowed over the continuing roar of the engine. "I'm going to try to contact Shacktown for a weather report. Be with you in a few minutes."

It was even colder here than at Ramsey, and Al kept the rotors turning slowly to prevent the engines from freezing up. Again, Will and Jeanne went straight out onto the ice while the others hurried into the hut.

Soon it was warm enough for them to shed at least their anoraks. Steve sat on a little table and unpacked the breakfast, while Penny and Tim crowded into the lower bed of the double bunk. The equipment hummed and chattered.

"What an ideal spot for a picnic," Penny said.

"Not many flies," Tim agreed. He looked around the cramped, windowless little room. "You know, I must be crazy, but I'm going to miss this whole lousy continent."

"It gets in your blood," Steve said. "Well, we'll be back next year."

Penny felt a brief, irrational envy of them all. Then she remembered the stink and squalor of Shacktown. God, that was too high a price to pay for some spectacular scenery.

Al burst in, a grim expression on his face.

"Get through?" Steve asked.

"I got McMurdo, not Shacktown. Just for a minute. They're having an eruption."

"A what?" Tim asked after a shocked moment.

"Mount Erebus is erupting—has been since early yesterday."

Penny remembered Erebus. She'd seen it as their plane approached Ross Island, a huge, gnarled mountain with a thick plume of steam trailing from its peak. McMurdo and its suburb, Scott Base, stood at the foot of the volcano, just where the edge of the Shelf met the waters of McMurdo Sound.

"Most of it's coming from the summit," Al went on, "but there's a new vent right on the shore, a few kilometers past Scott Base. They're getting great chunks of rock falling all around them. A Coast Guard icebreaker in the Sound was hit last night and went right to the bottom. They've closed down Inner Willy." That was Williams Field, the airstrip bulldozed into the surface of the Shelf; an auxiliary strip, Outer Willy, was twenty or thirty kilometers Grid North of Ross Island.

Steve got up from the table and pressed buttons on

the seismograph. The screen lit up in a flicker of colored lines and changing numbers. The others watched him in silence.

"Right—this must have been when it started," he said at last. "A strong shock at 0500 hours—then another twenty minutes later—and another—damn it, they keep getting stronger." He turned to Al. "You couldn't raise Shacktown?"

"Not a whisper."

"We've got to get back right away. Even if Inner Willy is closed down, Outer Willy should be okay. They'll be evacuating everyone as fast as they can, and we've got to let them know we need to get out as well."

"Okay. What about the shot Will and Jeanne are setting up?"

"Call 'em back. We don't have time for it." He hastily changed tapes on the seismograph while the others finished their meal. In less than two minutes they were back in their anoraks and heading for the door. Steve switched off the light and heat, leaving the hut illuminated only by the glowing dials of the instrumentation. Al opened the door.

The hut trembled, as if a violent gust of wind had struck it, and then lurched violently. Al lost his balance and fell through the doorway. The plywood walls began to creak; a chair slid across the floor and fell over.

"Out! Right now!" Steve shouted. He grabbed Penny, lifted her, and shoved her through the doorway; she nearly fell over Al, who was scrambling to his feet. Tim followed an instant later. Three hundred meters away, Will and Jeanne were struggling up the icy slope from the glacier, their gear abandoned. Except for the creaking and rumbling of the hut, everything seemed very silent; only after a few seconds did Penny become aware of a profound vibration in the rock beneath her. From the glacier below came a sudden sharp bang, then another and another, until each blurred into the others' echoes.

"Get into the helo," Al said. Penny and Tim started to obey when the mountain shuddered violently and they lost their footing. Clumsily, Penny got to her hands and knees and looked around for Steve. He was still inside the hut, watching the seismograph. He was smiling.

He's crazy, Penny thought. Crazy. Bonkers. The word made her giggle. A hum filled the air, like wind in a forest. The rock shuddered again and the hut snapped off its foundations with a shriek of torn metal and splintering plywood. The windmill toppled over, clanging on the twisted aluminum roof. Then the walls parted and the roof collapsed.

Al got up again and lunged toward the wreckage, but Steve came out by himself, feet first and unhurt. He was clutching a tape under his arm—the tape Tim had just put on the machine.

Penny turned to look at the helo. It was skidding away from its landing site, moving erratically down the shallow gradient toward the glacier, and toward Will and Jeanne.

Penny screamed: "The helo!" she couldn't hear herself. The hum was turning into a deep, rolling roar, growing louder every second, like an endless peal of thunder. Once she had watched a rocket lift off from Cape Canaveral; this was worse, much worse. It went on in a mindless, meaningless blur of sound that drugged and stupefied.

Another shock hit, rousing her enough to reach to Al and make him look away from Steve, toward the helicopter. She saw his eyes widen. Then he was on his feet, lurching toward it. It had found a steeper slope, and was now not just skidding about but sliding steadily downhill.

Al reached the helo, yanked open the door, and hauled himself inside. A few seconds later Penny could see him in the cockpit; the rotors quickened, but the engines were muted against that strange unending thunder. She shut her eyes against the downdraft from the rotors. The downdraft increased, throwing snow as fine and sharp as powdered glass against her face. The helo had lifted off, and was hovering just overhead.

Penny could not get up. It was easier to lie face down on the rock, to wait for the rock to stop shaking and the thunder to die away. A long time seemed to pass. Then someone took her arm and pulled her to her feet.

"I'm blind!" she screamed. Hands guided her deeper into the freezing wind, lifted her onto a floor that swayed and trembled more than the ground itself.

Someone must have shut the helo's door, because the wind stopped and the thunder lessened slightly. Penny let herself be lowered into a seat. She felt someone push back her hood and gently remove her sunglasses. Warm hands were cupped beneath her eyes; warm breath fell on her eyelids. They stung, then swam with tears. Steve's face appeared above her and slowly came into focus.

He put his lips next to her ear, and his voice came from far away: "Your eyelids froze." She nodded. He touched her cheekbones. "Frostbite. Don't worry." She pulled off her mitts and held her hands to her face. Steve sat back beside her, and the helo lifted abruptly.

Tears poured down her face and over her fingers; she found herself shuddering uncontrollably. She was dimly aware of Jeanne and Tim in the seat opposite her, and supposed Will must be up in the cockpit with Al. The endless roar diminished as they climbed, but was still too loud to permit speech.

When her eyes stopped watering, Penny put her sunglasses back on and looked out the window. Far below, the Beardmore was covered with a dazzling white haze that glinted prismatically here and there. On the horizon, the mountains had lost their sharp edges; mists and clouds were forming around them. Beyond them, over the polar plateau, a high overcast was growing. The helo turned and she glimpsed clear skies over the Shelf.

The intercom system wasn't working. Penny found

a pencil and paper in one of her trousers pockets, scribbled a note, and gave it to Steve: *Is this the surge?*

He nodded. *Quake was bad,* he wrote beneath her question. *7.5 at least.*

Why the noise?

Glacier sole full of stones—scraping over bedrock.

She looked out the window again, toward the unseen ice sheet that fed the Beardmore, the Shackleton, and hundreds of other glaciers. Up there the ice is over two kilometers thick, she thought. What could stop it once it began to move?

Will came in from the cockpit. Something about him seemed odd even to Penny's dulled perceptions. He leaned close to her, inspecting her frostbitten cheeks and nose. Smiling a little, he leaned forward and kissed her. She put her arms around his neck and kissed him back. —The crazy bastard's delighted. He's positively delighted!

Will turned to Steve and gripped his shoulders in an awkward hug, then shook Tim's hand, and then kissed Jeanne. She had been sitting curled up, leaning against Tim with her eyes shut and her hands over her ears. When Will kissed her she reached out as Penny had, embraced him, and began to cry.

He held her for a long minute; the sun, shining through the window behind him, made a halo of his curly red hair. A ministering angel, Penny thought, but in the same moment Will detached himself, gave Jeanne a businesslike pat on the shoulder, and left her to go rummaging in a chest at the rear of the passenger compartment. He got out some acoustic earmuffs and handed them out to the others. Penny put hers on, and with the sudden drop in the noise level she realized her body was as clenched as a fist. She took a deep breath and made herself relax.

Seeing the scrawls on Penny's paper, Will took her pencil and wrote quickly: *I want to get down near the ice.*

Steve mouthed: Why?

Check the speed of the surge.

What about noise? Steve wrote.

Earmuffs should help. Won't be long. OK?

Steve nodded reluctantly.

Penny looked at the terse questions and answers they had written. —Is that all we have to say about this?

Will went back into the cockpit, and almost at once the helo began to descend. As they approached the glacier surface, the noise grew loud enough to make them nauseous. They were near the Grid West edge of the Beardmore, but the glacier was invisible under the ice haze. Then they were low enough for the downdraft of the rotors to blow much of the haze away in the area directly beneath them; it was only a couple of meters deep. The helo hovered, and they could see the ↙ ʔotic surface of the ice moving steadily toward the Shelf. It was like nothing Penny had ever seen before. Perhaps a planetoid, rotating its shattered surface under an orbiting spacecraft, might present a similar image. Blue-gray blocks slid into view out of the haze, sank, rose, and fell apart. Splinters of ice speared upward and toppled, to be replaced by crevasses then crashed open and shut and open again. For a moment the helo's downdraft combined with the wind to wrap everything in swirling glitter; then the air cleared again as an ice thrust heaved up almost close enough to touch. Steve timed a particular ten-meter lump as it slid by beneath them; then, as the helo rose again, he scribbled a calculation or two. Will returned from the cockpit.

Abt 3 kph? Will wrote.

Steve nodded. *Faster in the centre than here.*

5-8 kph in centre?

Not yet. Soon—maybe faster when surge really gets going.

Penny grabbed the pencil: *Half ice sheet will go in 1 week at that speed.* Hollin had calculated that in his paper on Wilson's surge theory.

Will and Steve looked at each other and then showed

the paper to Tim. Tim wrote: *Maybe. Depends how many glaciers involved.*

The helo swept over the flank of Mount Kyffin; its mantle of snow and ice had slid away, leaving bare brown rock at its peak and avalanche scars down its sides. When Penny turned to look at Mount Kaplan, it too seemed barer than it had been. They flew out across the mountains, over a small glacier that was moving in a jumble of broken ice. The dull roar of the surge was broken every few seconds by a distant screaming sound as ice and rock shattered each other. When she could remember to, Penny took a few photos, but the view from the window had an almost hypnotic quality that kept her staring open-mouthed.

Then they were over the Shelf, and the Shelf had cracked.

These were no mere crevasses. For some kilometers out from the coast, the Shelf was grounded on the floor of the Ross Sea, but even the enormous weight and anchoring of seven hundred meters of ice could not withstand the surge. Some of the fissures were already over a hundred meters wide, and glowed blue in their depths. A long network of cracks ran roughly parallel to the coast; others ran Grid South until they vanished in the glare of the sun. The thunder of the surge lessened. From the Shelf came occasional creakings and detonations, like a great wooden ship caught in a storm.

The helo circled one of the north-south fissures. Blowing snow obscured the gap until the wind abruptly changed, and they looked down into a blue-black abyss. Penny saw glints of light far down in the darkness, a suggestion of something moving, and realized after a moment what it was: the waters of the Ross Sea, open to the sky for the first time in a hundred thousand years. The glimpse was brief: great slabs of ice, fifty meters thick and a hundred long, calved off the sides of the fissure and crashed down into the darkness.

Penny turned to see Steve using her Nikon to take pictures; his face reflected nothing. The helo flew on. Will came back again, more elated than ever, and scribbled a frantic exchange with Steve:

Fracture's very clean—shelf more homogen than I thot.

Think fissures will stay open? Steve wrote.

No (?) Surge will push shelf out to open sea, all packed together. How fast?

Will shrugged.

Has Al raised S'town?

Will shrugged again, then left to check with Al. He came back shaking his head.

Penny had a sudden hideous vision of a fissure opening up right under the station: the flash of daylight in the tunnels as the roof caved in, the boom of the breaking ice, the huts falling far down into the blue darkness. —Quit it! Stupid neurotic chickenshit moron fantasies. They'll be all right. They'll be all right. Worried sick about *us*. What a time we'll have, sitting in the mess hall comparing notes.

Notes. This had been going on for almost an hour and she hadn't even made any notes. She found some more paper and tried to organize her thoughts; after five minutes she gave up and slumped wearily back into her seat. Steve gently took the paper from her lap and began scrawling figures. But after every calculation he drew a line through what he had just written.

—He's in the same predicament. Trying to make sense out of this with black marks on a piece of paper.

She leaned against him, resting her head on his shoulder. Her face was beginning to hurt badly. Steve absently patted her hand.

A crosswind gusted off the mountains and made the helo sway. More gusts followed. The helo rose and fell; the overcast had spread clear across the sky. Dry snow began to hiss against the window, driven from the glaciers and avalanches by katabatic winds blow-

ing down from the plateau. Penny saw long snakes of
snow crawl across the Shelf, thickening rapidly until
the surface vanished. Then they were flying through
a roaring sunlit fog, a whiteout.

Al lifted the helo above the blizzard, back into
pale sunlight. The blizzard swept under them, its upper
layer almost as sharply defined as the Shelf had been
until a few minutes ago. Like a layer of cloud, it
stretched in all directions, from the mountains to the
Grid South horizon.

The world had vanished. There seemed nothing to
do, nothing to say or write that was not grotesquely
absurd and futile. They would not get back to Shacktown. They would not be rescued by the Americans
at McMurdo. This world of empty blue and formless
white was going to kill them in a little while, and they
would leave no trace. Penny thought of Scott, Wilson,
and Bowers, dying on the Shelf side by side, with
love and sorrow for one another and the hope that
friends would someday find their bodies, that their
letters and diaries would link them at last with the
living and make some sense of their deaths. —We
won't have even that much. Just scrawls on a couple
of scraps of paper, and some reels of magnetic tape
lost in the snow. And no one will ever find us. Ever.

Time passed. Jeanne went into the cockpit and returned almost at once. She mimed a radio conversation.

Shacktown? Steve wrote. Jeanne grinned and nodded. *20 km,* she wrote.

A little later they began their descent. The wind
and snow enveloped them again. If Al lost Shacktown's
TACAN signal, they would be in trouble at once. The
light dimmed from a blinding white to a deep, feature-
less gray. Penny removed her earmuffs and found she
could stand the noise; the helo's engines sounded almost normal, but there was still a low background
rumble interrupted by sharp cracks that must be
caused by the Shelf's continuing breakup.

—A few more minutes. Then we'll be home, safe

and sound after all, piling out in the hangar, groaning and laughing, hugging people, running down through the tunnels to the mess hall, finding out what happened to them *oh shit*—

The helo had been flying at an altitude of only five meters; Al had thought it was much more. Below them, a fissure had opened and then closed again, creating a pressure ridge about five meters high, and invisible in the whiteout. The Huey raked its belly on the ridge, shearing away its landing gear, and snapping its fuel line and some of its control cables. It lost power instantly, plunged to the surface beyond the ridge, and slid over a hundred meters before coming to rest.

Snow rattled against the helo's crumpled sides, and the wind was suddenly very loud. Somewhere far away, the Shelf broke again with a long, reverberating boom.

3

~~~~~~~~~~~

THE SHELF

By 1000 hours the Otter was fueled, warmed up, and ready to fly as soon as Al got back. Howie O'Rourke took out the big D8 bulldozer to clear the skiway; the Otter wouldn't need it, but it would help a Hercules. Plowing was a slow, noisy, cold, and boring job, and when he turned the D8 around at the end of the skiway Howie swore furiously. The dome and Shacktown's other surface structures were almost invisible in a thickening ice fog. Looking up, he saw the sky growing overcast. It would be a pissoff if they got another blow—not just because the evacuation would have to be postponed, but because he would have frozen his butt for nothing and would have to freeze it again when the weather cleared up.

In the reactor control room, Herm Northrop was going methodically through shutdown. It was a slow, cautious process, and the station would not have to switch over to its emergency generator for at least four more hours. By then, Al should be at McMurdo. Assume at least three more hours for a Hercules to be readied and flown in. By 1800 hours the core would have to be stored in its transport module, a lead-and-steel cylinder over two meters long. The module would then have to be wheeled through the tunnels and out to the plane.

Herm was not afraid of flying. But he hated the thought of a plane going down with a core aboard.

"By God, *I'm* not sorry," Terry Dolan announced to his wife. "This time next week, we'll be lyin' on the beach in Sydney, thinkin' how to spend our money." He was making soup in two huge pots, while his last batch of bread baked in the oven. It would be enough to keep people fed until they pulled out.

"It's all going in the savings," Suzy said firmly. "Every penny. And *you* might loaf on the beach, but I'll be looking for a job soon as we get home."

"Suit yourself, love. Just pray the unemployment's all gone."

"People got to eat, don't they? Always work for cooks."

Katerina Varenkova had been too efficient. With all her belongings packed by 0900, she had had nothing to do since then but smoke, and the air in the infirmary was now almost opaque. If the West was so convinced that cigarettes caused lung cancer, why did it produce such good ones? She would miss them.

Strange to think that she might be seeing Ivan soon —at Vostok, or Mirny, or perhaps back in Leningrad. They might well have evacuated Vostok already; it was the most remote of the Soviet bases, and the coldest place on earth—not a good spot to be in during the worst Antarctic summer on record. Compared to Vostok, this place was a vacation spot. Here there was no need to gasp for air on an ice sheet three kilometers above sea level, doing research with ancient equipment, fighting the cold with unreliable diesel generators and bearskins—bearskins!—hanging in the doorways to fight drafts. Here these pampered babies lived snug and relaxed, complaining because there was no mail and the TV projection screen was scratched. And all for propaganda.

They were pleasant individuals, most of them, and some were good scientists, whether their governments cared or not. She would miss Hugh and Herman, and one or two others. But it would be good to be among Russians again, and to lie laughing in bed with Ivan.

Sean McNally was down in the mine, shoveling snow onto the conveyor belt that led to the melter. He had long since stopped reflecting on the irony of a nuclear-powered snow melter that had to be fed by manual labor. It did seem a bit much to be doing it on the day they were to evacuate, but Carter Benson had been adamant.

The snow wasn't even glaciologically interesting. This muck had all been laid down in the last two hundred years; the real snows of yesteryear were down a lot farther, and it was the Little Climatic Optimum of the tenth and eleventh centuries that had brought him here.

While the conveyor belt rattled and flapped, Sean dug steadily, humming along with the Pachelbel tape on the cassette player he'd brought for company.

Bruce Robinson, the radio operator, came into Hugh's office without knocking. Hugh and Carter looked up from an evacuation checklist.

"I just got almost a full minute from McMurdo."

"Good man!" Hugh said. "D'you tell them Al's coming?"

"Didn't seem much point in that." He dropped a message form on Hugh's desk. It took very little time for the two men to read it.

"My goodness," Hugh murmured. "Willy Field closed down. Ash and bombs falling all about."

"It's just Inner Willy," Carter said. "Outer Willy's a good twenty kilometers away—it must be open."

"Yes, but they're not likely to have a Herc sitting about—more likely they're evacuating McMurdo itself, and hard-pressed to do it with the aircraft they've got. Well, Al will still go." Hugh sighed and rubbed his long red moustache. "This has not been our summer, I'm afraid. Who's minding the radio? Roger?"

"Yeah. We'll keep trying to get back in touch with them."

"And the helo."

"Uh-huh." Bruce looked at his watch. "They oughta be back in less than an hour. It's 1100."

Out at the drilling hut, engineer Gordon Ellerslee and mechanic Simon Partington cleared the hole of the last cables and pipes. Gordon packed away three samples of sea water in plastic flasks.

"That's that," he grunted. "Some other crazy bastard can drill the hole next year. I'll be back in Alberta, bitching about the heat and the blackflies."

"Come off it," Simon laughed. He was a tall, thin New Zealander, fair-skinned and a bit boyish for a man of thirty. Gordon was only a couple of years older, but looked more like forty-five; he was already balding at the temples. Plastic surgery hadn't entirely erased the scars gained in a Fort McMurray beer-parlor brawl long ago. "You'll be back," Simon went on. "Same as me. Two weeks back home, and you'll be begging to come back."

"No wonder you Kiwis are a twelfth-class country. You're all too dumb to find your own assholes with both hands and a map. Gimme a hand with this crap, will you?"

Howie was almost back to the hangar. A bit of wind had sprung up, and the ice fog was blowing away. He was looking out toward Grid Northeast, trying to spot the helo on the off chance that it might be coming back early, when his eye caught a flicker of motion off to his left. He scraped a mitt across the inner windshield; the heater wasn't working properly on the left side, and the glass had frosted over. He squinted through the clear patch.

A wave was running over the surface of the Shelf.

Howie could see it plainly; it lifted sastrugi into sudden prominence and dropped them again, making the surface twinkle. The wave was probably no more than a tenth of a meter from trough to crest, but it was there, moving swiftly from the mountains on the Grid North horizon.

As it passed the station, just a couple of seconds after he had first seen it, Howie felt a sharp jolt, as if the D8 had collapsed a snow bridge over a crevasse. There was another shock, and a third, all within five seconds. The bulldozer shuddered and skidded. Howie killed the engine, swung open the door of the cab, and stepped out onto the right track. He jumped to the surface, his legs sinking into soft snow almost to his knees. The vibration could still be felt.

A hundred meters away, Shacktown's two radio masts collapsed simultaneously with a metallic roar. A moment later there was a louder crash, and Howie turned to see the drilling tower falling onto the shed. He looked up at the dome, only a few meters away, and saw Colin Smith staring blankly down at him.

A third crash made Howie turn again. Not far from the radio masts, a gap had appeared in the surface. Howie walked toward it, staying on the hard-packed surface of the skiway. In a minute he stood at the edge of a rectangular pit. At the bottom, buried in powdery snow, was the ruin that had been the radio shack.

"Oh. . . ." He kicked the snow, sending a miniature avalanche down into the pit. "Oh shit."

Herm Northrop's chair threw him across the control panel, then slid back and fell over. The fluorescent lights flickered but stayed on. Herm got to his feet and gripped the edge of the panel, ignoring the floor's vibration as he watched the readouts. If anything in the cooling system had been seriously damaged, he would have to go at once to emergency shutdown.

After what seemed like a long time, his electric kettle and teapot fell off a nearby table. Books cascaded from their shelves. Through the lead-lined door to Tunnel E, Herm could hear muffled crashes.

Thirty seconds after the last shock, the reactor building was creaking as it resettled itself; the floor continued to tremble slightly. Herm took off his glasses and polished them on his necktie. Then he righted his chair, sat down, and studied the control panel slowly and meticulously. Everything was normal. He got up and opened the door to the cold porch, went through, and looked down the tunnel.

Shadows pounced at him and retreated as the tunnel lamps swung back and forth. Boxes, crates, and drums that had been stacked along the walls were piled over the duckboards. Far down the tunnel, something fell with the sound of breaking glass.

Herm went back inside; his glasses misted over at once. "Oh, for goodness' sake," he snapped, yanking them off. He bent myopically close to the telephone and punched Hugh's number. After five rings, someone picked it up.

"Yes."

"Oh, is that you, Carter? It's Herm."

"Anything serious?"

"Oh, not really. The reactor's all right. What was that—an explosion?"

"Damned if I know. Maybe it was Steve's earthquake. Hugh's out checking the whole station."

"He'll have trouble reaching me. The tunnel's blocked."

"Did it collapse?"

"Heavens, no. Just the stuff stored along the walls. It's a pretty mess."

"Good. We'll get to you as soon as we can. But the end of Tunnel A fell in on the radio shack."

"*No.* Anyone hurt?"

"Don't know yet. I'll get back to you."

Herm put down the phone. Then he put on his glasses, retrieved the kettle, and made himself a pot of tea. He had to hold the pot with both hands while he poured, and even then some of the tea spilled. Herm wasn't sure whether he was scared or merely excited.

Somehow, Suzy carried Terry from the kitchen to the infirmary. Katerina was in the doorway, zipping up her anorak.

"He's burned. He's burned. Oh God, he's burned."

Katerina helped carry him inside. Terry was in shock; his trousers were soaked with the soup that had splashed boiling from the kettles when they fell off the stove. Beans, rice, tomatoes and onions steamed on the table as Katerina carefully scissored the soaked cloth away from his legs.

"Oh God, he looks terrible," Suzy whispered. The skin on Terry's thighs, groin, and belly was heavily blistered, and coming off in bloody patches.

"I have seen worse. Don't worry, he will be all right soon. Please, now, Suzy, go back to the kitchen. I will call you."

She worked steadily and rapidly. Terry was breathing hard and seemed only remotely aware of what was happening.

Katerina wished the floor would stop vibrating.

The drilling hut was half-demolished by the collapse of the tower, but Gordon and Simon were unhurt and got outside without much trouble. The wind was picking up a little; snow drifted around their feet.

"Bloody masts are down," Simon observed.

"Bitch of a job to get 'em back up again. Hope they leave it for next year. I'd like to get outa here."

"So would I. Well, let's see what the hell happened."

As they rounded the hangar, they saw Howie approaching the personnel door.

"You guys all right?" he panted.

"Sure," Gordon said. "Bet it's a mess downstairs."

"Didja see the wave comin' across the Shelf? Weirdest thing I ever saw."

"All we saw was the bloody hut falling down around us," said Simon.

"Well, there was a wave. I'm not shittin' you."

As Howie yanked on the door, a sound like far-off thunder rolled down on the wind from the mountains.

Hugh was racing all over the station, but the radio shack was his main worry. The metal roof plate above it had fallen right through the top of Hut 1, along with several hundred kilos of snow; Bruce and Roger were somewhere inside. Several men were already frantically digging into the debris. Ground drift was increasing, blowing more snow into the tunnel, but within half an hour a narrow passageway had been made to the other side of the roof plate. Ray Crandall, the smallest man available, had crawled through to the ruined hut.

Roger Wykstra was crouched under a desk in the darkness. When the flashlight glared in his eyes, he said: "About fucking time. Who is that?" Roger's long, thin face was blue with cold, but he looked more irritated than frightened.

"Ray. Where's Bruce?"

"Under that wall. I think he's hurt. He was yelling for a while, but he's been quiet for a long time."

"You okay?"

"Thought you'd never ask. Yeah, I'm all right."

"Can you get out of there? Need any help?"

"Yeah, I can get out. Do you think it's safe?"

"Hell, no. But it'll take both of us to get Bruce out."

"Christ. I sure don't want to bring any more crap down on us. Well—" He crawled out. It was impossible to move except on hands and knees, and in places they had to crawl flat on their bellies. It was intensely cold, and Roger was wearing only jeans and a sweater.

They found Bruce pinned between the floor and the fallen wall. Roger crawled in on top of him and heaved the wall upward a few centimeters. Ray gripped Bruce's arms and pulled cautiously. Bruce gasped and screamed.

"My arm, you dumb bastard! Leave it alone!"

"Which one, which one?"

"Left. Jeez, it must be broken."

"I'm sorry," Ray said shakily. "God, you scared me when you yelled like that." He was a gentle, timid man, more at ease with computers than with people, and he dreaded upsetting anyone.

Painfully and slowly, they dragged Bruce clear and got him to the passageway. Ray turned him over and slid him headfirst to the men waiting on the other side.

None of the huts had been knocked off their stilts, but their interiors were in chaos. The labs had been wrecked, and many instruments had been smashed. A pipe leading from the water reservoir had broken, flooding much of Tunnel D and turning the duckboards slippery with ice. Hugh Adams clambered over piles of tumbled crates and fuel drums for several minutes before finally reaching the stairs leading up to the hangar.

Here, at least, there had been little damage; the vehicles and the Otter were unscathed. As Hugh was finishing his inspection, Carter arrived. The geophysicist's round face was tense, but he showed no sign of panicking. Hugh was glad of that. They went outside and walked around the surface buildings.

"Doesn't look too bad," Carter said. "The drill hut's not as badly damaged as it seems—a week's work ought to put it right. The ventilators all seem fine."

They headed down the skiway toward the pit in Tunnel A. "It's the radio shack and the masts that worry me," Hugh said. He sounded out of breath. "We've got to get the roof plate back in place as soon as possible, and put up at least one of the masts."

"I agree about the roof—leave it like that and by next year the tunnels will be filled with snow. But why bother about the masts? It's not really necessary if we're about to evacuate."

"I doubt that we'll be able to—for some time. Oh, we'll send Al off, but it's not likely the Americans will be able—" he caught his breath again—"to give us any help." He turned to look at the mountains, but they were lost in windblown snow. This was more than just ground drift.

"We'll be in the milk bottle soon," Carter said. "Al had better hurry."

The ice trembled under their feet, and the wind carried more strange thunder. "Steve ought to be pleased," Hugh murmured. "He called this one bang-on."

They reached the edge of the pit and looked down. A couple of men, unrecognizable behind sunglasses and frosted beards, were still digging out the roof plate. The edge of the tunnel had collapsed, allowing the plate to fall. Hugh studied the raw edge of the pit.

"It'll be awkward getting the plate back up," he said at last. "But it can be done. If only the radios aren't too badly smashed. Hullo down there—that you, Tom?"

One of the men looked up. His beard was flaming orange: it was Tom Vernon, the station's diesel mechanic. The other man was George Hills, the carpenter, wearing a heavily patched anorak.

"Hi, Major," Tom called out. "What is it?"

"I want every available man out here right away—to get the plate back up. And hurry! It'll be Condition One in half an hour."

"Right," Tom nodded. He and George turned and disappeared down the tunnel.

The job went faster than anyone had expected. The plate was winched up behind the D8 and manhandled into place in less than ten minutes. Hugh had thought that the collapse of the tunnel wall would mean a sloppy fit, but the edges of the plate still overlapped the tunnel by a comfortable margin.

"That's because the tunnel's a lot narrower than it was when the wall caved in," Carter said as the plate was almost in place. He pointed down: "See? There's hardly any space between the hut walls and the ice."

"Hm. We'll keep an eye on that, and shave away the ice if we have to." Hugh paused and caught his breath. "God, I'm done in. I'm going downstairs for a bit of a rest."

"Good idea, Hugh. Hell, get some sleep if you can."

"Maybe."

Snow swept thickly around them now, in flakes so fine and dry that they glittered like dust motes in the dimming sunlight. As Hugh turned, hunched against the wind, Colin Smith materialized out of the growing whiteout.

"Hugh. I got Al on one of the old Angry-6 transceivers, just a couple of minutes ago. He was only about twenty, thirty kilometers away. Then I lost him."

"Who's running the rig now?"

"Reg Lewis."

"Well, keep at it. He may still be receiving even if we can't hear him. Bloody old sets are damn near useless anyway." He walked back to the hangar's personnel door, taking each step very deliberately. In the machine shop, he paused for a moment and then went to the phone.

"Katerina? Hugh. I'm afraid I'll have to take you away from Terry and Bruce. Just for a minute or two. Could you—meet me in my room? I believe I'm having a heart attack. Thank you."

He put down the phone. Good job he hadn't told her where he was; she'd have told him not to try clambering through the mess in the tunnel, and somehow he didn't fancy the thought of the men coming back inside and seeing him like this. Better to drop dead in the tunnel and be done with it.

"You have taken a foolish risk," she told him a few minutes later. "It seems to have been a very mild heart attack, but you could have made it much worse. Even so, you will have to rest for several weeks."

"Good. I'll go to Fiji for a month." His voice was hoarse.

"You are sarcastic. But you must rest."

"There's too much to do."

She made him lie down in his bunk, and took off

his mukluks. "Plenty of people can do whatever must be done." She grinned wryly at him. "We old people must learn to slow down."

The blizzard and whiteout lasted almost eighteen hours, sustained by katabatic winds that gusted up to 130 kph and rarely fell below 70. All night long, the station shook. No one got much sleep.

Howie O'Rourke spent most of the night preparing one of the Sno-Cats so that he could search for the helicopter party as soon as the weather cleared.

Terry Dolan and Bruce Robinson yelled and swore until Katerina gave them tranquilizers and a stern lecture.

Suzy Dolan lay in her bunk, waiting silently for the next shock to hit.

Sean McNally had to dig his way out of the snow mine. Everyone had forgotten about him. He was too tired to be angry, but he was sorry to have lost his Pachelbel tape.

Hugh dozed in and out of frightening dreams and still more frightening wakefulness.

Katerina walked down the tunnel to look in on him every few minutes. The men clearing the tunnel asked how he was. "Sleeping well," she said.

Herm Northrop, after a long day checking the CANDU and getting its output back to normal, got through Tunnel E before it was cleared and went to the mess hall. He made himself a meal of three big sandwiches, a bowl of Terry's soup, and a pint of ice cream. Then he made himself three more sandwiches, filled a thermos with coffee, and went back to the control room.

Ben Whitcumb worked over fourteen hours straight in the tunnels. He went to bed at 0200 and fell asleep in his clothes, sitting up on the edge of his bunk. Geologist Max Wilhelm, his roommate, came in an hour later and gently stretched Ben out before climbing into the top bunk.

Colin Smith spent most of the night in the dome, alternately making weather observations and trying to raise the helo on the old ANGRC-6 transceiver. Over the endless wind, he often heard distant booms, rumbles, and metallic clangs. Sometimes he almost persuaded himself that the noises were those of an approaching helicopter. They weren't.

4

THE HELO

The helo smelled of gas. Al sat very still in his seat, catching his breath. He had been thrown pretty hard against his safety harness, and his ribs ached. Nothing was visible through the cracked windscreen but a boiling grayness of snow moving at 100 kph. He unsnapped his harness and made sure the Search and Rescue and Homing distress signal was on. Not that it was likely to be picked up. Thank God for that brief contact with Shacktown—at least they'd have a rough idea of the helo's location.

"You all right, Al?" Will's voice was almost lost in the wind. He looked dazed.

"Sure. Been through worse." He forced his body to relax. "How about you?"

"A bit shaky. But I'm not hurt."

They got out of their seats and stumbled into the cabin. The smell of gas was much stronger here. Al moved quickly from one person to the next, checking them over and getting them on their feet. No one was hurt, but they were all shaken up and slow to react.

"Get your survival packs," Al ordered. "Get your survival packs. Then get out."

"It's cold," Penny complained. "It's cold out there. I want to stay here."

"Come on, Pen." He gripped her shoulders, his hands clumsy in bearpaw mitts, and pulled her out of her seat. "We might have a fire. And if we don't,

42

we'll freeze in here." He thumped the wall. "Helo's a heat sink."

The wind was almost as deafening as the surge had been. They groped their way out of the helo, each dragging a backpack full of survival gear; Steve stubbornly brought his seismograph tapes and Penny's camera as well. The surface here was a topographic nightmare of drifts and sastrugi, with nothing high enough to give shelter against the wind. There was some protection in the lee of the helo; they huddled there while Al slowly circled the crash site, up to his knees in drift. He glimpsed the pressure ridge as a ghostly line in the whiteout.

"There," he shouted, and started plodding along the helo's skid track toward the ridge. It meant walking straight into the wind, but the others followed without a word, bent almost double to stay on their feet.

It took them almost fifteen minutes to reach the ridge, though it was only a hundred meters away. In the lee of an almost vertical mass of ice, Al, Tim, and Steve zipped their three survival tents together while Will and the women crouched in a hollow nearby. Steve crawled into the tent; a few long minutes later, it glowed orange from the light of a primus stove. The others crept inside at once.

The tent was scarcely high enough for them to move around in, even on all fours, and was just wide enough for them to lie side by side. Al assigned each of them a spot and told them to unroll their sleeping bags. "Then get your anoraks off and get into your bags. Two at a time; it's too crowded for everyone to do it at once. Penny and Jeanne first."

Penny felt dreamily clumsy, but she managed. The sleeping bag seemed even colder than the outside, and for a long time she shivered convulsively. Almost like a high, she thought. Your brain goes off duty and your spine takes over.

By the time everyone was settled, a pot of stew was steaming over the primus. The steam made frost crystals form on almost everything but the top of the tent, which was flapping violently in the wind.

"Hoosh smells ready," Steve said. Without getting out of his bag, he dextrously poured stew into plastic mugs and handed them round. "Get it down quick, while it's hot."

It was unbelievably delicious, though Penny had trouble holding the mug still enough to drink from it. The heat from the stew thawed the frozen tears on her nose and upper lip. She gave back her mug for a refill, and when that was gone accepted a greasy bar of pemmican and some hard, sweetish biscuits. It hurt to eat—every breath made her fillings ache—but gradually she felt warmer. Her hands and feet began to hurt.

Jeanne, lying between Penny and Will, said: "Will? Are we going to die?"

"Certainly not."

"What?"

"I said certainly not! Damn that flapping tent."

"Papa Al, is Will right?" Jeanne sounded very scared.

"He's right, Housemouse." Al reached across Penny and patted Jeanne's sleeping bag. "We'll be fine. Shacktown knows where we are, and the SARAH is still transmitting from the helo. Soon as the wind drops, they'll send out a Sno-Cat and we'll go home in style." In the light of the primus he looked very tired and old. "Finish your lunch and take a nap."

To save fuel, Steve turned the primus down to a faint glow; the tent darkened. The wind's noise lessened a little as snow drifted over them. No one said much. Jeanne went to sleep, cuddled against Will.

Shivering in her bag, Penny tried to decide on an angle for the story. Do it ironically, she told herself. The brilliant seismologist surprised by the earthquake he'd predicted. The escape from one treacherous shelter to another, each in turn destroyed, until a flimsy nylon tent was all they had. And they would have to escape again, to the doubtful safety of Shacktown. Then where? It would make a grimly amusing story.

She was suddenly aware that Al, lying beside her, was crying. She turned to him and touched his shoulder, trying to comfort him as he had comforted Jeanne. He was facing the wall of the tent; his weeping stopped at her touch, and he rolled over to face her. His eyelids were caked with ice.

"I really messed us up, Penny," he whispered. "I'm sorry. Too old for this kind of work. I'm sorry."

"It's okay," she said. "It's okay."

One by one they fell asleep despite the wind and the occasional tremor in the ice. Steve and Tim lay side by side on the far side of the tent from Al and Penny. Their faces were close together, and they spoke softly.

"If McMurdo's out of action," Tim said, "we're screwed. There's nowhere else to go. At least nowhere the Otter could reach, especially in bad weather."

"I know."

"What'll we do?"

"Depends on how Shacktown survived the quake. If it's okay, we can winter over."

"Steve, for God's sake—you've got your bloody surge, and we've seen what it's already done to the Shelf. It's floating out to sea. How are we supposed to winter over on a goddam iceberg?"

"With luck." Steve said nothing for a while. "If Shacktown isn't habitable, we can still rig some kind of emergency shelter on the surface. If old Shackleton himself could do it, so can we." He rubbed some of the frost from his mustache and beard. "Anyway, we've got more immediate problems. Go to sleep."

"I'm too hyper. And scared. By the way, congratulations on your quake. Your reputation is made."

"Why thank you, thank you. I owe it all to my brilliant assistant. . . . God, Tim, wasn't it beautiful? Wasn't it just beautiful?" They chuckled softly together, like boyish pranksters.

Millions of tons of snow blew across the Shelf that afternoon. By 1500 hours the wind had increased until its roar made sleep impossible. The tent was not too cold, thanks to the shelter of the pressure ridge and the insulating layer of snow. Around 1600, Will went outside for some ice, which he melted to make tea and soup. They had their meal without saying much—the wind was too loud—and settled into their bags again.

At 1700 the wind suddenly dropped. An occasional gust hummed over the ridge, but it was at least possible to talk.

"I shouldn't have had so much tea," Penny said. "I've got to go."

"It's the cold more than the tea," Al said. "And the ladies' room is right outside." He was his old self again, calm and businesslike. "Take the ice ax and chop yourself a little hole in the ridge, so you're out of the wind. You can freeze your sphincter if you're not careful."

"That's not all I can freeze," Penny muttered.

"I'd better come too," Jeanne said.

They had to dig their way out. The whiteout was fading, but it was still hard to find the horizon. A drift had built up over the helo until just one rotor was showing. The air was bitterly cold and full of snow. Penny chopped at the rock-hard ice until she had gouged a shallow niche. It seemed to take forever just to loosen her trousers, and pulling them down was agony. Jeanne squatted beside her. Their urine crackled and sputtered on contact with the ice, freezing almost instantly. When they crawled back inside, Will gave them each a hug.

"Well," he sighed, "if you two can do it, so can we."

Sobbing and giggling, Penny burrowed into her sleeping bag. "I n-n-never f-felt less p-penis envy in my life."

Inevitably, the traffic in and out let a lot of snow into the tent. Much of it got into their sleeping bags, where it melted. Penny found herself shuddering un-controllably, and could scarcely hold the biscuits Will gave her.

"We aren't so b-badly off," he told her. "When Bowers and Wilson and Ch-Cherry-Garrard made their w-winter trip to Cape Crozier, they h-had to th-thaw their way into their bags w-with their own body heat, inch b-by inch."

"Get stuffed," Penny moaned.

By 1800 hours the wind had picked up again, and it blew all night. They slept, woke, ate, and slept again. Penny dreamed she was in the tent and woke unable to tell dream from reality. There was always the wind, and sometimes muffled voices; there was the glow of the primus and the glitter of frost on the tent. Once during the night she wanted to reach up and touch the sloping wall of the tent, but did not: she was afraid that if she did the snow above them would collapse the tent and bury them alive.

Silence woke them all a little before 0600 the next morning. After more stew, pemmican and tea, Al got two fluorescent-orange pennants out of the survival packs and went outside to plant them at the top of the pressure ridge. When he came back there was an odd, excited expression on his face.

"Come on out. It's clear, and not too cold—no wind, anyway."

Everyone had full bladders, and followed him out-side without much delay. While they stood or squatted by the wall of ice, they looked around. The Shelf was a gently undulating plain, gleaming white in the light of the sun. Even the buried helo scarcely stood out.

"What the hell is this pressure ridge doing here?" Jeanne asked Will.

"Dunno. Unless we're right on a fracture zone—"

He looked as if he'd been hit. Then he floundered up the path Al had made to the top of the ridge. The others trailed after him, their breath crackling in the cold stillness, and stood in silence as they looked out toward Grid Southeast.

Less than twenty meters from where they stood, the drifted crags of the pressure ridge came to an end. Beyond them was a gap over two hundred meters wide, whose bottom could have been seen only by standing nearer the edge than anyone cared to go. Across the gap, the blue-white ice cliffs of the next island reflected the sun from a hundred great facets; at the top of the cliffs was a pressure ridge like the one they were standing on.

"We could have flown right into this cliff if I'd been coming down a little more steeply," Al said. "Or hit the ridge on the far side there, and gone all the way to the bottom."

As he spoke, a chunk of the opposite cliff—about forty meters thick, twenty meters high, and a hundred meters long—creaked, snapped, and fell. It must have hit relatively thin ice at the bottom and broken through it, because its impact threw a dazzling geyser of frozen spray high above the Shelf. The noise would have seemed very loud to them even twenty-four hours earlier.

"And *that* could have happened to us last night," Tim observed. "Or in the next thirty seconds, for that matter. We'd better get the hell away from here."

Al pointed Grid North. "There are the mountains. I'd say we're only ten to fifteen kilometers Grid East of Shacktown. We could walk it."

"Could be hard going through the drifts," Will said. They were already moving back down the ridge.

"Sastrugi look bad," Al said, "but the surface shouldn't be too rough. Probably a good hard wind-crust in most places."

"What if we get another blow?" Tim asked. "Just stop and camp?"

"Right. But we shouldn't need to. Ought to be home and dry before suppertime."

"I'm game," Penny said. "Anything's better than soaking in that bag."

It took fifteen minutes to take down the tent and

pack their gear. Five minutes later they were walking past the buried helo, with Al and Steve in the lead. Al had been right; the wind had compacted the snow into a hard crust, slippery in places but otherwise as easy to walk upon as a sidewalk.

No one spoke. Even on a good surface, it was hard to travel in ten kilos of clothing with an eight-kilo survival pack on one's back. Penny's nose ran, forming an icicle on her upper lip that couldn't be removed without taking off skin as well. As they began climbing a slope, she had to breathe harder; the cold air in her lungs made her cough. When she exhaled, her breath crackled as it froze.

The first two kilometers were fairly easy, a steady march over long, shallow gradients. Then they came into a relatively high area where the wind had carved the surface into sastrugi, and footing was treacherous. Now they had to scramble and slide, and in places they could get through only by chopping steps into the hard, slick sides of the sastrugi. After an hour, Penny's feet and hands were numb. She realized she had fallen behind the others, and hurried up the slope of the next rise. At the top she coughed until she couldn't stand upright. There was a salty taste in her mouth, and red spots in the snow by her feet.

"Steve—Steve! I'm in trouble!"

He turned and came back to her while the others waited.

"I'm coughing blood."

Steve put his arms around her shoulders and guided her down the slope. "It'll be okay. You're moving too fast, breathing too deeply. The air's starting to freeze your lungs. Don't walk so fast that you start panting. You'll be fine."

"I'm scared."

"It's all right. I'll stay with you."

They walked and climbed slowly, trailing after the others. The sastrugi field seemed to go on forever. The crests were blindingly bright; some of the troughs between them were deep in shadow. It was hard to see where to put her feet, and she fell several times, but Steve always caught her.

"Your face looks pink," she said to him.

"So does yours." He looked closely at her. "It's sunburn. We'll all be pretty badly burned by the time we get home."

"At least I can't feel it."

Around 1000 hours, Al called a halt. They ate some biscuits and sweet chocolate, and Will melted snow for tea. He poured it into their mugs at a rolling boil, but it cooled rapidly—Penny's first sip was scalding and the last only tepid. At least it warmed her enough to make her feet hurt.

"Can I have some more?" she asked.

"No, but you can have some hot water. Too much tea and you'll dehydrate yourself," Will said. "Not to mention freezing your bottom."

They moved on. The surface was softer here; snow was deep and powdery in the lee of each sastrugus, and in places they waded knee-deep. Penny felt less dependent on Steve, but didn't let herself get too far away from him. She noticed Jeanne keeping close to Will. —Tough kid. She looks like hell, but she's not complaining. Jeanne seemed to have got over whatever had made her sick yesterday morning.

Penny's throat and chest hurt. Even though she kept to a slow pace, she was sweating; the sweat kept freezing, breaking off her skin, and gathering at her waist and boot-tops. It was worst inside her padded bra, which trapped the ice on her breasts. When she rubbed a forearm across her chest, she could hear the ice crackle, but couldn't feel anything except a steady ache. At least they'd warned her to expect this, back in Manitoba at the training camp, or she'd have started screaming—frozen lungs or not.

One foot after another. The sastrugi were replaced with a stretch of hard, flat windcrust, but after only a couple of hundred meters they found a belt of deep crevasses cutting across their path. The first few were narrow cracks, easily crossed in a stride, but after that the gaps were four and five meters wide.

"I don't remember crevasses like these anywhere close to Shacktown," Al said.

"They're old," Will answered. "Must've had thick, hard snow over them till the quake."

"Everybody stay well away from the edges," Al ordered. "We'll just have to detour."

It was like traversing a maze without walls: a hundred meters' progress cost three hundred in cautious zigzags. As the sun climbed to its zenith, the depths of the crevasses turned from black to a deep glowing blue. They moved slowly. Al, Tim, and Will, roped together, tested the surface with telescoping aluminum rods. If the snow resisted a hard push, they advanced; if it yielded, they stopped to find another path.

Penny was beginning to feel drowsily detached from herself, and to daydream about the dry warmth of her bunk. A tremor ran through the Shelf, no different from a dozen others they had felt since the crash. This time, however, the snow under Will collapsed into a crevasse five meters wide. As he fell, Al and Tim were yanked off their feet and dragged downslope, head first, toward the edge.

Steve lunged forward and caught Tim's ankle with one mittened hand; with the other, he drove his ice ax deep into the snow. Penny and Jeanne stumbled up to him and gripped his shoulders.

"Thanks," Steve panted. "Will! You all right?"

"As long as I don't look down."

"Does the edge of the crevasse look solid?"

"No—it's crumbling—" An instant later, a meter-wide belt of snow vanished and there was a hard jerk on the rope that nearly pulled them all in. Al and Tim were right at the edge now, their hands and knees digging in for purchase.

"I'm right against the wall of the crevasse," Will called.

"Can you climb back out?" Al asked.

"Lost my bloody ax. Al, can you lower another rope?"

"Can't move or I'll go in on top of you."

Penny let go of Steve and crawled the two meters to the edge of the crevasse. Lying beside Al, she tried to untie the rope looped around his shoulder. Her bearpaws were too clumsy so she pulled them off, and then the leather gloves underneath. The wool shells still on her hands were little protection, but at least she could use her fingers. Untying the coil of rope, she carefully unwound it from Al's shoulder. He grinned and winked at her.

"Good going. Now lower it to him."

Will caught the end of the rope. After a few endless minutes, he knotted it to the first one and rigged a sliding loop.

"Right. Ready or not, here I come."

If he climbed too fast, or too abruptly, he might yank the others in, or further collapse the edge of the crevasse. Penny lay across Al's back to hold him securely. She saw Jeanne doing the same thing with Steve. Tim was carefully working his elbows and knees deeper into the snow, his face set.

It took Will almost ten minutes to pull himself to the surface. As he reached the top, Al gripped his wrists and helped him over the edge.

"You've got some frostbite," Al said conversationally.

"More than that—I could hear my ears freeze. They snapped like potato crisps." Will managed a smile as he crawled past them onto safe ground. Al and Tim, relieved of Will's weight, inched backward on their bellies. Penny knelt by the edge, pulling on her gloves and bearpaws. Her hands hurt so much she wanted to scream. Instead, she looked down into the blue-black depths of the crevasse, and whispered: "Fuck you. You'll never kill us."

Long before they got out of the crevasse field, they saw the Sno-Cat prowling along its edges, looking for a safe path. When they reached it, Howie and Simon welcomed them with handshakes and embraces. It was long past noon.

"How far are we from Shacktown?" Al asked.

"Only about three kilometers," Simon answered. "Just over that rise."

"Why can't we see the masts and the drilling rig? I was starting to think we were lost."

"Masts are down. So's the rig," Howie grunted.

"Christ," said Will.

"Wait'll you see the place. We've moved all the furniture," Simon smiled. "C'mon, let's go."

The cab of the Sno-Cat was unheated, but still warmer than the outside by four or five degrees. Penny squatted against the rear wall of the cramped cab, wedged between Tim and Steve. The roar of the engine made talking difficult, but she was too tired to talk anyway. Steve caught her eye.

"You were damn brave."

"Didn't feel brave." She leaned against him and abruptly fell asleep.

5

THE GREENHOUSE

The tunnels looked about the same, though the supplies along the walls had obviously been stacked in haste. Carter Benson met them at the door to Tunnel E, where a work crew was still clearing up. His round face brightened when he saw them, though he seemed half-entranced by exhaustion.

"There you are at last. God, it's good to see you all! Everyone well?"

"We're cold and tired," Will said. "How's Hugh?"

"They told you, did they? He'll be fine if he gets enough rest. Poor guy—we may have to strap him down to make sure he gets it. Look, go and get something to eat. Then have Kate give you a quick look-over, and get to bed yourselves."

"There's too much to be done," Steve objected.

"It'll keep. Off you go now."

There were few signs of damage in the lounge and mess hall: a lamp missing, books still strewn on the floor, pictures hanging crooked. Suzy welcomed them with kisses.

"How's Terry?" Al asked her. "Howie told us he'd been hurt."

"Silly old bugger got scalded by his own soup. Katerina says he'll be all right, but his legs—his legs—"

Jeanne hugged her. "He'll be fine, don't worry."

"Oh God, if you'd seen—the skin's just gone, all raw and b-bleeding." She caught her breath and wiped her eyes. "On top of everything else he's got a damn

54

crybaby for a wife. And here you are—what on earth kept you? You all look done in. Sit down, sit down—what'll you eat?"

Katerina came in as they were eating. She looked businesslike as ever, with her dark hair neatly brushed and her white jacket freshly ironed. She studied each of them expressionlessly.

"Do your ears hurt?" she asked Will.

"Oh—a bit." He grunted when she touched one.

"A bit, eh? A lot, I think. But they will be okay. Any frostbite? Yes, everyone a little bit. And your hands? Penny, let me see. Yes. Not so good, but not bad. And you are all very sunburned. Well, I will want complete examinations right away. Al first, then Steve, then Will, then Tim. Penny and Jeanne after."

"Why not ladies first?" Tim asked.

"Ladies are tougher."

"Sexist," he muttered.

After the examinations Katerina was satisfied that there were no serious problems with most of them. Tim was surprised to learn that he had fractured his left wrist.

"Never felt a thing," he protested as she set the bone and put a cast on it. "Everything else hurt so much, I never noticed." He studied the cast with disgust. "How the hell am I supposed to work with this thing on?"

"You are resourceful; you will find ways."

Al was dehydrated, sunburned, and exhausted, but otherwise in good shape. So were Steve and Will. Penny's frozen bronchia made her cough, and her voice was almost gone, but Katerina saw nothing that a few days' rest couldn't repair. Jeanne was so tired she seemed to sleepwalk, and obviously needed rest also.

"Go to bed. And stay there," Katerina ordered them. Penny and Jeanne needed no urging, but the others simply went to the showers, changed their clothes, and dispersed to help the work teams.

"They are impossible," Katerina told Hugh when she went to see him late that afternoon. "Suicidal."

"Nonsense. I think they're wonderful." Hugh grinned evilly. "Ought to follow their example."

"Do not make me more upset, Hugh. Please."

"I'm sorry, Kate. You *are* upset."

"Yes. I worry too much."

"Well, don't. Now—unless you want to see me get up and go to work in the snow mine, bog off to the kitchen and have a nice cup of tea and a smoke with poor old Suzy."

Her smile was startlingly warm and beautiful, enough to make Hugh think it was a good job she didn't reveal it often; it reminded him of his wife's. He felt hideously lonely and impotent, lying in this chilly little room.

"Very well. I will see you later. *Don't get up.*"

Hugh lay back, staring at the ceiling and waiting for Carter to arrive with the latest report on the clean-up. His chest hurt.

Penny woke up around 2300 hours that night, and for a nightmarish moment did not know where she was.

"Pen? You all right?" Jeanne's sleepy voice was comforting.

"Yes." She could scarcely speak above a croak, and her face and hands hurt like hell. "How about you?"

"God, I ache all over. And I'm starved. Let's go get something to eat."

The bunkhouses were so quiet that they supposed everyone had gone to bed early. But when they entered the mess hall, they could hear voices in the lounge: deep, serious male voices that made Penny hesitate to intrude. There was no boisterousness, no boyishness in the rumble of the voices, not even much intensity. There was only the dispassion of men unwillingly but unavoidably in danger.

Penny and Jeanne slipped into the lounge. Almost everyone was there except Terry; even Hugh was lying quietly on a sofa. Carter Benson was standing by the blank TV projection screen, looking haggard.

". . . and that about sums up the present condition of the station. Not good, but it could be worse. Our chief concern will be repairing the radio shack and getting the transmitter working again. Hullo, kids. Have a seat.

"Any more questions? Good enough. Steve tells me he's had a chance to study the tapes from remote 12, and he can tell us just what happened up there."

There was a soft rustle in the room as the men shifted in their seats, lit cigarettes, or swigged beer. Steve got up.

"I'll keep it short. You know Tim and I have been studying earthquake swarms, and that I suspected we were in for a major quake. I thought it might even cause a surge of the ice sheet—part of it, anyway. And in the last few weeks there were signs that the quake might be coming soon. We had meltwater under the Shelf, with radon gas dissolved in it. Also, pressure-wave velocities were increasing; that's often a sign that a quake is due.

"What I didn't realize until now is that the quake and the surge created each other. You see, when rock undergoes strain it expands and opens up microscopic pores. That helps stabilize the rock. Then water percolates into the pores, and when the rock is saturated, the quake occurs. It looks now as if the ice sheet put a strain—a really enormous strain—on a series of faults on the far side of the Queen Maud Range. Tim and I are pretty sure the faults mark the edge of a plate boundary. Because there was so little liquid water available to soak down into the rock, the faults were locked, maybe for centuries. But meltwater began to form, partly from the pressure of the ice and, maybe, from the heat that the ice sheet has been slowly absorbing for the last ten thousand years. The meltwater began to soak into the rock, and when the rock couldn't absorb any more, water began flowing out under the ice into the sea. So the ice sheet made certain that any quake would be a big one, big enough to create a surge.

"According to the tapes, the quake was centered between Otway Massif and Roberts Massif, just over the mountains. It was fairly shallow—only about fifteen or twenty kilometers down."

"How strong?" Hugh asked.

"At first I thought it was about 7.5 on the Richter scale. But in fact it was an order of magnitude larger—8.4 or 8.5. Roughly as strong as the Alaska quake of '64. It's got something else in common with the '64 quake. Most of the damage done to Fairbanks was caused by soil liquefaction. The ground under the city lost its stability and flowed like thin mud. The ice here seems to have done something like that."

"Wait a minute, Steve," said Gerry Roche. "You've always said a surge would ride its own meltwater, and make more by friction."

"That's happening. But the Beardmore settled too fast—and moved too fast. The only explanation I can come up with is that a good part of the base of the ice sheet just turned to mush and carried the upper layers down the glacier valleys. No one's ever seen so much ice subjected to such a quake, but now we know that it behaves like an unstable soil."

"How fast?" Hugh said.

"We estimated that the center of the Beardmore was moving about five kilometers per hour—maybe more." He paused and looked at the ceiling. "The Beardmore is a hundred and sixty kilometers long. So it must be spilling its whole length into the Ross Sea every thirty-two hours. If the surge is widespread, and moving at the same speed, maybe half the total volume of the ice sheet could be in the ocean in two or three weeks."

"D'you know how much ice you're talking about?" Gerry asked incredulously.

"Roughly thirteen million cubic kilometers. Enough water to refill the North Atlantic."

Will Farquhar raised his hand. He looked both exhausted and excited.

"Wilson and Hollin predicted that would happen,

twenty years ago. The ice will spread out, all around the edge of the continent, maybe as far as the Antarctic Convergence."

Sean McNally interrupted. "That would make one hell of a heat sink, Will. You'd double the albedo of the southern hemisphere."

"I know."

"Hey, what's albedo?" asked Tom Vernon.

"Reflectivity," Sean explained. "If we got a new ice shelf that size, the southern hemisphere would reflect twice as much sunlight back into space as it does now."

"And that," said Will, "means the new ice shelf would be self-sustaining; it would cool the southern hemisphere enough to keep itself intact. Now is the time to invest in Brazilian coffee futures."

There was a brief burst of laughter.

"There'll be some more dramatic effects than that," Steve said. "The whole Pacific basin has probably had some bad tsunamis. You can't dump billions of tons of ice into the ocean without creating terrific waves."

Carter Benson said: "Let's stay a little closer to home for a moment. You're suggesting that the Shelf —the ice right under us—is going to move north."

"It already is."

"Then what happens to us? To this station?"

"We'll move north, too. At a guess, about a kilometer or two per day."

"That's pretty damned fast," Carter said. "At that rate, Shacktown would be out in the Pacific in a year, if the Shelf hasn't completely broken up by then."

"I don't think it'll disintegrate," said Will. "More likely the Shelf will break up into big floes—islands— with not much open space between them. The surge ice will be all broken up, but it should consolidate fairly fast. This winter the whole mess will freeze together—if the surge has slowed by then—and we'll have the beginnings of a supershelf. I expect Shacktown will be somewhere in the middle of it."

"By then we'll be evacuated," Sean said.

"Don't count on it," Steve replied.

"Oh, come on, Steve—"

"We know Erebus started erupting just before the, uh, icequake. McMurdo was in trouble, and Willy Field was being covered with volcanic ash. If the Shelf is pushing up against Ross Island, it may wipe McMurdo right off the map."

"Christ," someone muttered.

"Bruce," said Katerina, "what are our chances of making contact with McMurdo?"

"Not good," Bruce said, sitting awkwardly with his left arm in a sling. "The main transmitter is so much junk, and we really need to get the masts up again. I might be able to luck out with one of the smaller transmitters."

"And McMurdo may not be able to help us anyway," said Carter.

"What about New Byrd, or the stations on the Peninsula?" Katerina persisted.

"We might get messages through, but they're no good as places to evacuate to," Bruce said. "Too far away. And not much chance that they'd have a plane big enough to fly in and get us."

"McMurdo is still our best chance," Hugh said. "Al, I know you've earned a rest, but the sooner you can go the better."

"No problem," Al said serenely. He was sitting in a chair with his feet up on a coffee table, puffing benignly on a cigar. But to Penny he seemed drained, almost numb with fatigue.

"Good," said Carter. "Colin, how long is this clear spell likely to last?"

The meteorologist shrugged. "At least twelve hours; more likely twenty-four. But I don't know what it'll be like at McMurdo."

"I may not even have to land there," Al said. "But once I'm close enough for line-of-sight radio, I should be able to find out how they're doing. And see if they can send a plane down to get us."

"How soon can you start?" asked Carter.

"Give me four hours' sleep—another hour to check out the Otter—call it 0530 tomorrow morning."

"Al, would you like some company?" asked Max Wilhelm.

"Love it."

"Good enough," Carter said. "Then I suggest the rest of us pack it in. We've had a long, long day."

"Wait a minute," said Ben Whitcumb. He stood up self-consciously, hands in his trouser pockets. "Uh, we've been talking as if no one else on the ice has problems. What about the people at Amundsen-Scott and New Byrd? They may be in even worse shape than we are."

An uncomfortable silence fell.

"Very true," said Steve. "Any suggestions, Ben?"

"I think we ought to fly out to them as well. See how they're doing, and give whatever help we can."

Two or three people snorted with annoyance. Steve ignored them.

"I think you're right. It'll depend on the weather, and the plane. Not to mention Papa Al. But McMurdo's got to be our first priority; if it's okay, we can consider possible rescue flights to other stations before we're evacuated."

"Of course, they might show up here first," Will said. "If there's a Hercules at the pole, and they evacuate, they might stop here to pick us up. I must say I don't feel much like a rescuer just now. Much rather be a rescuee."

There was another burst of laughter, and some applause. Penny saw the men's tension vanish. —Good for Will. He knows how to cheer us up. She remembered his calm and endurance in the crevasse, and felt comforted. Carter finally ended the meeting, and everyone straggled off to bed.

Jeanne touched Will's arm as the meeting broke up.

"Hullo. Can we talk a bit, if you're not too tired?"

"Sure. Shall we go have a drink?"

"No, I just want to talk, somewhere quiet."

"There'll be no one in the lab."

The lab was still a mess; they had to pick their way over broken glass and scattered equipment. Jeanne sat down on a cot sometimes used when observations had to be made all night at frequent intervals. Will sat down beside her.

"Tell me something," Jeanne said. "When you were down in the crevasse—what was it like?"

His smile changed. "Ah. Well, it wasn't the first time, you know. But the times before, I thought I knew what I was doing. It was frightening, I'll admit. But you know, Jeanny, it was really quite lovely down there. Bloody cold, but even so—the light in the ice is the purest blue you'll ever see, and the ice seems to glow. The sky looks a long way up, and down below it's just—black. Nothing. You can't tell how far down it might go. When those bits of the edge fell in, I couldn't hear 'em hit bottom. But then I was cracking my skull on the wall at that point."

"You sounded so calm."

"Did I?" Will laughed. "After the quake, and the crash, I was getting almost used to it all—weren't you?" Then, looking around the disordered lab, he added: "This is worse, in a way. I don't even want to think about the drilling rig."

"Yes."

Will turned sideways to face her. "All right, House-mouse. What's on your mind?"

"You'll think I'm pretty stupid."

"Come on."

"I'd—I want to move in with you, Will."

He looked carefully at her. "I'll be damned. You're not joking."

"No, I'm not joking."

"Well." Will looked both pleased and alarmed. "Well. It's a lovely idea, isn't it? But it'd just upset everyone to no purpose—including me. There'd be jealousy, envy, resentment—"

"That Canadian girl last year—she moved in with Bob McCullough, and no one minded."

"Perhaps not. But it was nearly the end of the summer, and we were all about to go home." He chewed his thumbnail. "I like you a lot, Jeanny. And you like me. But you're not the sort to fall madly in love; you are certainly not madly in love with me."

"No—not in some soppy girlish way. But I do like you. And I need you. Ever since the quake, I've been—" she covered her face with her hands and leaned against him, shuddering. "Oh, Will, I keep thinking this is all a dream, all a dream. But it doesn't quit, and I'm so bloody frightened."

"Yes, yes." He stroked her curly yellow hair. Her fingers were peeling from the touch of frostbite she'd suffered. She smelled sweet and clean. "Yes, yes. I know."

"God—I feel rotten doing this to you," she murmured. "As if you didn't have enough trouble, falling into crevasses and freezing your poor ears, you've got me blubbering all over you."

Will laughed, and kissed her gently. "All right. Look. Go back to bed. In the morning, if you haven't changed your mind, and I haven't either, I'll talk to Carter about it. Maybe he can give us that empty room McCullough had."

She hugged him.

"I won't change my mind, I promise you."

"Ough, you're choking me, you brute. Now up you get. I'll walk you home, if I may."

She had been up only an hour or two, but as she slid into her bunk Jeanne knew she would have no trouble getting back to sleep. Tomorrow, once they were settled, she could tell him what she was really frightened about. He'd understand. God, he'd better understand.

Katerina Varenkova lit a Rothman off the butt of the last one, and poured herself some more brandy.

"Those things are lethal, you know," Herm Northrop remarked. His dark eyes gleamed behind his rimless glasses. "I'm always astounded to see a doctor smoking."

"Communists are brave people. And in-vul-ner-able."

"Not to our capitalist carcinogens. Nor to their own alcohol."

"You are saying I am drunk?"

"Why, I believe I am. Katya, you are drunk."

"Good. I deserve to be drunk. Since yesterday morning I have two or three hours of sleep. I am not a young girl; I cannot stay up so long. But Terry and Hugh need attention. The emergency supplies for McMurdo, I must pack them. So I stay up. I have Big Eye anyway, unless I drink brandy. Then I get some sleep, or I am no good to anybody."

"At least you're not being under-used."

"That is true. I am very busy. I will stay busy."

"Good. So will I." He raised his styrofoam cup. "To us—the workers of the world."

"To us."

It was quiet in the infirmary. Behind a partition, Terry, drugged against the agony of his burns, slept heavily. A single lamp, flickering with power surges induced by solar flares, glowed on the desk next to Katerina. Herm sat in an uncomfortable armchair, looking avuncular as always but a bit drunk as well. He regarded the lamp suspiciously.

"I don't mind the flickering," he said, "but I do worry about the reactor's electronics. The silly thing might decide to shut itself down. Or go for a walk."

She seemed not to have heard him. "Herman—what will happen to my husband?"

"I don't know, Katya. But I'm pretty sure he and the others will pull through all right."

"And why?"

"Vostok's a long way from all this, isn't it? A good thousand kilometers or more. And it sits on three kilometers of ice—goes down below sea level, if I'm not mistaken. That won't move very easily. In any case, they can fly out to Mirny Station. Good lord, with those monstrous tractors of theirs, they could *drive* out if they liked."

"Yes. That is so." She obviously didn't believe him, but she brightened a little. "Poor Vanya. He is probably worrying over me. And your wife—she will be worrying over you."

"I suppose so." He realized he hadn't thought about his wife since the quake. Toronto seemed very far away, farther and stranger than Vostok.

Penny went to the greenhouse after the meeting. The plants seemed unchanged, but after a while she noticed that a few were missing—probably knocked off their shelves by the quake. The long fluorescent day went on for those that remained, and the air held a faint scent of sweet peas despite the ventilation fans.

She got out her notepad and began to reconstruct the events of the last two days. Her hands still hurt a bit, and the right one was peeling badly with frostbite; it reminded her that what she was describing had really happened. So did the sunburn on her face, which was the worst she'd ever had.

She wrote steadily, ignoring her own doubts about the adequacy of her words to convey what they had gone through at Beardmore and on the Shelf. When she got a chance, she would develop and print the photos she had taken, but even they would fail to show the true scale and power of the surge. Maybe nothing could.

An hour passed quickly. She heard footsteps, and Steve walked in.

"Hi, Penny."

"Hi. Isn't it past your bedtime?"

"Too wound up. And Tim's snoring and talking in his sleep." He sat down on the bench next to her, his back against the table on which Penny was working. "I'm sorry—am I interrupting?"

"Nothing serious." She patted his hand. "How are you?"

". . . I'm not sure. Scared and happy."

"Mm. I can understand scared, but—"

"Well, I was pretty accurate about the quake, and too conservative about the surge."

"Uh-huh. Very expensive vindication for a crackpot theory."

Steve nodded somberly. "Yes, it is. And this is just the down payment."

"I guess so. What next?"

"Mass extinctions. A new ice age. A temporary rise in sea level of ten or twenty meters. More earthquakes and volcanism."

"Can I quote you?"

"Don't be sarcastic. It suits you too well."

"Sorry. But it isn't going to be quite that bad, is it?"

"I think it'll be very bad. Since the Roche Event, the whole planet has taken a huge dose of radiation. It's been aggravated by the solar flares, which have damn near finished off the ozone layer." He smiled faintly at the blisters on her cheeks and nose; he had them too. "The ozone will recover eventually, when the sun quiets down, but until then we'll take far more ultraviolet than we're used to. And until the magnetic field builds up again—which will probably take generations—we'll also get a lot of ionizing radiation."

"Which means increased mutation rates and reduced fertility rates, at least for land animals."

He nodded. "Bad time to be a big vertebrate. It'll affect sea life as well. But those are things we'll be worrying about a year or two from now, as the cows and pigs start dying off. It's the long-range effect that really scares me." His voice was flat and unexpressive: "The new supershelf will start the ice age. The sheer volume of ice going into the sea will cause the rise in sea level. With some help from increased melting. A rise of ten or twenty meters will drown every major seaport in the world, and submerge a good percentage of usable farmland. After a century or two the sea level will drop again as the glaciers start expanding into ice sheets. So much for Canada and northern Europe, and maybe the USSR. The redistribution of ice and water will put more strain on faults, so we'll have more earthquakes, and more eruptions. The volcanic dust in the atmosphere will help cool us down even more." He shrugged.

"Then we're finished, aren't we?"

"Nonsense—it's not the end of the world, Penny."

"Dope! I mean us, here."

"Oh. No, not that either. We may be stuck here over the winter, but we'll probably get home somehow."

"Uh-huh. How?"

"Well—weather or no weather, they'll want to know what's going on down here. By spring there may be more people in the Antarctic than ever."

She thought for a moment. "You know, no matter how bad it is out there, they'll never understand what we're going through."

"No, I guess they won't. We probably won't understand it ourselves, once we're back."

He leaned over and kissed her, tentatively at first and then with something like fierceness. There was a pleasant, faintly acrid smell to him, and she felt her sexuality waken for the first time in weeks. Her responsiveness surprised them both. After a long moment, she pulled away.

He smiled, without complacence or arrogance, and kissed her again. It was the same smile she had seen when the quake began, the smile of astonishment and delight of a man seeing the world marvelously shape itself to obey his private vision.

They made clumsy, gentle love on the greenhouse floor, between the ice and the flowers and the nodding green leaves.

6

~~~~~~~~~~~~

THE OTTER

Howie and Simon winched the Otter out of the hangar into the sunlight. The morning sky was clear; there were light winds from Grid Northeast, and the temperature was -35°C. Al went smoothly, almost absent-mindedly through preflight checkout and engine-starting procedure while Max Wilhelm squinted into the sun. Someone was up in the geophysics dome, but no one else was up to see them off.

"If we hustle, we can be back before anybody's up," Al said as he started the first engine.

"I hope we're back before *I'm* up," Max muttered.

The engines started without difficulty, and Al taxied out onto the skiway. The blizzard had blown right across it, so there was little drift; Howie's work with the D8 two days before hadn't been entirely in vain. Carrying nothing more than the two men and three fifty-kilo emergency packs of food and medical supplies, the Otter moved lightly and easily. It bumped briskly along the skiway and lifted off.

"Camera ready?" Al asked. Max nodded. In his lap was a Nikon with a 150mm telephoto lens.

"Nothing much to see yet," he remarked.

"Even so, take a picture every three or four minutes."

"What for?"

"It'll give us a better idea of what's happening to the Shelf. You should be able to get a couple of good shots in just a minute anyway."

"Okay."

Al followed the Sno-Cat tracks back to the crevasse field, and then tried to find the crash site, but it was lost in dazzle and shadow. As they flew low over the pressure ridge, Max stared down in astonishment at the abyss beyond.

"Take pictures!" Al ordered. He changed course slightly to follow the gap between Shacktown's island and the next, while Max shot a dozen frames. In some places the gap was up to five hundred meters wide; in others it narrowed to a crack one could step across, but it never entirely vanished. The depth of the gap was hard to measure: too much ice had calved off the floes. But there was one short stretch where the bottom was evidently covered with only a thin crust of bergy bits, and the cliffs rose over fifty meters to the top of the Shelf.

Max put down his camera at last. "You were very lucky," he said.

"Yeah. Sloppy good luck. I've had a lot of it." Al lit a cigar. "When I was a kid in the Navy, fresh out of training, they put me in a Search and Rescue outfit in Vietnam. We sat on a carrier offshore, keeping an eye on the traffic. Guys were going down almost every day—sometimes it'd be a fighter pilot coming back from the North, but usually it was some artillery spotter or a gunship crew. We figured we had about half an hour, tops, to get to them before the VC did.

"Well, one morning a Huey gets shot down. Four guys in it. We go roaring off, another chopper and me, to collect them off a hillside, and darned if they haven't come down in the middle of a North Vietnamese regiment. I get close enough to see about two hundred guys racing up the hill, and all of a sudden I've got no oil pressure. Some of those guys could really shoot.

"So I veer off and manage to bring the chopper down about three kilometers away, almost on top of some U.S. Marines. The other chopper goes in, lands next to the Huey, and takes a mortar round. Killed instantly. I never did find out what happened to the guys in the Huey."

Something in Al's tone made Max turn to look at him. "Did you feel bad about not being able to save them?"

"Oh yeah, for a while. A couple of months. I took some dumb chances. You start feeling guilty, y'know? And you think your buddies might think you're scared. I wasn't. Heck, I didn't even believe in the law of gravity. Anyway, I got over feeling bad. But that's what I mean by sloppy good luck."

"Perhaps your real luck there was in outliving your feelings. I think about those days, and all the feelings come back as strong as ever."

"You weren't in the war, were you?"

"No, no. I was still in Europe. But I remember one day in 1968, in the spring. I was only twenty-three, just a year out of university, without a job, and it looked like the revolution was about to happen in Paris. In Vienna in those days, we were all radicals. So I decided to go and join the revolution. I spent the night before I left with a very sweet girl, a Swedish girl named Kaj. In the morning she walked me to the station, and that is what I remember: the smell of the air that morning, and the sound of our footsteps—it was very early, there was no traffic yet—what her hand felt like in mine. She said to me, 'You'll have such a good time you'll never come back.' And I said, 'Nonsense, I'll be back in the fall.' But she was right, you know? By fall I was in New Zealand. I never saw her again, never wrote to her, but I think of her almost every day and it makes me feel as happy and young as I did that morning. And sad also."

"That's the longest speech I've ever heard you make," Al smiled. Then, after a pause, he said: "I know what you mean. With me, it's the last time I saw my daughter. May 11th, 1975—her birthday. She was four years old."

They flew over several more immense fractures, as

well as huge fields of seracs—the topographical night-mare caused by intersecting crevasses. Some were like miniature mesas, steep-sided and flat-topped; others rose from shadowed crevasses in razor-edged blue spires and ridges. In one place, they could see the edges of a fracture part, close again, and grind together in a cloud of wind-driven snow and ice fragments. The noise of the collision, even a thousand meters below them, was a blend of booms and shrieks that drowned the roar of the Otter's engines.

"There's Erebus," Al said after a while. "The smoke up ahead."

The flat horizon was beginning to blur, lost in gray-ness. Off to the left, the peaks of the Royal Society Range glittered sharply. Al tried to raise McMurdo, without luck.

"It's snowing," Max said. "—No, it's ash." A fine, grayish-white powder was swirling off the windshield. He clicked off the remaining shots and rapidly re-loaded the camera.

They passed a few kilometers Grid West of Minna Bluff, a narrow promontory jutting into the Shelf from the mainland. Scott, Wilson, and Bowers had died not far from here; they would scarcely recognize the Shelf now, it was so contorted and shattered. Just beyond Minna Bluff were Black and White Islands, clearly visible despite the growing haze. The Shelf had ridden up on the islands' Grid North shores, and in some places had already moved over the lower slopes to the far side, like a wave breaking over rocks. In the lee of the islands the ice had parted, creating long leads of dully gleaming water.

Now Erebus was dead ahead, its slopes obscured by ash and smoke. From its crest a black-and-white pillar of smoke rose boiling into the sky, only gradually yielding to the wind and smearing across Ross Island and the distant edge of the Shelf. Orange flares of light spurted through the smoke, and in three or four places lava streams picked their way delicately down-hill. A deep, unending roar filled the air; the stink of sulfur was strong. A few kilometers Grid West of Hut Point Peninsula, beyond the site of Scott Base, a steep black cone rose from the shoreline. It was well over a hundred meters high, and like Erebus it was pouring smoke and ash into the sky.

"A satellite cone," Max shouted, pointing to it. "God —it must be growing faster than Paricutín did."

The new volcano was wrapped in mist; as the Shelf moved up its black slopes, ice melted, vaporized, and then froze again as ice fog. But when the wind was right, they could see a red flare at the cone's summit, pulsing like arterial blood and bright enough to throw shadows down the smoking slopes. In this world of white and blue, black and gray, the flare looked oddly artificial: crimson and orange here were the colors of man-made things.

"Did you see Outer Willy?" Al yelled.

"No." Max was taking photos with tense deliberation.

"We must be too far Grid West. There's Inner Willy."

Something bounced off the windshield, and a moment later a hailstorm seemed to have struck them. The ice below was shattered into countless crevasses, and was a dirty gray color Al had never seen before. Willy Field swung below them, recognizable only by the geometric patterns of its buildings. The iceway and skiway were gone, buried under ash and crumpled by the moving ice. Al saw the blackened remnants of a big Hercules, its nose tilted into a crevasse, its spine broken.

Visibility was down to perhaps three kilometers in the direction of Ross Island, but Al could make out enough of the shoreline to see that Willy Field had moved well down McMurdo Sound, past Hut Point. He circled twice, trying to raise someone on the radio. At first static was the only reply; then a blurred voice sounded in his earphones.

"Otter Five-Three, Otter Five-Three, this is McMurdo. Do you read me? Over."

"McMurdo, this is Otter Five-Three. I read you. Over."

"Is that you, Al? Harry Rasmussen here. Are we glad to hear from you! What is your position? Over."

"Harry! Hi, old friend. We're over Hut Point, coming over McMurdo Station for a look around. Are you guys okay? Over."

"Al, there ain't no station. There's about fifty of us up here in the old reactor buildings on Observatory Hill. The ice is only a few hundred meters downslope from here. Over."

It grew very dark, like late twilight. Far away to Grid North, Al saw sunlight gleaming on the Shelf, but it seemed like a vision of another world. This world was thunder and night and the stench of sulfur.

The rattle of ash and stones on the fuselage intensified, and Al began to fear for his engines. Even a pebble striking a prop or being sucked into the engine could knock them out of the air. He stared into the gray mist below as they swept low around Hut Point.

Harry had been right. Where the station had stood, there was now only a jumble of seracs and pressure ice that ran far up the shore and piled thickly around Observatory Hill. At the edges of the ice Al and Max could see brightly colored debris: a smashed orange tractor, a pastel-green wall torn from some hut, a twisted panel of aluminum, all of it jammed between the ice and the rock. Gusts of wind, rising off the Shelf, stirred up clouds of ash and snow.

The Otter curved around Observatory Hill less than two hundred meters from its summit. Through the gloom they could just make out the main reactor building, its flat roof drifted over with ash. Three or four men stood in the lee of the building, their orange parkas unreally vivid; they were waving frantically.

"Harry, do you need any food or medical supplies? Over."

"Christ, yes! Repeat, yes. We've got more than twenty people hurt, some pretty bad. And not much food. Over."

"Well, we'll try a drop. I'll circle twice and drop three bundles. I'm sorry, but they'll have to come down at once. I can't risk more runs. Over."

"Great, Al. Just great." He coughed for several seconds. "Air's pretty bad down here. Hey, how's Shacktown? Over."

"Okay, so far. Harry, where's everybody else? Over."

"Most of 'em flew out right after the eruption started. After our planes reached New Zealand, the Kiwis sent down every big plane they had. They had to land at Outer Willy—we ferried people out there by helo. Boy, Al, you've missed some of the best fucking flying anybody ever saw. Over."

"I believe it. So what about you characters? Over."

"I don't know, Al. There hasn't been a helo from Outer Willy since yesterday afternoon. Tell you the truth, we're scared shitless. Some of our guys may not make it if they ain't taken outa here pretty damn quick. Over."

Al pressed the button on his mike and then released it. He didn't know what to say. Then he turned to Max.

"They need our medical stuff. On the next pass, I need you to drop all three bundles. Snap 'em to the static line. Then slide the door open and make sure it's secured. I'll yell when the bundles should go."

"Good." Max unstrapped himself, carefully stowed the camera, and went into the passenger compartment.

Visibility was getting worse. Something the size of a grapefruit arched across the Otter's path; Al said "Uh!" as he watched it vanish below the nose of the plane. Even a graze by something that big could kill them.

The Otter made its final approach. Judging from the clouds swirling around the reactor building, winds at the surface must be coming from Grid Northeast at about thirty kph. Al adjusted course and speed.

Wind howled into the flight compartment, sulfurous and filled with a gritty, bitter-tasting dust. *"Now!"* Al screamed. He glanced back over his shoulder into the passenger compartment and saw the last of the bundles slide down the static line and out the door. Max made his way to the door and slid it shut; when he got back into his seat, his cheeks were streaked with frozen tears.

Al banked the plane and watched the bundles drop. One had lost its chute and streamed in, a tiny orange speck that vanished into the ash-encrusted ice. The other two drifted down to land within half a kilometer of the reactor buildings, upslope from the ice.

Al thumbed his mike. "Okay, Harry, your supplies are on the ground and I see some people going out to retrieve them. Uh, we lost one bundle. Sorry. Anything else? Over."

"Thanks, Al. Listen, any chance of coming back with your old Huey? At least we could get some of the worst cases off of this goddam hill. Over."

"Wish to God I could, Harry. But I wrecked the helo right after the quake. Over."

"Drunk again, huh? Well, old buddy, thanks for everything just the same. And keep in touch. Even a postcard now and then. Over."

"Will do. And when they do fly you guys out, don't forget to mention that we're still out on the Shelf. We need rescuing too. Over."

"Okay, Al. Good luck to all of you. And thanks again. See you in Christchurch next week. Over."

"I'll buy you a beer, Harry. Over and out." Al turned to Max. "Ready to go home?"

"Almost." Max pointed at the shrouded bulk of Erebus. "I'd like to look at the crater. Would it be safe?"

"Sure, if we stay upwind and fairly far away."

He turned the Otter back over the Shelf and across McMurdo Sound, then followed the mainland coast Grid South toward the open sea. The glaciers of the Royal Society Range, at least, did not seem to be surging, but most of them were relatively small and unconnected with the continental ice sheet.

The plane rose until, at four thousand meters, it was above the summit of Erebus. Though the air was very thin, it was at least clean. Al squinted up at the pillar of smoke.

"We should be able to get in fairly close if the wind doesn't change. But I'll just make one pass."

"Good. One will be plenty."

Al dropped the Otter's nose a few degrees, and the plane began a long, shallow dive. As they neared the crater, he found himself keeping his eyes on the instruments. The smoke and ash had seemed to be rising as slowly as from a small campfire, but at close range the ejecta were moving with terrifying speed. The sound was almost as bad as that of the surge, and shook the whole aircraft.

Now they were so close that the entire field of vision was a moving, mottled, gray-black wall, billowing in oily clouds. The Otter banked steeply to the right, giving Max a clear view of the crater. He snapped photos rapidly for several seconds. Then, above the constant roar there came a sharp detonation, followed by a flash of red-orange light and a shock wave that nearly flipped the plane over. Al fought to steady it, and then looked down.

About a quarter of the rim of the crater was collapsing, sliding down into the lava of the caldera far below. In a fiery parody of calving bergs, the avalanche overwhelmed the caldera; glowing jets of lava shot up around the edges of the smothered pit. Thousands of tons of ice, carried down in the collapse, flashed into steam, rose as clouds, and fell again as snow. The crater grew even darker; the roar subsided to a deep, almost subsonic growl.

Max turned from the window and gestured frantically toward the Shelf. Nodding, Al put them on a course straight for home. He tried to find Observatory Hill as they passed over it, but it was lost in fog and smoke. The new volcano was still erupting violently in irregular bursts.

"The worst hasn't happened yet," Max shouted.

"The main crater has blocked itself up. More lava will find its way out through the satellite cone. And it's too close to those poor buggers on the hill."

Al stared out at the broken blue-white surface of the Shelf as it slid slowly under them. As he watched, the ice darkened and turned pink: the sun, though fairly high in the sky behind them, was shining redly through the dust of Erebus.

"I should've tried to find a landing site," he said. "There must have been someplace to put the plane down. *There must have been.*"

"Al, Al, if there had been they'd have told you. There was no place. Not for an Otter."

Al checked his bearings and glanced at the mountains off to the right. "We've passed Outer Willy again. Even if no one's there, there must be a helo. I could fly back in that and at least get out the worst cases."

Max looked at him thoughtfully for a moment. "That's up to you, Al. Just remember the people at Shacktown too. Without you, the rest of us are as good as dead."

"I know what I'm doing." He turned the plane in a long arc until Ross Island again stood on the horizon before them. "Outer Willy's probably moved about as far as Inner Willy has," he said. "So we should see it a couple of kilometers Grid South of where it ought to be. Keep your eyes open as we come up to Black and White Islands."

"Right."

This time Al found the field without difficulty. The Shelf around it had fractured into a rectangular island about five kilometers long and three wide. The skiway and buildings had received a light dusting of ash, but otherwise the field seemed undamaged. Three bright-orange helicopters stood near the GCA hut; not far away was a Hercules, evidently poised for takeoff but unmoving. Ski tracks showed that aircraft had recently left; but the ash on and around the Hercules was ominously undisturbed. Nor were there any signs of life: no steam vented from the huts, and nothing moved. Al buzzed the field at fifty meters, then climbed a little and circled.

"Nothing. Everyone's left." He shook his head, uncomprehending. "How could they? How could they?" Then he lined the Otter up with the skiway and prepared to land.

Max began to feel afraid. They were coming in from Grid North, so rapidly and steeply that it looked as if they might crash into the abandoned Hercules. Both men were watching the skiway intently, so the flash on the horizon was only peripherally visible, an orange flicker that might have been the glint of sun on metal. Max looked up.

"Al, pull up. Pull up fast."

Al stared at him, then followed his gaze.

The satellite cone—and most of Ross Island—were invisible. Over the Shelf moved a shockwave of blackness, traveling at a speed half that of sound. Above it, a ragged black cloud was climbing through the murky sky, spreading as it rose. Whatever light might be inside the cloud was lost in its oily thickness, dense enough to make the smoke of Erebus seem like a morning mist. Within sixty seconds, the new cloud had risen to an altitude of ten or twelve kilometers, and at its top was perhaps ten kilometers wide. It blotted out the sun; Ross Island and the Shelf around it sank into darkness.

Al caught his breath, unable to understand how so much matter could be moved so high, so far, so fast. For a dizzying moment he lost all sense of scale and distance: surely it must be a smaller, closer, slower eruption. Instinct alone made him level off, climb and bank steeply over the deserted huts of Outer Willy, turning for the safety of Grid North.

"The satellite cone—" Max whispered, and then the shock wave hit. The plane shook violently, rose, and began to nose down. Al wrestled the controls, knowing that they might be flipped over if he didn't bring the nose up.

Suddenly it was past. The air was still turbulent, but the Otter was again behaving like an aircraft and not like a leaf in the wind. Far off to the right and left, sunlight glistened on ice, but for many kilometers around them the Shelf was darkened by the shadow of the cloud. A second shock, less violent than the first, jolted the plane and was gone.

"The satellite cone," Max said again. "The satellite cone. It must have collapsed to well below sea level—water flooded in—like Krakatoa." Like a sleepwalker, he got out of his seat and moved into the passenger compartment. From the windows at the rear, he watched the cloud rise and spread and sink back into itself. He watched for a long time, until the plane finally outran the shadow of the cloud and the sun glared serenely into his eyes. Then he went back to his seat and sat in silence.

Halfway back to Shacktown, as they were passing over a heavily fractured region, Al saw a long dark streak cutting at an angle across a field of high sastrugi. They went down for a closer look, but Al knew what it was: a crashed Hercules.

There was not much left of it but a spray of blackened metal fragments half-melted into the ice. Only the tail section was intact, and the letters RNZAF were clearly visible. Debris was strewn for a couple of kilometers; Al circled the site three times at low altitude, but no survivors could be seen.

"Wouldn't expect any in a hit like that," he mumbled. "Well, Max, that was our rescue party."

"How do you know?"

"They were on a course for Shacktown, and they went down less than thirty-six hours ago—there was hardly any drift on the wreckage."

"Why did they crash?"

"I don't know. Maybe some mechanical problem—they probably tried to set down for repairs and plowed into the sastrugi. Something like that." His voice shook a little, and he looked sadly down at the crash for one last time. "They deserved better than that."

Penny and Steve lay amiably in each other's arms in their new cubicle. It was at the end of the bunkhouse, next to the Dolans', and as private as any room in the building could be. Still, they talked in murmurs—partly to avoid disturbing Suzy, but mostly for the pleasure of it. It was the evening of Saturday, February 9.

"It hurts when you kiss me," she complained.

"I'm sorry. Can't get affectionate without getting rough." He kissed her again, very gently. "Poor old Pen. That's the worst sunburn I've ever seen."

"Yours is almost as bad."

"I know. We must look like a couple of amorous pomegranates." His nose was blistered and peeling, and his cheeks—what little had been exposed between his beard and his sunglasses—were almost maroon.

"Oh well," he sighed. "It must be the same for a lot of people."

"Why—the ozone?"

"Yes." He was silent for a few seconds. "Millions of people must have been badly burned by now—worse than we are. Especially in the tropics, but everywhere. God knows what's happening to animals and insects." He touched her hand very gently. "Frostbite hurt?"

"A lot." She pulled the hand out of their sleeping bag. "Jesus, look how it's peeling. Steve—are we really going to have to winter over?"

"Looks like it." He didn't sound disturbed. "Max's photos made it finally seem real to me—even more than watching the surge." The still-damp photographs of the Ross Island eruption had been the subject of a long, grim meeting in the lounge that evening.

"But they've got to send more planes," Penny said.

"Mm—not so sure," he mumbled sleepily. "They'd have to fly in dangerous weather, with no radio, and no good landing zone between Christchurch and here. The Kiwis have sent one plane and it hasn't come back—for all they know, it picked us up and crashed at sea." After a moment, he went on: "They probably have enough to worry about at home, and not just the ultraviolet. The surge must have caused some bad tsunamis, and maybe the volcano did too. Every coastal city in New Zealand would be hit—just about every city around the whole Pacific, for that matter."

"Well—they'll still want to know what's happened down here."

"Eventually. Anyway, so what? It's not so bad. We're through the worst of it, and there's plenty to study." He grinned. "You'll get a book out of it."

"If it's not ancient history by the time we get out of here." She felt annoyed by his acceptance of their predicament: it seemed unpleasantly stolid and passive of him to regard the disaster as just something to be studied. But it was so good to be in bed with him, with no need for long underwear, that she swallowed her resentment almost at once.

Next door, Suzy heard the rhythmic creaking of the bunk and felt an annoying stab of envy and self-pity. Poor old Terry was lying in pain in the infirmary, and all she could think of was sex. She put in her earplugs, turned over, and went unhappily to sleep.

"It'll sound unromantic, Jeannie, but I'm worried about something," said Will.

"You're afraid I'll get pregnant?"

"Yes."

She chuckled and patted his face. "Don't worry, love. Don't worry."

Something in her voice surprised him: a mixture of fright and amusement. "What—"

"I'm already pregnant."

"Are you, now."

"Please don't be angry with me, Will. I couldn't stand that."

"Oh, I'm not angry, but I must say I'm impressed."

"Impressed by what? Women do get pregnant, you know."

"Not and march twenty kilometers over the Shelf from a wrecked helo."

"They do if they've got no choice." But she felt flattered.

"Why on earth didn't you tell us?"

"I thought I could manage all right. And I didn't want to be fussed over, or make everyone feel they ought to slow down for my sake."

"Och, you're mad. Mad. The worst machos are always women."

Later, Will drowsily said: "And who's the father?"

"No one here. A fellow in Christchurch. Old school chum. We spent a couple of days together before Christmas."

The firewatch patroller clumped down the corridor. Don Treadwell's death-rattle snore changed pitch.

"Damn silly of me, really. I missed my period, and felt ill, and all that kind of thing, but I figured I might just as well get on with my work and worry about everything else when I got back home. And then—everything happened, and I got scared. And I needed you. Does that sound awful?"

"No. I think I'm complimented. But you'll have to tell Katerina, you know. And no arguments—you'll do what she tells you. You know—if we don't evacuate—if we're stuck here till spring—when is the baby due?"

"September, I reckon."

"You could be the mother of the first native-born Antarctican."

Hugh Adams lay staring in the darkness. —Easy does it. Get upset and you'll only take longer to get back on your feet. And you're enough of a nuisance now.

He went on staring at the dark until he fell asleep.

Ben Whitcumb sat up drinking beer and reading in the lounge. Gordon Ellerslee, half-drunk, swayed in from the mess hall.

"Hey there, ol' Benny Rabbit, whatcha readin'?"

"Some mystery."

"You look kinda depressed. Something eatin' you?"

"No, no. Just tired. Too tired to sleep."

"Whatcha think of all this sex and lust and general wick-dipping we got going on around this here scientific research station?"

"I've got enough to worry about without that."

"You sound kinda pissed off, Benny Rabbit. I'll bet you're jealous as hell."

"What are you talking about?" Ben snapped.

"Big Red, who else? Man, just think what she must be doin' to old Steve right about now. Mm-mm! Makes you wish you'd gone in for seismology, doesn't it?" Gordon laughed. "Gotta admit Steve sure knows how to make the earth move, eh?"

Ben closed his book and stood up. "Thanks, Gord. You're making me sleepy already."

A few hours later, Colin Smith sat in the dome, watching the sun slide above the horizon. The sky was cloudless, but brilliantly tinted in shades of red, pink, orange, and yellow. The ice and the mountains reflected the colors, which changed almost from second to second. The dust of Erebus was already widely scattered across the Ross Sea.

The sun, rising through crimson haze, was a sharp-edged yellow disc. There were mottled regions all over it, of a darker yellow with a tinge of brown. Colin watched in silence, absently aware that his whole body was shaking. He had never before seen sunspots with his own eyes, unaided.

All through the morning of February 10, tremors ran through the station. Nothing was damaged, but Howie had a bad moment in Tunnel D when all the newly stacked crates and drums began to sway, and a miniature snow flurry fell gently from the frosted steel ceiling. Howie stood still for two minutes, his breath steaming in the light of the swinging lamps overhead. Then he went on down the tunnel to the lounge.

Al was sitting in an armchair, his slippered feet

on a coffee table. He had had thirteen hours' sleep, a hot shower, and a big breakfast; now he was contentedly lighting his first cigar of the day.

"Morning, Howie."

"Hi, Al. You're lookin' pretty goddam comfortable."

"If you're through in the hangar, I won't be comfortable for long."

"Well, she'll fly. But she looks like you tried to fly her through a mountain. Pretty bad up there, eh?"

"Yeah. Yeah. We were lucky; could've sucked a big chunk of pumice into one of the engines. Well, you go find Carter and tell him we'll be on our way in a few minutes."

"Steve goin' with you this time?"

"Yeah. Max says he's bored with flying."

"Gonna take Penny too?"

"Don't I wish!" Penny yelled from the mess hall. She appeared in the doorway; her face was peeling, there were blisters on her nose, and her thick red hair was tied back in a disintegrating bun. "I've been put on permanent KP."

Steve and Carter came into the lounge; Steve was carrying a stereo camera and a portable videotape recorder. He glanced at the monitor screen in the corner of the lounge. "Still looks good outside."

"Yup. Let's get going."

"Have fun, you two," Suzy called from the mess hall. "Don't be late. No stopping off for a quick drink on your way home."

Al shook his head sadly. "You know, the Antarctic used to be so nice before they let women in." He blocked Penny's punch and said to Steve: "See you in the hangar in ten minutes."

Penny wanted to kiss Steve goodbye, but knew better; it wasn't done in front of others, least of all in front of men without women.

He waved at her. "See you, Pen."

"See you." But she felt irritated at his casual attitude; if he couldn't kiss her, he could at least look as if he wanted to.

The day was almost cloudless, but there was an autumnal quality to the sunlight as the Otter lifted from the Shelf. Even now, at noon, the sun was not far above the horizon, and the dust of Erebus dulled the sky like a faint overcast. Al set a course for Axel Heiberg Glacier, about fifty kilometers Grid West. It was one of the shortest and steepest glaciers in the range, and would get them up to the polar plateau in the least time.

Though both men kept earmuffs nearby, the deafening noise of the surge seemed to have abated. The Shelf below was broken in long, surprisingly straight lines, and the gaps between the islands seemed to Al to be larger than they had been yesterday. The most dramatic change, though, was along the coast: the landward edges of the islands were already six or seven kilometers offshore. The steep sides of the islands were up to fifty meters above the chaos of broken surge ice that filled the gap between Shelf and land.

"Looks like the worst pressure ice anyone ever dreamed of," Al shouted over the growing roar from below. Steve nodded and put the videotape camera to his eye.

The glaciers were moving fast, carrying immense blocks of ice into the sea faster than the Shelf could move. This ice piled up in the gap until in some places it actually rose higher than the surface of the Shelf. Steve watched one raft of ice, a hundred meters wide and five hundred long, nose under another berg and lift its landward end right into the air. For a few seconds, it loomed over the jumbled surface like a monstrous cannon aimed at the mountains; then it snapped of its own weight and fell in a glittering cloud. The surge ice absorbed it and moved onward; from the air it reminded Steve of the "chaotic terrains" in photographs of the surface of Mars. He smiled without amusement: precise and elegant physical laws were the cause of this chaos, as spectacular a proof of entropy as one could hope for—or fear.

They reached the mouth of Axel Heiberg and began

to gain altitude. Here the noise was still bad, and they were grateful for the earmuffs. The glacier—the one which Amundsen had ascended on his way to the pole in 1912—looked like a rapids filmed in slow motion. The surface at its center was moving at a stately ten to twelve kilometers per hour, and almost as fast along its edge. On either side the mountains were slashed and scarred, and most of the snow on them had already avalanched to merge with the glacier. The crevasses seemed narrow but deep, contorted into elongated U's by the speed of the surge. Occasionally the moving ice struck some obstacle below the surface, and bulged upward for a few seconds before riding over it. The air was almost windless, and very little of the glacier was obscured by the kind of ice haze they had seen on the Beardmore just after the quake.

Neither man spoke for some time. The Otter climbed hundreds of meters in a few minutes, following the rising terrain. As they approached the ice falls near the top of the glacier, Steve swore in surprise: where the ice had once hung still as it imperceptibly crept down the cliffs, it now shot out, sending great blue-white chunks, some the size of apartment buildings, toppling free to drop a hundred meters.

Then they were over the plateau, and the mountains slipped behind them. Ahead was a white emptiness, little different from the Shelf but far vaster. Both men were familiar with the plateau, and at first it seemed unchanged. Then Al pointed straight ahead.

"It's moving."

Steve had been taping a crevasse field; when he took his eye from the camera, he saw that the field had no end. The plastic ice far below the surface was too compressed to break, but the upper layers were shattered into thousands upon thousands of narrow parallel crevasses. Here and there they crushed themselves out of existence as the ice struck some buried mountain. The noise was like constant distant thunder; the sun seemed slightly dimmed.

"It can't be like this all the way to the pole," Steve yelled. Al looked at him and shrugged.

Steve slumped in his seat and shook his head. Al checked his bearings and altered course a few degrees; a shaft of sunlight fell through the side window and gleamed on the instruments. Steve watched dust particles sparkle in the sunlight and then vanish.—*We get a few moments in the light, and we see some marvels, and we go into the dark again.*

They almost missed Amundsen-Scott Station. The surface at the pole was heavily crevassed, and there were few visible vehicle tracks. Al spotted a dark blur and flew lower. Near the top of a wide crevasse was a twisted mass of metal that retained a vestige of geometry: the remains of the geodesic dome that had covered most of the station.

"They must have gone into the crevasse and then burned," Steve said. "Go around again."

The Otter orbited the pole six times, just a few meters above the broken surface. There were no signs of life, and no place that looked safe enough to land on. Apart from the dome, a few tractors and a collapsed rawin tower were all that was left of the station. Steve taped their last orbit and said: "Let's go home." He stared down at the ice, watching its shadows lengthen as the sun dropped lower.

Al looked at the altimeter. It should have read 3500 meters; instead, it indicated they were only 3100 meters above sea level. The ice sheet had already dropped here by 400 meters.

"Going to be a long winter," he said quietly.

7

LAPUTA

The day after the Otter's flight to the pole, the weather went bad again for three straight days. When it cleared, Al and Max made a quick sortie back to Ross Island. The explosion of the satellite cone, they found, had created a steep-walled new bay on the Grid Northeast shore of the island; Scott and McMurdo Bases were gone. Hut Point Peninsula was now linked to the rest of the island only by a blackened isthmus of steaming rock. The Shelf went on forcing its way into the new bay, where it melted and froze again in a self-sustaining blizzard. The floes—ice islands, really—of the broken Shelf were deeply drifted with ash and pumice, especially downwind of Ross Island.

Part of the Shelf was bypassing Ross Island and moving down McMurdo Sound into the open sea. Al thought he saw Outer Willy, far to the Grid South, but since Erebus' main crater was erupting again he didn't dare fly close enough to make certain that he'd seen the abandoned airstrip. But he and Max both saw Scott's old hut near the shore of the Sound, intact despite its nearness to the volcano. There was no sign of life anywhere—on the island, the ice, or the mainland.

On their return, Al and Max made two low-level circuits of Shacktown's own island. It was relatively small, a rough rectangle slightly over a hundred kilometers along its north-south axis, and about fifty kilometers from east to west. To the Grid South, the island drove against a somewhat larger one; to the Grid East and West, ice-choked leads separated it from other islands. To the Grid North, a squarish island about fifty kilometers on a side was welded to Shacktown's island by a seam of pressure ice; beyond was the surge ice, still pouring off the continent.

That was the last of the reconnaissance flights. Gerry Roche and Howie O'Rourke took one of the Sno-Cats out on February 12, and traversed the island from one end to the other. They found surprisingly few crevasse fields: pressure from the surge seemed to have crushed most of them, creating treacherous sink-holes and sastrugi-like surfaces. Wherever one island touched another, pressure ridges were growing; at the Grid South end, the ridges were up to thirty meters high and three hundred meters wide. The noise of the grinding, splintering ice kept the men from venturing too close to the island's edges, especially since here, at least, there were many new crevasses. They set off some seismic shots that indicated the island was still in one piece, and collected ash-filled snow samples.

By the time they returned, on February 15, Shacktown was beginning to resume its routine. Steve fussed over his instruments in the seismographic tunnel; Carter and Gerry watched the slow, slow growth of the earth's new magnetic field, and the odd behavior of solar protons striking the atmosphere in almost straight lines. Colin Smith watched the weather and compiled twice-daily forecasts that were usually bad and usually accurate.

Penny was working in the mess hall the night after the Sno-Cat returned. Around 2030 hours, just as the seminar was getting organized next door, Steve and Max wandered in, talking animatedly. She envied them their energy.

"Hi, Pen. Are we too late for supper?"

"I saved some for you. What took you so long?"

"We've been looking at Gerry and Howie's snow samples," Steve said.

"They have a lot of debris from Erebus," Max added eagerly. "We should get even more as we move north." He took a little plastic bag from his shirt pocket and drew from it a damp paper disc, speckled with fine gray-brown dust. "This is volcanic dust. Very characteristic of Erebus. And if there is this much in the snow around us, then there must be—God—tons and tons, millions of tons, in the atmosphere downwind of Ross Island. Maybe even more than Agung put into the atmosphere in—when, '62? '63?"

Penny poured three cups of coffee and followed them to their table. Max went on:

"If the dust in the stratosphere is on that order, it will be a bad winter in the southern hemisphere."

"Because the dust will block the sunlight?" she asked. He nodded.

"It'd be bad even without the dust," Steve said. "The surge is still going on. According to Gerry, we're moving four or five kilometers a day—at that rate, we'll be past Ross Island in six months. And the ice islands north of us will be cluttering up the Southern Ocean almost as far as New Zealand."

"Six months from now will be the end of August," Max said, shaking his head. "By then the surge will be all over, and we'll slow down as sea ice forms, yes?"

"Maybe. But not for long. The surge ice will take months to reach equilibrium." He rubbed at the peeling skin on his nose. "It'll be interesting to see what happens."

Max laughed. "You know, in German we have a word, *Schadenfreude*. It means—mm—taking pleasure, joy, in disaster."

"That's our boy," Penny agreed. "Jolly Jeremiah. I don't know which is more disgusting—your pessimism or your scientific detachment."

Steve didn't rise to the bait; his eyes were fixed on the photomural of a New Zealand sheep station. Penny waved a hand in front of his face, and he blinked.

"Sorry—I wasn't listening."

"God, you're hopeless. You know, you remind me of those scientists in *Gulliver*. The ones on the flying island, remember? They had to be hit with bladders to bring them back to reality."

"The Laputans." Steve smiled. "Yes, I guess I am a bit like that. A lot of us are. They drove their wives crazy, didn't they? The women used to sneak off the island to have affairs with ordinary men."

"Some girls have all the luck," Penny said.

Later that evening, Max suggested at the seminar that their ice island be officially named Laputa. Hugh then offered Lilliput for the island Grid North of them, and Blefuscu for the one Grid South. The islands to the east and west were called Lagado and Balnibarbi. "But I won't hear of anyplace being named Brobdingnag or Glubbdubbdrib," Hugh warned.

Jeanne and Will wasted no time before examining the ruins of the drilling hut with Gordon Ellerslee.

"Pretty bad, eh?" Gordon observed.

"But not impossible," Jeanne said. "The roof needs reinforcing, but the rig doesn't seem out of alignment. Gord, how long would it take to get us back in business?"

He gaped at her. "Jeez, I dunno. Ten days, two weeks, maybe. But why bother, Housemouse?"

"We need that hole open again. We can't just sit and do nothing, and the hole will tell us a lot about what's going on—won't it, Will?"

"It will."

"Shit," Gordon mumbled. "By the time it's ready, we'll be pulling outa here. Why should Reg and Simon and me bust our asses for nothin'?"

"Och, it'll not be for nothing," Will assured him. "We may be here longer than you think. And if we *are* evacuated, it'll be that much less work next year. Leave that roof like that and the shed'll be full of snow in three months."

"It ain't worth it, Will. I got better things to do."

"If you can't do it, Gordon, just say so. We'll understand." Jeanne looked levelly at him; he rubbed his scarred, broken nose.

"Aw, I can do it, all right. But it'll be a waste of time."

"Good old Gordie!" Jeanne chuckled, hugging him. "What would we do without you?" Looking past Gordon's arm, she sent Will an exasperated glance; this kind of manipulation disgusted her.

The look turned to faint alarm when Gordon showed reluctance to let her go, and she avoided his eyes when he freed her at last.

The radio shack was repaired, though it remained chillingly drafty. Bruce and Roger spent days rebuilding the main transmitter with cannibalized parts. The antennas, however, were a major problem, and only a clumsy jury-rig could be set up during the impossible weather of mid-February. The radio operators tried to transmit to the outside, despite Gerry's warning that it would be easier to bounce a brick off custard than a signal off what was left of the ionosphere.

The technicians went from one job to another in a flurry of swearing and grunting for a couple of weeks, while the scientists gathered data and happily quarreled about their findings. On the night of February 20, Gordon ate supper with Reg, Simon, and Tom Vernon. As they ate they grumbled about the futility of their work.

"Well," said Gordon at last, "we can piss and moan all we want to. Why the fuck don't we *do* something?"

"Any suggestions?" Simon asked.

"Yeah. Tell you what—pass the word there's a meeting tonight in the machine shop. Just the techs. The scientists'll be busy impressing each other in the lounge —won't even notice. But we gotta get our asses in gear if we want to get outa this dump."

An hour later, most of the techs were in the machine shop, a large hut tucked in a corner of the hangar. Powder-fine snow glittered under the hangar lights, somehow driven into the station by the winds of the latest blizzard.

"We got a problem," Gordon began. "The fucking scientists think this mess is the luckiest thing that ever happened. They're already counting on a couple dozen Nobel Prizes or something. They all talk about how much they want to be rescued, but they're working their asses off—"

"Working *our* asses off, you mean," Simon interrupted.

"Really," Gordon nodded. "Really. Steve Kennard and a couple others are already saying we're sure to winter over, but they aren't losing no sleep over it."

"Losing sleep other ways," Simon said. No one laughed. Like most men in the Antarctic cold, the techs had little sex drive, but it was still frustrating to see other men living with women.

"Well, hell," Gordon went on. "What are we supposed to do? Just work all day and hope to God this fucking overgrown iceberg don't break up under us?"

Tom Vernon rubbed his red beard until it stood out from his face like a misplaced halo. "How are we supposed to get out of here, Gord? On skis?"

"Shit, I'm just a goddam stupid driller. But I know we got a good plane here—" He gestured out the window toward the Otter. "And the best fucking pilot on the ice, and plenty of gas. Why can't Al fly out toward New Byrd, set up a fuel dump, and then hopscotch out to the Peninsula? Jeez, it ain't *that* far. From there he could fly to South America if he had to."

Tom sucked his teeth. "I don't know—sounds pretty dicey. He'd have to make a couple of trips to set up a dump—come back—fly out again—find the dump—refuel—go on without knowing what he was in for. Papa Al—he's not crazy, Gord."

"Shit. Some guy flew all over the ice in a little Cessna or something, must be twenty years ago now. If he could do it, so can Al."

"Then, uh, why doesn't Al suggest it?" asked George Hills.

"He's fucking shellshocked, that's why. He don't volunteer for a goddam thing any more. But he'll go if he's asked."

"It's worth trying," said Simon. "Beats sitting here with our thumbs in our bums and our brains in neutral."

"Let's wait—a few days anyway," Tom suggested. "God—what if he went off—got pranged somewhere—and then they got down here from Chee-Chee to fly us out anyways. I'd feel pretty—pretty awful about something like that."

"Think how you'll feel if we all starve together," Gordon shot back.

George ponderously shook his head. "It's too early for that kinda talk, Gord. Let's wait, like Tom says. If it really looks like the scientists want to stay no matter what, then we can go talk to Hugh."

"I'll give 'em a week, and that's all," Gordon said. He looked grimly around the room; each of them nodded.

It was longer than a week. In a delayed reaction to the icequake, there was a rash of practical jokes. "Regular bloody silly season," Suzy growled to Penny, who only nodded. When male inanity was so patent, it hardly bore discussing. Someone planted a large frozen trout in the snow mine; the outside monitor in the lounge was wired into the videotape player, making it seem as if the station had been transported to the American West. But most of the gags were less imaginative: sugar in the salt shakers, ice in sleeping bags. Ben Whitcumb's clothes vanished one morning while he was housemouse; they turned up next day in a corner of the hangar, frozen in a solid lump.

The day after that particular gag, Hugh was up

early having a cup of coffee in the mess hall with Penny. No one else was up yet.

"Haven't seen much of Ben lately," he remarked.

"He hardly ever comes out of his room these days unless he has to," Penny said. "Sometimes Max has to take him a sandwich because he won't even come in for a meal. It's that schmuck Gordon."

"Mm. Riding him pretty hard, isn't he?"

"You ought to do something about it, Hugh. Gordon bothers Jeanne too."

"Ah, that I didn't know. How?"

"He's always making eyes at her, touching her, that kind of thing. Not when Will's around, though."

"Well . . . he's always chaffing you, too."

"That's just it!" Her own intensity startled her. "He clowns around with me, and it's a pain in the ass, but it isn't serious. With Jeanne it's—groping. Scary."

"Does Will realize it?"

"I don't think so, no." She cut him off before he could speak. "And don't just groan about the folly of letting women on the ice, Hugh. Gordon's the problem, not Jeanne or me. He'd be a problem anywhere."

Hugh said nothing for a moment. "Well, we'll sort it out."

That same morning, Carter Benson sat down in Don Treadwell's closet-sized office and carefully went over the food inventory Don had prepared for him.

"This doesn't look good," Carter said quietly.

"I know," Don agreed. "There just isn't enough food for a whole winter and maybe part of the spring. Not unless we go on rationin'."

"Then we will, of course. But it'll depress everybody. Might even be dangerous. Damn it, you need four thousand calories a day just to cope with the cold, let alone do anything in it."

"In winter? We won't be doin' much outside work."

"Fair enough. Unless there's an emergency."

Don's smile was wry. "An emergency? Here? You're jokin'."

Carter's round face went pink. "Yes—silly thought, isn't it? What could happen? Anyway, thanks for the inventory. I'll talk to Hugh about it. You coming to breakfast?"

"Sure."

Each of them sat down to scrambled eggs, a small steak, fried potatoes, baked apples, and four slices of whole-wheat toast with butter and orange marmalade. Halfway through his meal, Carter lost his appetite. He went on eating until his tray was empty; it seemed to take a long time. Don, usually a hearty eater, was equally slow. When they took their trays back to the kitchen, they stopped and watched Penny and Suzy scraping mounds of food off other trays and into the garbage hole.

"What's the matter with you two?" Suzy smiled. "Something you et?"

Steve went quietly into Hugh's room. It was a little larger than the bunkhouse cubicles, but was cramped and cluttered by filing cabinets, crowded bookshelves, and a desk strewn with old printouts. Hugh was sitting up in bed, a notebook propped against his knees.

"Hullo, Steve. Have a seat."

Steve settled into the swivel chair by Hugh's desk and crossed his arms. Hugh noted the uncertainty in the gesture. "How are you feeling these days?" Steve asked.

"Much better, thanks. I wish I didn't tire so easily. But each day's an improvement on the last. How's life treating you?"

"All right. I'm working too hard, but it's all fun."

"You know, I do believe you're already wintering over."

"Shouldn't I be?" Steve smiled. "Don't tell me the plane's waiting outside!"

"There's bugger-all outside. . . . Look, old son. You seem to've adjusted faster than most of us to this pickle we're in; are you aware of the morale problems we're developing?"

"Yes. There's not enough public bitching."

"Mm! A lot of it going on in private, though. Have you given any thought to what it would be like to winter over with most of us living like monks and some of us—"

"God, yes."

"Terry and Suzy—no problem, everyone's used to them, and Terry's still in sick bay anyway. But these romances you and Will have got yourselves involved in—they're bothering some of the fellows."

"I know. Ben Whitcumb can hardly stay in the same room with Penny. And Gordon's jealous of Will, and takes it out on Ben."

"Ah. . . . D'you suppose you and Will could, mm, suspend your liaisons till we're out of here?"

"I can't speak for Will. For myself, no."

There was silence. Steve went on: "First, I like Penny very much. We've been through a lot together."

"Fair enough—"

"Second, and more important, if we stop living together somebody else—maybe two or three of the men —will be tempted to try moving in on her. The same would be true of Jeanne if Will left her. If we start fighting over women, there really will be a murder."

"Well, then, what do we do?"

"We keep as busy as possible. And we get Gordon off Ben's back."

"I think I can manage that."

After dinner that evening, Hugh called Gordon in to discuss some of the technical aspects of repairing the radio mast. He listened attentively to Gordon's complaints about the time required to get the drilling rig operating again.

"I can see your point," Hugh said. "But I think you should press on with the rig before starting on the masts. After all, we might get through with the jury-rig antenna Bruce is using now, and the Kiwis might even fly in without a radio contact. The bloody weather makes working on the masts almost impossible anyway. But the drilling rig is really important, and I think you've done miracles with the repairs so far. Nobody else could've done so much, so fast."

"Well, it's what I know how to do," Gordon shrugged, agreeably flattered. "And, uh, if you think the rig's important—"

"Christ, yes."

"—Okay, don't worry about a thing. Another two, three days and we can start opening the hole again. Then I can go to work on the masts, and they shouldn't take more'n, oh—two, two and a half days."

"By God, that's the best news I've had in a long time. Excellent!"

"Say, Hugh—long as I'm here—you thought any about maybe sending Al out again? Like to New Byrd Station?"

"No—certainly not in this weather. Al hasn't suggested it, has he?"

"No, no. Just an idea some of the guys been kicking around."

"Mm, well, I'll certainly think hard about it now you've raised the suggestion. By the way: there's one more thing I wanted to get your advice on. Bit delicate, and I think you're the fellow to take care of it."

"What's that?"

"Some of the younger fellows are giving our American friend Ben a bit of a rough time. They look up to you, you know. Think you could put the brakes on 'em? Just a little?"

"Well, uh, well—"

"You're an old hand on the ice. You know how important good morale is—now of all times."

"Sure, Hugh. Sure, I understand. Well, I'll do whatever I can. Just leave it to me."

"Good. That's a load off my mind."

The drilling rig went back into operation, but getting even one of the masts up was impossible: during the last week of February and the first week of March,

Colin's instruments never recorded still air. Average wind velocity was 62 kph, with a high of 180, and the temperature never rose above -30°C. There was almost no respite from the resulting whiteout. In such conditions, outside work had to be done in five- or ten-minute bursts, followed by half an hour of rest and warmth.

Hugh invented scores of new inside jobs, and kept everyone too busy to worry. The nightly seminars became twenty minutes of brief weather reports, duty assignments, and idle speculation about the outside world; those who were still awake after that rarely lasted long enough to get in more than an hour of even the station's most time-honored leisure pursuits, drinking and Monopoly.

On the evening of March 10 the seminar was even more perfunctory than usual; the only surprise was Colin's prediction of clear weather for the 11th. As everyone was about to adjourn for a beer or bed, Ben Whitcumb stood up and cleared his throat.

"I've got a suggestion," he said.

Carter was presiding. "Sure, Ben. Let's hear it."

"We seem to've given up reconnaissance flights since the second trip to McMurdo. I know the weather's been pretty bad, but we've had a few good days. Colin's just said we're due for another good one tomorrow."

"Where d'you wanna go, Ben—Hawaii?" Ray Crandall asked.

"How about New Byrd?" Ben answered. "It's not all that far—"

"Eight hundred kilometers," Al interrupted through a cloud of cigar smoke.

"Okay. That's in range; the Otter's got extra fuel capacity. New Byrd—it's a big station, three times our size. If they're okay, they'll have plenty of fuel for Al to get back on."

"And if they're not okay, I can walk home," Al muttered.

"Say, that's a pretty good idea," Gordon said.

"Y'know, Al could even refuel and go on to the Peninsula. Then we'd be sure of getting evacuated before winter."

Though Gordon had been leaving him alone lately, Ben didn't look pleased with his new ally. "Hey, I'm only suggesting a reconnaissance, not a flight across the whole doggone continent. For all we know, New Byrd is wrecked, just like Amundsen-Scott. But there *might* be some help for us, or help we can give them."

Carter looked uncomfortable; Hugh, sitting up on a couch, impassively stroked his mustache.

"Ben," Steve asked, "what's the best result you can foresee from this flight?" His face was as inexpressive as Hugh's.

"Uh, I guess a quick evacuation, if they're intact and they've got a big enough plane. Or radio conditions could be better there, and they could call in help for us."

"What if the station's wrecked, but there are survivors? Does Al bring them back here?"

"Sure."

"I just wish I could've got those guys off Observatory Hill," Al put in. "Sure I bring 'em back, Steve. What's your point?"

Steve turned to Don Treadwell. "How's our food holding out, Don? Have we got enough to last until spring?"

"Well now, that's kind of, ah, hard to say, you know?" Don looked at Carter, who nodded slightly. "If we stay at normal rates of consumption, we will be out of food by the end of September. And we won't be eatin' well in August."

"Suppose we got eight or ten new people?" Steve asked quickly.

"Then we are out of food almost two months earlier. The middle of winter."

"Steve, are you suggesting that we just forget about helping anyone who needs help?" Al asked.

"No, I'm not. But we'd better be aware of the consequences."

"Steve sounds like a convert to Dynamic Self-Reliance," Carter remarked dryly. There was a flutter of laughter. "Ah, he has—he's raised a point I've been meaning to bring up soon anyway. We're going to have to start rationing. It's a hell of a note, but it's the only way we're likely to get through to spring."

"The implication," Ben said, "is that you don't want Al to fly anywhere if he might bring back inconvenient people."

"Oh, Christ!" Carter snapped. "Don't be pigheaded. If there were a *hundred* people at New Byrd, we'd take 'em all, and you know it. And we'd eat the bloody sweet peas in the greenhouse if we had to."

"Carter's right, Ben," Steve said. "The problem with a flight is the risk of losing Al and the plane."

"Great!" snarled Gordon. "We got a plane, but we can't use it. That makes sense."

There was a moment's silence before Hugh spoke. "There'll be no flight to New Byrd. The risk is too great for the benefit we might get out of it. And now I suggest we adjourn."

That night, Penny picked a fight with Steve as they lay in bed.

"You didn't need to cross-examine the poor jerk. You could've just said what Hugh did."

He lay very still beside her in the darkness. "Ben was getting support from Gordon, and Gordon represents almost half of the people here. He could have talked the rest of us into the idea, before we all understood what we were getting into."

"I still think it was crummy of you."

Steve turned away from her, and she automatically moved with him to keep close to his warmth. It was hard to stay combative when her breasts touched the taut, smooth skin of his back, but she worked at it.

"Pen, you don't understand. Ben's idea is a good

one. But it's too risky. If we knew there were survivors at New Byrd, I'd volunteer to go with Al to help load 'em aboard. Gordon doesn't give a damn about that; he just wants to get out, and Ben's suggestion was a smokescreen for him."

"Well, what's wrong with getting out, may I ask?"

He sighed. "Even if Al could get all the way to the Peninsula, and then get in touch with home, there's no chance now that we could be reached until September or October, especially with this weather and no radio. Then we'd be stuck here with no plane and no pilot; what if a real emergency breaks out during the winter? How could we get anyone out?"

"You're talking complete bullshit. First, you don't *know* that we can't be reached until spring. Hell, it isn't even winter yet, and they've been making winter flights down here for twenty years. Second, this *is* a real emergency. How could things get so bad that we'd have to send Al for help? And if they did get that bad—like the island was breaking up or something—what chance would he have of getting anywhere?"

"Okay, love," he answered slowly. "Pretend you're a hotshot pilot in a Hercules, sitting up in New Zealand at Harewood. You know there's a couple of dozen people three thousand kilometers away who need rescuing. You don't know exactly where they are. You can't contact them by radio. You have no idea what the weather's like anywhere between New Zealand and the South Pole. Your compasses are all cockeyed. Your plane's electronics go bonkers now and then when another solar flare hits. And you and your crew have flown in the Antarctic before, so you know what you're getting into. Are you going to roar off to the rescue?"

"If I had the balls God gave my grandmother, I sure would."

Steve guffawed, turned over, and hugged her.

"You don't get off that easy," she said. "There's some other reason why you don't want to send Al."

"Two reasons. The first one you won't like. I don't

want to leave. At least not till spring." He paused, as if choosing his words carefully. "There's too much to learn here. And the risks of wintering over aren't *that* high. I think most of the scientists feel the same, but we don't talk about it much. The technicians want to get the hell out, and I don't blame them, but we've got an opportunity here that'll never come again, and I don't want to miss it if I don't have to."

"I think that's fine, Steve, but I don't like watching you manipulate everyone just so you can stay and play with your seismographs."

"The second reason is Al," Steve went on, ignoring her. "He didn't say much tonight, right? He'll go if he's asked, but he doesn't want to. The poor bastard's exhausted—and he's the one who's responsible for us. Not Hugh, not Carter, not anyone else. If Al makes a mistake, we're finished. Tired men make mistakes."

". . . Okay. That I'll accept."

Thinking of Al made her think of all of them, of their fragility and transience. She could feel the strength in Steve's arms as he held her, and remembered how that strength had sustained her in the long walk from the helo. All that strength could be mocked and annihilated by the blind violence of the ice and the wind.

Bad weather seemed to have settled in for good. Day after day, snow and high winds made outside work difficult or impossible. Howie and Gerry tried another traverse, but bogged down in soft snow within three kilometers of Shacktown; it took them three days to dig out their Sno-Cat and crawl back in a near white-out.

Daylight was going swiftly now. They would lose the sun completely in mid-April, though for some weeks after that there would be a long twilight until the sun sank well below the horizon. People reacted in different ways to the approach of winter. Some, like Suzy, seized any chance they got to get outside in daylight, even if the sky was overcast; others, like Ben, retreated to their cubicles to read, sleep, and wait for the next day to come. Gordon Ellerslee did some quiet plotting.

On the afternoon of March 22, Al and Howie were doing some maintenance chores in the Otter's flight compartment when Tom Vernon climbed aboard.

"Say, Al—when you get a minute—some of the guys want to see you—in the machine shop."

"Got a poker game going?"

"No—just want to ask you something—any time you're free."

"Okay, give me ten minutes."

Tom tramped out and Al turned to Howie. "Any idea what it's about?"

Howie nodded his dark, shaggy head. "I think they want you to go to New Byrd."

"Oh, for gosh sakes. Well, let's get this finished first."

A few minutes later they got out and walked across the oil-stained ice floor of the hangar to the machine-shop hut. Most of the station's techs were there, crowded into the far end by the door that led down to Tunnel D. Gordon was sitting behind a desk, leaning against a wall solidly papered with old *Playboy* and *Penthouse* gatefolds.

"Hi, Al. Howie. You guys want a beer?"

"Sure," said Al. Howie shook his head, and leaned silently against a filing cabinet. Someone found Al a chair, and he settled into it across the desk from Gordon. Simon handed Al a bottle of Kiwi Beer.

"We been talking things over, Al," Gordon began. "And we all think something's gotta be done about getting us outa here."

"Uh-huh."

"It's nearly winter. Pretty soon we'll be stuck in this shithole till October, maybe longer. Hugh said the other day we shouldn't try for New Byrd, but he doesn't have any other ideas. Anyways, we figure the old man's just doin' what Carter and Steve tell him to do. Like he isn't really himself these days, you know?"

Al swigged his beer.

"So we figure it's time we decided things for ourselves. The scientists wanna play with their toys, and if that means *we* gotta risk getting killed, they don't give a shit."

"Hear, hear," said Simon.

"Anyways, what we wanna do is, go to Hugh and tell him he's relieved of his job, and we'll have a committee take over until we're outa here. Uh, the first thing the committee would do, is authorize you to take the Otter to New Byrd and maybe to the Peninsula."

Al smiled. "Uh-huh."

"Colin says we're due for another break in the weather. Maybe forty-eight hours, starting sometime tomorrow. You and Howie been keeping the Otter in good shape, right? Shit, it's worth a try—we'd be crazy if we don't give it a try when we got the chance."

"Just about sure to be our last chance, too," Simon added.

"Really!" Gordon agreed. "Now or never. It all depends on you, Al. Y'know, I bet you're itching to fly again after bein' holed up all this time, eh? All you gotta do is say you'll go, and we'll tell Hugh."

There was a long silence while Al finished his beer.

"You're talking to an old Navy man," Al said with a burp. "But you're suggesting I join in what amounts to a mutiny."

"Now, just hold on—"

"You hold on, Gordon. Everybody here signed a contract with CARP, and that means everybody agreed to accept the leader CARP appointed. That's Hugh, and Hugh said no flight to New Byrd."

Gordon stood up and leaned across the desk; he loomed over Al like a tree. "Goddam it, Al, this is life or death, not some picky little contract problem. We sure want you on our side, but if you don't want to go along, we'll fucking well *make* you go along."

His eyes locked with Al's for an instant. An instant later, Al's beer bottle flew past Gordon's ear and shattered against the wall behind him. Gordon flinched and turned automatically; turning back, he found Al standing in front of the desk. Al slapped Gordon twice, the second time hard enough to knock him off balance. The Canadian crashed to the floor behind the desk.

Al turned slowly, looking coldly at each of the men. No one moved.

"The party's over," Al said, his voice thick with anger. "As far as I'm concerned, this meeting never happened. But if you guys pay any more attention to this . . . idiot, you're as stupid as he is." He jerked a contemptuous thumb at Simon, who looked almost as stunned as Gordon. "Get him on his feet."

When Gordon was unsteadily upright again, Al looked up into his face. "Don't ever threaten me again, Gord. Or anybody else."

Gordon nodded slowly. He had bitten his tongue when Al slapped him, and blood glistened on his lips.

Al went through the door into the cold porch, and down the steps to Tunnel D. Howie, after giving Gordon a glare of disgust, followed. One by one, the others left quietly until Gordon and Simon were alone in the machine shop.

"Jeez," Gordon mumbled, "the old fucker's really fast."

That evening, Will and Jeanne sat on the bed in the infirmary, watching Katerina light a cigarette.

"You are indeed pregnant. And you say conception was about three months ago?"

"Almost to the day," Jeanne nodded. In her baggy pants and sweater she looked no different, but her face was a little fuller.

"Over twelve weeks. Why did you not tell me sooner?"

"I—didn't think I'd have to. I thought we'd be back in New Zealand by now, and then—one thing led to another." She looked embarrassed. "I'm sorry, I should have, I know."

"You realize we are likely to be here until perhaps October or November, on short rations."

"Yes."

"Under the circumstances, I recommend you have an abortion. You have already endangered yourself enough. There is no need—"

"I understand, Katerina. But I'm not having one."

"Ah. Why do you decide this?"

"Well, I sort of like being pregnant. I feel really super, at least now. And I'm dying to see what the baby will be like."

"That is absurd and trivial. You endanger yourself and everyone else, including the fetus."

Jeanne laughed. "After all we've gone through, we're not going to be wrecked by a little baby, are we?"

Katerina rubbed her face tiredly, put out her cigarette, and looked thoughtfully at Jeanne and Will. The girl was obviously the stronger of the two, though perhaps she didn't realize it; Will had obviously known of her pregnancy for some time, yet they hadn't come to Katerina until Jeanne had decided to. Despite the childish flippancy in her remarks, Jeanne was a tough young woman who knew her own mind.

"I think you are making a mistake, but I will do all I can to, to—shrink the mistake. We must work out a diet for you, and exercise plans, and I would like you to come to see me twice a week at least."

"Whatever you say," Jeanne grinned, and Katerina smiled back.

Someone came running down the corridor from the lounge, his big, booted feet making the floor shake. Roger Wykstra swung open the door, so hard that it struck Will's shoulder a painful blow. Roger ignored Will's surprised protest.

"Katerina—we got contact with Vostok. Your husband wants to talk to you."

8

VOSTOK

The lounge, mess hall and kitchen were deserted; everyone had headed for the radio shack as soon as they heard the news. Roger almost had to force a path for Katerina through the crowd.

Carter Benson and Al Neal were standing by the transmitter, firing questions which Bruce relayed. The answers were faint but clear, in heavily accented English. Bruce broke off when he saw Katerina.

"Here's your wife," he said into the mike. Then, to her: "You know how to use this?"

"Yes, yes." She held the mike tightly. "Ivan? Vanya?"

"Hello, Katya," he replied in Russian.

"Oh, it's so good to hear you! Is everyone safe?"

There was a staticky pause. "I don't know. I was just telling your friends—most of the station was evacuated by tractor two weeks before the catastrophe. We don't know if they reached the coast, or what's happened at Mirny. Five of us stayed behind to close down the station. They were going to fly us out, but no plane arrived."

"Ah—and everyone there?"

"Vitali Alexeyevich and Nikolai Mikhailovich are dead. The magnetics lab collapsed in the catastrophe. At least it was quick for them."

"And yourself? Who is with you?"

"We have some frostbite. Yevgeni Pavovlich is the worst off; Kyril Matveivich is the healthiest. I'm in between. Your friends say they will try to fly here to get us, but I don't think they should. Half the airstrip is gone. There are crevasses all around us."

"Vanya—if there is a hope, they'll do it. Oh, I—I don't know what to say. I'm so happy I want to cry."

"Katya, we're losing your signal. Can you still hear me?"

"Yes, just barely. Do you need to say anything more to the leader here?"

"We will be grateful for his help, but only if there is no risk to his people. Weather here is clear and cold, -60 degrees. If they do fly in, it should be soon. Shall I repeat?"

"No, I heard you. Vanya, I love you."

"I love you."

His voice faded. Bruce tried to renew the contact, but it had vanished.

Katya turned and embraced Carter. "Oh, he is alive, alive!"

"Isn't it wonderful," Carter laughed. "Wonderful. Al, did you get the information you need?"

Al nodded. He turned around at a ring of intent faces. "Let's go talk in your office for a minute, Katerina."

As they entered the office, Katerina glanced at the clock on her wall and realized that it had been less than ten minutes since Roger had come running down the corridor. A little absently, she wondered what had happened to Will and Jeanne.

"It feels so strange. Like a dream, you know?"

"I know. I'm really happy for you, Katerina."

"A drink! Would you like some brandy?" she asked brightly.

"Love one—a little one. Thanks. I shouldn't even have this one if I'm going to be flying in the morning. Look, Katerina. We'll get the Otter ready tonight, and we'll leave first thing tomorrow. Promise me one thing."

"Yes, of course."

"Don't get your hopes too high. I may not be able

to get there. Or I could get there and not be able to land. I'll do everything I can. But it may not be enough."

She put her hand on his. "I understand. I understand."

It was almost midnight when Al and Carter went to Hugh's room, which was quiet and chilly after the noisy bull session they had just left in the lounge. Hugh, looking better than he had in weeks, sat up in his battered swivel chair. He smiled at Al.

"Dicey business, this flight," Hugh said. "How d'you plan to get there and back?"

"Varenkov says they've got plenty of JP4 in one of their storage huts, so we should be able to refuel. Just in case we can't, I'll take six or seven drums along in the passenger compartment."

"Fair enough. Is the Otter up to a flight like this?"

"Yeah. But I'm going to need a lot of JATO bottles. At 3500 meters, the Otter takes off like a crippled brick."

"Okay," said Carter. "What can we do to help you get back?"

"Keep the TACAN switched on, and pray that I can pick it up. And set up some signal fires along the airstrip. We'll be coming back at night, almost for sure."

"You'll need at least a couple of the chaps to help you," Hugh said. "Any preferences?"

"I'd rather do it alone, Hugh."

"Out of the question."

"Then just one. No more."

"It ought to be a scientist," Hugh said. "This may be the last trip we make over the continent; pity to overlook the opportunity."

Al laughed. "With friends like you, the scientists don't need enemies. All right. Steve again?"

"I'd prefer Will," Hugh said. "He'll understand what the ice is doing."

"Jeanne's not going to like that."

"No doubt. Well, he'll jump at the chance. Go and ask him. Anything else?"

Al shook his head slowly.

"Good. For heaven's sake, get some sleep and leave the mechanics in peace tonight."

Will and Jeanne were sitting in their cubicle, talking quietly, when Al knocked on the door, opened it, and walked in.

"Hi. Will, you want to go to Vostok?" They both gaped at him. "Hugh said you'd love to."

"Good God," Will muttered. "Hadn't thought about it—other things on my mind. It'd be great fun, but—" He looked questioningly at Jeanne.

"Don't ask *me* to make up your mind for you," she said firmly. "I know that old male trick."

Will spluttered with laughter, and kissed her. Then he looked up at Al. "What time?"

"About 0830. Sunrise will be just before 0900, and we'll need all the daylight we can get."

When Al was gone, Jeanne reached out and touched Will's face with both her hands. "You bloody bugger, you'd better come back alive if you know what's good for you." She pressed her fingertips into his cheekbones and kissed him hard.

The hangar faced Grid South, so that its doors would be in the lee of the prevailing winds off the continent. When the doors groaned open the next morning, the sky was a wild array of reds and oranges that turned the surface of Laputa to a glowing ochre. There was steady 10-kph breeze from Grid Northwest, and some drift across the skiway. Floodlights illuminated the mouth of the hangar, where the Otter was being winched out.

"Looks like good weather," Will yawned. "We're in luck."

Al grunted. When the plane finally stood outside the hangar and the doors shut behind them, he studied the dawn sky for a long minute. Then he handed Will a clipboard.

"Let's go through the starting procedure, okay?"

Will stared at him. "You must know it better than you know your name."

"Yeah, well. This is no time to forget something." Al sounded embarrassed.

"Good enough; glad to oblige." Will snapped on an overhead light, coughed, and recited:

"Parking brake."

"On."

"Pilot's static selector."

"Normal."

"Radio and electrical equipment."

"Off."

"Circuit breakers."

"In."

As the checkout went on, Will felt a sting of anxiety. Was Al losing his nerve? He pushed the thought out of his mind by concentrating on the list. It seemed to take a long time to reach the last item.

"That's it." Will looked expectantly at Al, who nodded and took a deep breath.

"Okay, let's see if this thing wants to go." Al dry-motored the right engine for five seconds. Then he waited for a minute until the battery was warm enough to permit starting. He held the start switch at RIGHT and watched the oil pressure slowly rise. When gas generator speed had stabilized, he moved the engine fuel lever to ON. The engine accelerated to a normal idle; Al released the start switch. Oil pressure steadied and the CAUTION light went out. An ice fog began to gather around the aircraft.

He repeated the procedure for the left engine, checking to make sure he had forgotten nothing. Warm air began to flow into the flight compartment. Will watched Al, trying not to seem obvious about it.

The Otter taxied out onto the skiway. Someone up in the dome waved to them; Al waved back. The plane accelerated between the long rows of empty fuel drums, tilted, and took off. Al set a course on Grid 50° and lit a cigar.

"Something the matter?"

"Yeah. I'm scared. Kind of late to develop a fear of flying."

"Do you know something I don't know?" Will asked.

Al laughed. "It'll be okay. I didn't get much sleep last night—makes me a little slow, but I'll be all right." He shook his head. "It hasn't been a good year for old Antarctic fliers."

He looked out to the left; the first light was glowing on the peaks of the Queen Maud Range, surprisingly far away. "Hey, we really have moved, haven't we?"

"You're right." Will glanced down, but the Shelf was still too dark to be seen clearly. "Laputa must be getting close to the Ridge."

"Guess so." The Ridge was a range of submarine hills that divided the Ross Sea into two relatively deep basins beneath the Shelf; in places, the Shelf was grounded on it. Will had studied the effects of that grounding during his first summer at Shacktown, three years before.

Neither man spoke for some time. Dawn broke, and the sun began its brief traverse along the Grid South horizon. The surface of the Shelf seemed unusually rough in the low-angled light; even small sastrugi threw long shadows, and crevasse fields looked grotesquely sharp. The sky was clear, but long streamers of cloud flew from the mountains across the broken islands of the Shelf.

"Look at the bloody pressure!" Will exclaimed as they neared the Shackleton Coast, not far from the Beardmore Glacier.

"What's wrong?" Al stared at the gauges. "What's wrong with the pressure?"

"Sorry—I meant the pressure ice. I've never seen such ridges. They look like mountain ranges." He lifted the videotape camera to his eye and shot thirty seconds' worth.

Wherever two islands were in contact, their edges were crumpled into steep ridges for hundreds of meters on either side, with crevasse fields running at right angles to them. In one place, Will saw that part of a ridge had disappeared as the submerged sides of two islands had crushed each other to bits, creating a kilometer-long chasm whose bottom was lost in darkness.

A few minutes later they sighted what seemed to be a real island rising from the Shelf just a few kilometers Grid South of the Beardmore's mouth. It glittered, white and blue, presenting an almost sheer face to the sun.

"What's that?" Al asked. "There's no island here."

"Not sure," Will said. "Must be two or three hundred meters high."

"Want to get a closer look?"

"Yes, please."

The Otter banked to the left and descended a thousand meters as it neared the island. They were still several kilometers away from it when they realized it was growing, rising higher into the air every moment while avalanches of shattered ice fell in lovely plumes like waterfalls down the island's vertical face. The rumble of the avalanches could be heard over the engines as the Otter leveled off near the crest of the island and flew parallel to the enormous cliff. Drifting snow and falling ice masked much of the cliff face, but it did not look like the side of a tabular berg, and the island itself was too narrow to be one.

"It's a grounded island, being pushed right over!" Will shouted.

"What?"

"Pull away to the right, fast!"

Even as the Otter banked, the island disintegrated. The cliff fractured and toppled in hundreds of places almost simultaneously, falling in a blinding white cloud that spread out over the Shelf at well over 100 kph. In less than three minutes, the island was only a mass of rubble, from which a few spires of ice rose here and there.

To the Grid North, beyond where the island had been, was the surge ice. It stretched away to the distant mountains, sparkling in the morning sun like quartz crystals. It had hills and valleys, patches of drift and serac fields that went on to the edge of vision. In some places it had overrun the Shelf, crushing or drowning some islands and sliding beneath others that rose until they broke under their own weight.

The Otter climbed again, until the Shelf and the surge ice shrank to a black-and-white jigsaw puzzle; they crossed the coast at Richards Inlet, about thirty kilometers Grid East of the mouth of the Beardmore. The Otter followed Lennox-King Glacier up into the Queen Alexandra Range, crossed the Bowden Névé, and then went up Law Glacier to the polar plateau. Everywhere the ice was surging, though less rapidly than Axel Heiberg had done a month earlier. The drop in the level of the ice made the terrain strange to Al: too many new nunataks, unfamiliar crevasse fields, and dagger-like ice thrusts. He scarcely recognized the Sandford Cliffs; facing the plateau, their steep black slopes had been almost buried by the surge. The cliffs receded under the starboard wing. Ahead was a glittering nothingness.

Al, mistrusting his compasses, shot the sun and got a good fix on their position while Will taped long stretches of the polar plateau.

"It's moving here as well," Will said. "The ice looks like the tapes that Steve brought back. Just seracs and crevasses and more seracs. . . . How are we doing?"

Al was plotting the plane's fuel consumption on a "howgozit" chart. "Better than I expected, but not as well as we should be. The fuel drums are too darn heavy."

"Bloody nuisance. Varenkov said they've got lots of JP4; no reason to carry our own."

"Maybe not. But if their fuel's contaminated, we could spend a long time filtering it."

"That's a thought. God, how are we going to land if Vostok's as chewed up as all this?" Will gestured toward the plateau.

"We'll manage."

The sun crept along the horizon, sometimes dimming behind banks of clouds. The plateau was an irregular mosaic of blues, grays, blacks, and whites; only around the occasional nunatak could it be seen to be moving. The ice-free slopes of the nunataks had a raw look to them, as if their sides had been scoured. Will looked at one nunatak through binoculars, and sucked in his breath. He took some telephoto shots and then studied the peak until it disappeared behind them.

"The surface is dropping," he said. "The surge was a good two hundred meters higher than it is now."

"That's almost as much of a drop as there was at the pole," Al said.

"You know, I begin to think that we've missed the worst of the surge. The Shelf acts like a buffer—slows down the ice and piles it up." He pointed to the horizon ahead. "No ice shelves to speak of out on that coast. The surge would go straight into the ocean like—like a kid shooting off the end of a slide. And there'd be a hell of a lot of it. The thickest part of the ice sheet is between here and the coast. . . . God help the poor buggers at Mirny."

The ice sheet seemed flat, but in fact it sloped steadily upward like a shallow dome hundreds of kilometers in diameter; Vostok was near the top of the dome. To maintain their height above the surface, they had to keep climbing, and Al watched their fuel consumption rise. The howgozit looked less promising. After shooting the sun again, Al calculated the amount of fuel they would have when they reached Vostok.

"Twenty liters."

"We could land somewhere and refuel from the drums," Will said.

"If we can find somewhere, I'm all for it," Al answered. "But it's bad down there. I'd hate to risk it, especially at this altitude. We might not get back into the air unless we used our JATO bottles, and I have to save them for Vostok."

"What then—take a chance, or go home?"

Al looked at his watch. "If we can find a place to land in the next ten minutes, we will. Otherwise we turn around or we dump the drums. And hope there really is enough JP4 at Vostok."

The surface below showed no clear space longer than a hundred meters. After seven minutes, Al looked questioningly at Will.

"We can't turn back, Al."

"I know. Okay. If we get rid of the drums, we should gain another twenty minutes' flying time."

"Good enough." Will pulled on the hood of his anorak, tied the drawstrings under his chin, and pulled his gloves on. Then he went into the passenger compartment.

All but four of the seats had been removed to make room for the drums, which were lashed down on their sides. There were eight of them, each weighing close to a hundred and fifty kilos. Will edged around them to the door, slid it open, and secured it. The wind made him squint, and he stepped back quickly. With the wind chill factor, the temperature near the door must have been close to -100°C. He moved cautiously around the cabin until he stood opposite the door, with the drums in front of him. Working awkwardly in his gloves, he unstrapped the first one and rolled it toward the door. It was much harder to move than he'd expected; the plane was at five thousand meters, and the air was thin.

Leaning back against the wall, Will heaved against the drum with his boot until it rolled heavily out the doorway and vanished. The Otter bucked slightly. He unlashed another drum and repeated the process. By the time half the drums had been dropped, he was panting hard and trying not to breathe too deeply. Al came back for a moment to check on him.

"Pooped," Will gasped.

"Yeah. Catch your breath and finish 'em off. We're running into a little weather."

"Right. Be done in a minute."

But it was more like five minutes before Will felt ready to go on. He unlashed the fifth drum, heaved it into place, kicked it, and lost his footing as the Otter lurched a little. The drum hit the edge of the doorway and caught there.

"Bloody hell." He sidled across the cabin and gave the drum a shove with his boot. There wasn't enough leverage, so he bent over and heaved at it with both hands. It spun with unexpected ease, and toppled out. Will sprawled flat as the plane tilted to the right and then back again, a little too far. He fell within a handsbreadth of the doorway and felt himself rolling over, as helpless in his bulky clothes as a Weddell seal. He was looking out at the far horizon, a straight white edge marred by a chain of distant nunataks. A kilometer below was the tortured surface of the ice sheet, glittering and sharp and very far away.

Instinct wanted him to bend his knees as if in readiness for the long drop; reason made him straighten his legs and fling out his hands above his head. Feet and hands struck the sides of the doorway. He groped for a handhold and found nothing. With a grunt, he flung himself away from the door, rolling over until he reached the fuel drums and could hook an arm through their lashings.

"Bloody *hell*," he muttered. His vision was blurred, and for a horrible minute he was afraid his eyes had frozen. At last the blue-painted drums and yellow nylon webbing came into focus. He pulled himself upright and shuffled around the remaining three drums. His hands were shaking so badly that he could scarcely undo the knots in the lashings. It took almost ten minutes to jettison the rest of the drums; then he slammed shut the door and went back to the flight compartment.

"What took you so long?"

"I got to admiring the view."

Al handed him a thermos of hot coffee, thick with condensed milk and sugar. Will drank it all and felt almost drunk as its warmth spread from his belly to his hands and feet. Revived, he found Al's howgozit. A new line had been drawn on it.

"I shot the sun again and found we were doing better than I'd thought," Al said. He looked embarrassed. "Looks like I stuck you with a job that didn't need doing. Sorry."

Will took a deep breath and let it out very slowly.

As they flew deeper into the continent, the ice sheet's surface grew less chaotic. Amid the seracs and crevasse fields, smooth patches began to appear, some of them hundreds of meters on a side. "They must be on one of those spots," Al observed.

"Have you picked up anything from them?" Another part of Will seemed to be speaking; his real self was still looking down through the doorway, reaching for a handhold that wasn't there.

"Nothing." Al checked their position and studied the fuel gauges. "We're so close we ought to be able to smell the borscht."

Will studied the terrain below. In all but the worst serac fields, there was something of a pattern in the surface features.

"Looks as if the ice is moving Grid Southeast—toward the coast. We're over the top of the dome. I'll bet they've moved farther than they realize."

Al looked at him, inscrutable behind his sunglasses. "We've got about seventy minutes' flying left. You'd better be right." He changed course, and they began a standard search-and-rescue sweep pattern.

Fifteen minutes later, they saw a short line of black dots across a clear patch. Al brought the Otter almost to the surface and circled the station. "They've moved almost seventy kilometers," he said. "I never would have believed it."

There was no sign of life below. The skiway was heavily drifted over and both ends of it vanished into crevasses. Al estimated that no more than fifteen hundred meters remained of the four-kilometer strip. A row of half-buried buildings extended Grid Southeast from the skiway; several of them had collapsed, and one had obviously been gutted by fire. A few vehicles, mostly big green Kharkovchanka tractors, were neatly parked about fifty meters from the buildings.

"See anyone?" Will asked. Al shook his head. He was studying the skiway.

"Bad. Looks bad," he said. "If I don't put us down right now, I'll be too scared to try."

It was a rough landing. The Otter dropped to the surface, bumping and skidding as it struck sastrugi buried like land mines under the drift. Al brought it to a halt not far from a crevasse field and turned it cautiously around. They taxied back to the buildings, and Al throttled back the engines.

"Don't strain yourself," he said. "The altitude and the cold will make you pretty clumsy. Let's hope we don't have to stay long enough to get acclimatized." He looked at the altimeter, and his jaw dropped. "Twenty-six hundred meters. That's wrong. That's impossible."

"This side of the dome must have surged even faster than the other side," Will said. "It must have, to move Vostok this far and drop the surface by a thousand meters."

"Mmh. Let's get going."

The air was very still, and very cold. A constant background rumble could be felt more than heard. Will took a few steps from the Otter and looked around. It was much like the Shelf, or most places on the polar plateau: a white flatness, disturbed here and there by sastrugi or drifts. The crevasse fields were invisible from here. Above them was an empty blue sky.

"Where are they?" he wondered. "They must've heard us."

"Probably in no shape to move. We'll find them."

The nearest building was a pile of wreckage. "The American Pavilion, they used to call it," Al commented as they made their way around it. "Used to be one or two guys from McMurdo here every year, back in the old days. We had some great parties here. We had a pissing contest once, right about here. It was fifty-five below. Your pee darn near froze in mid-air."

They trudged on between the buildings and the Kharkovchankas. They were immense, like railway cars on caterpillar tracks. Each was ten meters long, five high, and five wide; Will recalled hearing that they could sleep ten men, and were divided into rooms—even a laundry.

"Gotta be in the main building," Al said. "It's down there, past the drilling sheds."

"Buggers must've liked walking a lot," Will wheezed. "Never saw such bloody urban sprawl." His face felt stiff and masklike, and even his eyelashes were delicately picked out in frost. His head ached badly.

"You never saw so many guys in such good shape as the Russians. Really solid." Al gripped the handle of the door to the main building's cold porch, and pulled hard against the drift that blocked it. After a minute of grunting and tugging, he got it open. They went through, leaving the outer door open to give some light.

The inner door of the cold porch opened into a narrow corridor. There was much of the same sort of clutter one found in any station; the chief differences Will noticed were stenciled Cyrillic letters on the crates, and brownish-black bearskins hanging over the doorways.

Al looked down the corridor. "Hello!" he shouted. "Anybody here?"

"Hello," someone called back faintly. "We are here, hello."

The two men blundered down the dark corridor. At its end was a door like all the others, but its frame was heavily crusted with frost. Will pulled aside the bearskin—it was as rigid as plywood—and fumbled with the knob. The door seemed frozen on its hinges, but yielded at last. They stepped into the station's mess hall.

Three kerosene lamps, standing on tables, were the only illumination. The floor was slippery with ice except at the far end of the room, where long batts of fiberglass insulation had been laid down; some of them were covered with blankets. A long, narrow window in one wall had been blocked off with more insulation. A little stove made the room just warm enough to be dank. There was a sour stink of kerosene and human waste in the air.

"Hello?" Al repeated, less confidently. The blankets at the far end of the room moved a little. A man's eyes glinted in the lamplight.

"You are here," he said thickly. "You are the Shackleton men?"

"That we are." Al picked his way across the slippery floor; Will shut the door behind him and followed.

"We are very glad you come," the man smiled. He was gaunt and pale; his thick gray-black beard was matted. "I am Ivan Grigorievich Varenko." And he slowly extended a bandaged, badly frostbitten hand. Al took it gently.

"I'm Al Neal. I think we met once, a couple of years ago at Mirny. And this is Will Farquhar. Where are the other men?"

Ivan tugged at the blankets on either side of him, revealing two sleeping men; they breathed shallowly, as if dreaming, and did not waken. Both looked as ravaged as Ivan himself. He nodded toward the one on his right, a very young man with a sparse blond beard and a half-healed scar across his forehead. "Yevgeni Pavlovich Shtein. Geophysicist." The other was middle-aged and moon-faced, with a beard as white as Al's. "Kyril Matveivich Borisov. Aircraft mechanic."

"Are they sick?" Al asked quietly. He and Will squatted awkwardly by the men's feet.

"We are all sick. Frostbite. Scurvy."

"Your wife told us you were well."

"I—I do not want to worry herself. If I say we need help, and you cannot help—what use? You know, I do not think you could reach us." The smile flashed again. "I am very happy you surprise me."

"Can you walk?" asked Will.

"No. Not well. For last week, I must crawl to radio." He nodded toward a table across the room, where an ancient field transceiver stood; it was hooked up to a hand-crank generator. Will looked at Ivan's bandaged hands and imagined what it must be like to operate the radio. "Every day, we try, we try. Until yesterday, nothing. I nearly stop."

Al looked at his watch. It was almost noon, Shacktown time, but only about 1000 hours local time. Sunset would be around 1630 or 1700 hours. There wasn't much margin for delay, and he didn't want to spend a night here if he could help it.

"Where are the fuel drums?"

"In green shed near airstrip."

"We'll have to refuel as fast as possible. Then we'll come back and put you on board. It shouldn't take more than an hour and a half."

They went back outside and walked as quickly as they could to the shed Ivan had mentioned. Its doorway was solidly drifted over; Will had to go back to the Otter for a couple of shovels, and they spent fifteen minutes digging their way in. Al looked inside and nodded.

"Well, well. Genuine JP4, all right." The drums stacked inside were stenciled US NAVY VXE-6. "I'll bet I dropped some of these myself."

"You're joking."

"Back in the old days, we couldn't do enough for each other, us and the Russians. But we didn't want to take their fuel for our own flights, so we used to airdrop a few drums every now and then, so we could fly out on our own gas. Then everybody got snarky, and we didn't come here so often any more. And the Russians were too proud to use what we left." He saw that the seals on the drums were intact, and broke one. A little clumsily, he tilted the drum and poured some fuel through a scrap of cloth.

"Looks okay. There might be some sediment on the bottom, but I'll check for that while we're tanking up. Let's get a move on."

They had to wrestle the drums outside and then roll them a hundred and fifty meters to the Otter. Seven drums would be needed to fill the Otter's tanks. Will cursed the plane for needing so much, and Al for misjudging their fuel consumption on the flight in. But at last they were ready, and the process of pumping the gas into the tanks took less time than he expected, even with Al's pauses to check for contamination. By 1545 Shacktown time, the job was done. Al looked up at the sky.

"Warming up. We're going to get some weather."

They went into the hospital building with flashlights —whose batteries did not quite freeze—and found a stretcher. It wasn't easy: the interior was a mass of collapsed partitions, overturned furniture, and broken glass. Then they returned to the main building.

"Now—who's going to be our first passenger?" said Al. He unrolled the stretcher.

"Kyril Matveivich," Ivan said at once. Kyril shrugged and grinned, showing several missing teeth, and tried to get up. His legs wouldn't support him; Will and Al had to carry him. There was a nasty, putrid stink from his boots; Al recognized it at once as gangrene. They wrapped him in blankets and carried him outside.

Kyril must have been inside for a long time; the sunlight made him grunt and shut his eyes, and his lids promptly froze together. But he made no complaint during the ten minutes it took to reach the plane. They got him inside and gently lifted him into a seat. Will pulled a sleeping bag out of one of the survival packs and gently drew it over Kyril's legs—partly to keep him warm, and partly to suppress the smell. Kyril looked around the cabin with obvious professional interest; he seemed to be pleased with what he saw.

"Khorosho," he nodded. "Otter wery good."

It took three more trips to load the airplane: two for Yevgeni and Ivan, and one for some boxes of scientific records and personal effects, including a small bronze bust of Lenin. Then the JATO bottles had to be attached.

"Want me to go through the checklist?" Will volunteered when everyone was strapped in.

"Don't bother," said Al, his hands and eyes moving smoothly over the instruments. He taxied to the far end of the skiway and turned the Otter around. It was almost 1500 hours, Shacktown time. The sky was rapidly growing overcast.

"Dos vidanya, Vostok," Al said.

The Otter began to move, slowly at first, and then accelerated. Near the end of the skiway, Al ignited the JATO bottles, and everyone was slammed back into his seat. The engines howled, sucking at the thin air, and then they were climbing at a shallow angle above the seracs. Will shouted from sheer exuberance; cheers and laughter came from the cabin.

"Those are three tough buggers," Will said.

"Yup. Good men." Al rummaged in his anorak and found some cigars. He put one in his mouth and handed the rest to Will. "See if anyone wants a smoke."

They circled the abandoned station, gaining altitude, and then turned Grid West-southwest. Smelling of gas, cigars, excrement, and gangrene, the Otter pursued the sinking sun.

9

PRESSURE

It was dark by the time they reached the center of the Shelf, but the TACAN signal was fairly clear. Al even made voice contact with Roger Wykstra, and told him that all was well but that the Russians would need immediate medical attention.

"Okay, Papa Al, I'll tell Kate. Uh, we'll start sending up a flare every three minutes until you start your approach. And the skiway will be marked by fires. Anything else? Over."

"Boy, all the comforts of home. Ah, tell Terry to throw some steaks on the fire, and no nonsense about rationing. We're all starved. Over."

"Will do. Mind your step, now. Over and out."

A few minutes later they saw the first flare sparkling like a star over the dim blue surface far ahead.

"Bang on course," Will said. "What a bloody navigator!"

"Nothing to it," Al grinned. "I just followed the smell of my own fear."

"*Your* fear? I've been pissing my pants all day."

A second flare went off, much closer now, and then two lines of orange light appeared: the skiway. Al circled, dropped, and landed with scarcely a bump.

Floodlights glared into the flight compartment as the Otter taxied up to the hangar, but Al and Will could just make out a group of dark figures milling about on the snow. The hangar doors drew open, and someone ran out with the winch cable. Two minutes later they were inside and the doors boomed shut.

Al got up and went into the passenger compartment. The Russians looked exhausted. He patted Ivan's shoulder, and then went to open the door. He saw Katerina walking steadily and carefully, picking her way over the greasy duckboards. Despite her bulky anorak and trousers, Al thought she looked very small. "Hey, Katerina!" he bellowed, his voice echoing off the hangar roof. "Come and say hello to your husband."

"He is pretty tough, that one," she said. "I thought he would be okay." She climbed the four-step ladder into the cabin, her smile bright.

"Katya—"

She caught her breath when she saw him in the dim light.

"Ah, Vanya—Vanya!" She fell to her knees beside his seat, gripping his arms and kissing his cracked and blackened lips.

Much later that evening, Katerina left the infirmary and went for a walk in Tunnel D. The walls glittered with frost. From the huts in Tunnel C came laughter and Max Wilhelm's uncertain tenor rendition of "Your Cheating Heart." The welcome-back party had moved from the lounge to the geophysics lab after Katerina had insisted on quiet in the infirmary. She was glad she hadn't dampened the celebration.

She turned back and went into Tunnel B, avoiding the cold porch nearest to Hugh's room; no need to disturb him—or his attendant—any further tonight. At the next door, she went in and walked down the bunkhouse corridor until she came to the room shared by Max and Ben Whitcumb. She knocked gently.

"Come in," Ben snapped. When he saw who it was, his expression softened.

"Hi, Katerina. Good to see you. Here, let me take your coat."

"Thank you." She sat down and looked around. The

cubicle was crowded with books, boxes of fossils, and cold-weather gear, but there was little to reveal the personalities of the men who lived in it. Ben had been sitting at his desk, reading a geology journal.

"I hope I am not interrupting?"

"Nothing serious. I'm reduced to reading Max's stuff these days. How is your husband? And his friends?"

"Resting. They are all very glad to be here."

"I'm glad too. It's like the old days, isn't it? When we all used to help each other."

"Yes. Not such very old days—you and I both remember them. Why are you not at the party?"

"Oh—I'm not much for parties these days. Too many people get on my nerves."

"Yes, it happens. I want to ask you for a favor."

"Sure."

"You have medical training."

Ben smiled. "Not exactly. Two years as an Army medic, that's all."

"It is more than anyone else has. Tomorrow I must operate on the men. I will need help."

"Amputations?"

"Yes. I am afraid so."

"Well, I'll be glad to do whatever I can."

"Thank you, Ben. I am grateful. About nine o'clock tomorrow morning."

Katerina went down the service corridor to Tunnel A. She walked through the deserted mess hall and lounge, and noticed a light on in the microfilm room between the lounge and the infirmary. Will and Jeanne were sitting at two readers, scanning old articles and reports.

"Hullo, Kate," Will said. "Your babies are sleeping like stones."

"Good. And what are you two doing?"

"Reading up on the Ross Sea Ridge," Jeanne answered. "This crazy man had two beers and dragged me away from that lovely party to fiddle with microfilm."

"And what is the Rossy Ridge?"

Will pointed to a map on the screen of his reader. It showed the Ross Sea, the Siple Coast, and Marie Byrd Land, off to the Grid West of Shacktown. "It's a range of hills under the Shelf. See, it starts here, near the Siple Coast, and runs Grid East all the way to here." His finger touched a spot about two hundred kilometers Grid South of Shackleton Glacier. "It's about five hundred meters below sea level at this point. In some places, a little higher—high enough for the Shelf to ground itself."

"Ah—I see what you are thinking," Katerina said. "Our island is how thick?"

"Between five hundred and fifty and six hundred meters," said Jeanne.

"And how far away are we from the Ridge?"

"Fifty kilometers. A little less than a month away," said Will.

Steve had been working on repairs to the drilling hut, and on digging two new tunnels for seismic equipment. Every night he pitched into bed and slept almost without moving; in the morning, he would wake and make love to Penny with an urgency that first excited and then worried her. It was as if some feeling—some joy or fear—could be expressed only in her arms. They would murmur amiably for a while afterward, and then get up to resume endless hours of work. She saw him when he came into the mess hall for meals—which wasn't all that often—and sometimes in the evening if she could get off work before he came lurching in to sleep.

The morning after the Russians arrived, Penny and Steve both slept late; the party had lasted all night. Penny woke around 0900. Steve, beside her, was too still to be asleep. Next door, Terry Dolan snored violently.

"Awake?" she asked.

"Yeah. Hi." He kissed her.

"What's on your mind?"

Steve yawned and stretched and said: "Winter."

"Oh ho ho," Penny murmured. "I thought you were looking forward to it."

"In a way I am. But it's getting close now. In two weeks we'll lose the sun."

"So what? I haven't seen much of the sun for ages anyway."

"It'll feel different, believe me. It was rough enough here last winter, with just nine of us and plenty of food and knowing the first plane in would be landing by the middle of October. This year there'll be thirty of us, on short rations, and no idea when we'll get out. *That's* what I don't like—the uncertainty, and what it'll do to everybody. . . . If Hugh weren't sick I'd feel better."

She felt uneasy as she walked to the mess hall; it was as if whatever was struggling in Steve had almost come out, and she had forced it back inside.—Hell, if he wants to wring his hands and be a prophet of doom he doesn't have to make *me* listen to it.

But it wasn't that, and she knew it. She was afraid he was going to tell her he was frightened, really frightened for his life, and that was one thing she didn't want to hear. Not ever.

Katerina and Ben were in the kitchen, drinking tea. Ben looked self-conscious when Penny came in, avoiding her eyes. Usually she felt sorry for him, and sometimes his moony expression disgusted her, but this morning his crush on her felt flattering. At least Ben wasn't grim and all-knowing, like Steve. "Morning," she smiled. "Can I make you two some breakfast?"

"That is very kind of you, but no. We must operate this morning. Afterward, we eat. The men will not be ready to eat until tomorrow, except maybe some liquids."

"Oh." Penny was taken aback. "Well, you know, call me if you need anything."

"Perhaps," Katerina went on, "if you keep people out of the lounge this morning, and shut the door from the mess hall to the infirmary, it will be helpful."

"Sure." She looked at Ben. "Are you helping? I didn't know you were a surgeon too."

"No, just an ex-medic." He looked as wretchedly proud as a schoolboy at his first dance after being complimented by his date.

Katerina finished her tea. "Let us begin."

They brought Ivan and Yevgeni into the lounge; the infirmary was too small to hold everyone during an operation. The men drowsed, woke, and drowsed again. Penny looked in on them once in awhile; they would look up and smile at her and then stare at the ceiling. Though they had been bathed last night, they still stank of sweat and gangrene, and occasionally a whiff of it filtered into the mess hall.

Kyril lost his right foot, part of his left, and all the fingers on his left hand. Yevgeni lost all his toes and the fingertips of his right hand. Ivan, the last, lost his left foot, his right big toe, and most of the fingers on his right hand; he also lost his ears.

It was past noon when the amputations were finished. The three men slept drugged in the infirmary; the lounge and mess hall now smelled of ether. Nevertheless, there was a crowd in the mess hall when Katerina and Ben came in. Carter sat them down at a table and patted their shoulders.

"Did it go all right?"

"Yes, very well," Katerina said briskly. "Ben was excellent. Very helpful. Quick and precise." Her hand reached out and touched his, gripped it hard for a moment.

Gordon Ellerslee finished his supper that night, got up, and went back to the serving line. "Let's have some seconds of that super stew, Terry!"

"Sorry, Gord. That's it."

"Aw, the hell you say."

"Come off it—we been on rationin' for a week."

"This ain't goddam rationing, it's slow starvation. I go out to the drilling rig every day, I freeze my ass off, I need the goddam food. Now, how about some seconds?"

There were almost twenty people in the mess hall. Their conversations stopped. "Hear, hear," called Simon.

Terry folded his arms and contemplated Gordon with detached annoyance. Suzy stood next to him, her face taut. Penny stood in the door to the kitchen.

"You've put away three thousand calories today. Just like everybody else who works outside. I don't hear anybody else bitching about it, except for that Kiwi asshole Simon." Terry stared at Gordon's big belly. "When that gut disappears—*and* that double chin—you might get some sympathy. But not from me. And you might even get seconds. But not from me."

Gordon slammed down his tray and turned away, his face purple. Carter stood up and came over to him. "Let's talk about it at the seminar, Gord."

"Talk about more'n that," Gordon growled. He stalked out of the mess hall and sat sulking in the lounge.

Carter opened the seminar with the usual routine announcements: tomorrow's housemouse and snow miners, Colin's weather forecast, and Laputa's current position—about 1.7 kilometers Grid South-southwest of yesterday's, and 125 kilometers Grid South of their original location. He asked Katerina for a report on the Vostochni, and everyone applauded when she said they were doing well.

"Something dicey is coming up," Will said. He explained the problem he foresaw as Laputa approached the Ridge. The others listened in silence; then Howie raised a hand.

"If this is gonna happen, how come we haven't stopped already? There's a lot of ice up ahead of us, and it must be hitting the Ridge too."

"Good point. First, don't forget the Shelf thickens as you go from the sea toward the land. A lot of the ice ahead of us is too thin to hit the Ridge. But over the last couple of weeks, you see an odd pattern in our rate of drift. We go a couple of kilometers one day, a kilometer the next, and the third day we scarcely budge. A day or two later, we move four or five kilometers, and then slow down again over the next few days. It looks to me as if each island is hitting the Ridge and grounding itself; then the ice behind it breaks it up into bite-size bits, and we all move three squares forward. Then the next island grounds itself, and so on."

"Beautiful!" Sean McNally said excitedly. "All these bloody thick ice islands get chopped up, so the debris covers a greater area and moves faster—and the super-shelf forms inside a year or two. You'd think someone planned it."

"I'm delighted that you appreciate the esthetic elegance of my hypothesis," Will grinned. "The Scots and the Irish usually understand each other in these matters. But it means we get chopped up too, and probably in the next six weeks."

Half a dozen people started talking at once. Katerina hushed them; Carter then pointed to Gordon, who had leaped to his feet and was determined to be heard.

"That settles it," he snapped. "We gotta get out of this place, right now. Hell, another three, four days and we won't even have sunlight. Al ought to leave at once for New Byrd; that's what I think."

"Wait a minute, Gord," said Will. "Remember, I said your drilling operation is important."

"Not now it isn't."

"It is. You see, we may be better off than we look. The bottom of the Shelf is as crevassed as the top—maybe even more so, now we've had such a pounding. It's just possible that the bottom of our little island may be, uh, rotten enough to break away without destroying the island. If—"

"If, if, if," Gordon jeered. "What if it's not?"

"We move to the mainland," Hugh said quietly.

"Perhaps to one of the Dry Valleys. And we winter there."

There was more uproar. Herm Northrop stood up. No one paid him any attention until he banged a beer can on the table.

"I don't care where we go," he said, "as long as we take the reactor core with us." He looked wryly pleased with the startled expressions on his listeners' faces. "It can't be left behind if our island is going to be broken up. The core is radioactive enough to poison the whole Southern Ocean."

"But you could seal it, Herm," Colin said. "And it could be picked up next year."

"Next year it might be at the bottom of the sea. Eventually the container would rupture. We simply mustn't let that happen."

Al Neal cleared his throat. "Herm, the core container is too big and heavy for the Otter. You'd need a Hercules."

Gordon was on his feet again, jittering with impatience. "Goddam it, that's another reason for sending Al out for help! I'm no ecology freak, but I sure don't want to see those rods down on the bottom, warming up the Ross Sea. Hugh—Carter—you gotta send him."

Hugh closed his eyes. "We'll consider it, Gordon. Meanwhile, get that hole drilled."

Jeanne had tentatively raised her hand a couple of times; now Carter nodded to her. She stood up, looking nervous.

"I don't exactly know if this is the time or place to mention it. But there's something else you might as well consider. I'm pregnant."

There was a moment's silence, followed by cheers, whistles, and tablepounding. Simon bellowed, "Good for Will!" and Will blushed violently. Jeanne blushed too. Hugh and Carter glanced at each other.

"Does Katerina know about this?" Carter shouted above the noise.

"Yes, I know," Katerina called from the door to the infirmary. "Please, more quiet."

"Sorry, Kate. All right, all right, settle down, everyone." Carter got them quiet and went on: "My own reaction to your news is, ah, modified rapture. We don't need all the details—"

"Yes we do," someone croaked.

"Belt up, there!" Carter roared. "Anyway, we'll do everything we can to keep you safe and well, Housemouse. It's a—a factor to consider." He looked very unhappy. "Does anyone else have any exciting revelations for us? I sincerely hope not."

"I want to talk about this rationing," Gordon said. "Hugh's being cagey about sending Al out, but it looks to me like you'll have to send him, Hugh. And if he goes, we'll be evacuated within a week or two. So there's no need for rationing, and we can start eating enough to do our goddam jobs."

"Gordie deserves to get stuffed if anyone does," Suzy Dolan muttered.

"I'm sorry, Gord," Hugh said. "Inside people get two thousand calories a day; outsiders get three. If we're evacuated, you can make it up in New Zealand."

Gordon was about to say something more, but everyone else applauded Hugh so loudly that he thought better of it. Katerina popped in again, looking furious.

"We must have quiet!"

"Meeting adjourned," Carter said. "Everybody out of the lounge."

The weather was, unexpectedly, very good: temperatures stayed below -35°C, the sky was clear, and there was very little wind. People found excuses to go outside, if only for a walk around the station. The moon, half-full, was bright; haloes often formed around it, and Penny once saw three moondogs arrayed across the sky. The Grid South horizon would begin to glow around 1000 hours. By noon the sky was pink or orange, and the sun made a brief appearance; twilight lasted until past 1500. It was never wholly silent outside. Distant rumbles and creaks came from all sides, and even the snow underfoot often vibrated. In the drilling shed, the whine and clank of machinery went on around the clock.

Al, Will, and Sean made a short flight around Laputa to survey its progress toward the Ridge. As Will had predicted, Blefuscu—the island Grid South of them—was breaking up: short-lived peaks were forced as much as a hundred meters above the Shelf before collapsing of their own weight. Deep crevasses opened up and crashed shut all around the pressure ridges, but they were encouraged to see that beyond the Ridge the Shelf still showed many extensive flat surfaces. Apparently the big ice islands were breaking into relatively small ones, linked by wide belts of pressure ice like scar tissue.

To the Grid North, Lilliput continued to grind against Laputa; beyond Lilliput was the growing area of chaotic surge ice, an uneven mass that rose up to two hundred meters above the Shelf. The Otter ventured as far Grid North as the Dufek Coast, which was almost unrecognizable under the glacial overflow. The remote station near the old mouth of Shackleton Glacier was gone, overwhelmed by ice, and many coastal hills were now nunataks.

"I'd love to see what it looks like up on the plateau," Steve said to Penny on the evening after the flight. "There must be whole mountain ranges exposed. Like Atlantis risen from the sea. Well, maybe we'll get a look at it in the spring."

"Christ, not again," Penny groaned, pulling away from him. The bunk seemed narrow and uncomfortable. "We've *got* to be out of here by then."

He grunted. "Well, maybe. But I'll be back."

"And what am I supposed to do while you're falling into crevasses and freezing your balls off? Knit baby booties by the fireside?"

"—Good lord, don't tell me *you're*—"

"No, no! I just—oh, forget it. Forget it."

"Come on, Pen, what is it?" His bafflement was obvious, and infuriating.

"I had some idiotic sentimental idea that we'd stay together when we got home," she said wearily.

"Ah. Well. I hadn't really thought that far ahead."

"Not about us, no. Just about coming back to this—this *place*."

"This place is important to me, Penny. It's the most important place in the world."

"And I'm not important, of course."

"Not in the same way, no. In another way, you're far more important, and you know it. Shush! But this is my work. My *work*. If you don't understand that, you don't understand me at all."

"I understand you, all right. I used to be married to someone exactly like you."

He turned over. "This is ridiculous. Good night."

The hole through Laputa was exactly 511.5 meters long. On April 20, after several attempts, Will and Jeanne managed to drop a gadget called a snake-eye all the way to the sea. It was technically known as a Mobile Remote Fiberoptic Underwater Observation Module, and was a considerable advance over the television cameras that had first probed the underside of the Shelf in the late '70s. The snake-eye looked like a miniature torpedo, just over a meter long and about as thick as a man's arm. Its nose contained a powerful lamp and three lenses, as well as instruments to measure temperature, salinity, and turbidity. Attached to a cable running up the drill hole, it could be steered—clumsily—by jets of compressed air from a tank in its midsection. The operator of the snake-eye sat at a console in the drilling shed, using three controls to steer it and six others to run its cameras and instruments.

Jeanne had a knack with the snake-eye, and Will automatically assigned her to the console. He, Gordon, and Simon stood behind her as the snake-eye finally got all the way down without mishap. The console video lit up, and the VTR went on.

"My God," Jeanne said. "Looks like chocolate syrup down there." The screen was a muddy gray-brown. "Awfully turbid." She lowered the snake-eye about ten meters and aimed its nose up at the ice. A swirl of bubbles glittered in the beam of the lamp, rising past the orange line of the cable. The bottom of the ice was a mottled gray surface; the bubbles crawled around on it like droplets of mercury, with a few finding their way back into the black circle of the drill hole. Jeanne lowered the snake-eye to the horizontal and turned it slowly through 360 degrees. The same mottled gray of old ice showed through the murk; the drill had come through into a crevasse.

Jeanne had to lower the snake-eye over fifty meters before it reached the true bottom of the island. She sent it cruising Grid South, pausing every few meters to turn its lenses upward. After it had traveled almost four hundred meters, and the cable was near its fullest extent, Jeanne sent it on a roughly circular clockwise course. Angled upward, it scanned a surface as bleak and scarred as some Neptunian moon's. Crevasses slashed deep into the ice, with sometimes only a meter or two between them. Mud had drifted into cracks and been trapped there, giving much of the ice a resemblance to clay. Countless ice fragments, broken loose, had refrozen to the island like stalactites.

"Not bad," Will said cheerfully when the circuit was completed. "I counted twelve major crevasses in eight hundred meters, and lots of little ones. We might just slide over the Ridge with a few thumps."

"Wishful thinking," Jeanne retorted. She began drawing the cable in, watching it wind around a rotating drum. "Our bottom's no different from the ice under Blefuscu. Those crevasses are wide, but they're not all *that* deep. And they'll start closing up when we hit the Ridge, instead of breaking off."

They looked at each other for a long moment, and then at Gordon and Simon. Will sighed and shook his head. "She's right, I'm afraid."

"What's it mean if the crevasses close up?" Gordon asked.

"They'll absorb some of the impact," Jeanne told him. "But only a little. Then we'll start breaking up, vertically and horizontally. Everything will be all jumbled up; we could end up with another chunk of ice on top of us, or we could turn turtle."

Gordon paced across the shed and back. "Christ. If this don't get 'em off their ass, nothing will."

Will looked at Jeanne. He touched her shoulder. "Gordie, I think you may be right."

Gordon's arguments, for all the weight they gained from the snake-eye, were blown away by a blizzard that swept over the Shelf that night, and lasted for days. The Otter was readied and Al was prepared but the wind never dropped below 100 kph, and often gusted to 300.

On the third day of the blizzard, Herm Northrop walked down Tunnel E from the reactor. Usually he was grateful for the CANDU's compactness and automated systems, which enabled it to run with only minimal supervision; but today he almost wished it would malfunction and give him something to do. He thought about the Ridge, and about what would happen to the core rods when the island broke up. He would have plenty of time to shut down and pull the core, anyway. The container might, with great luck, be buried in sediment before it could rupture. (Jeanne, however, had given him no comfort on that point: there was very little sediment anywhere under the Shelf, and the Ridge, being steadily scoured by the ice, was likely to have none at all.) If it *did* rupture it would, as Gordon had said the other night, warm the Ross Sea.

Herm's eyes widened behind their rimless glasses. He stopped, turned, and went back down the tunnel a little way. Along one wall, several big reels of heavy-duty power cable were stacked amid boxes and crates. The cable had been there, useless surplus, since the station had been built. There must be six or seven thousand meters of it, a sop to environmentalists' anxieties about having a reactor too close to the station. Herm ran his gloved hand over the cable while he did some sums in his head. Then he trotted down the tunnel and went looking for Gordon Ellerslee.

That night's seminar was the first attended by the Vostochni, who sat in a corner with Katerina translating for Yevgeni and Kyril. They had recovered with astounding speed, and if they were depressed by their amputations they gave no sign of it.

The Shacktowners, however, looked grim as they heard from Colin that the blizzard showed no signs of ending, and from Will that Laputa had moved almost five kilometers in the past twenty-four hours—an indication that Blefuscu's destruction was complete and that Laputa's turn was next. A depressed silence fell over the lounge. Gordon stood up.

"I've got a suggestion. Actually, it was Herm's idea, but he checked it out with me and it sounded pretty good.

"We got about three million miles of old HV-12 cable piled up in Tunnel E. If we stripped the insulation off of it and shoved it down the drill hole in a big loop, or maybe even two or three loops, and ran a hell of a lot of juice through it, we might be able to loosen up some of the ice under the island."

"Sort of like an immersion coil?" Terry Dolan asked.

"Yeah," laughed Gordon. "The world's biggest goddam immersion coil. If we switched station power over to the diesel generator, the CANDU could give everything it's got to melting the ice."

"And that's a great deal indeed," Herm put in. "As you all know, the whole station—with everything running—only draws about a tenth of the reactor's maximum output."

Somebody whistled. Will said, "It's an interesting idea, but you can't just shove the cable down there; you'd have to deploy it right up against the ice. But it'll just sink."

"I think the snake-eye could probably deploy the cable," Herm said, "and if we rig floats along the cable—perhaps styrofoam, or even wood—it'll stay pretty close to the ice. I don't think we'd need to melt very much ice—just enough to weaken the ice between the crevasses so that they'll break off as we hit the Ridge."

Jeanne said, "It might work over a very limited area, Herm. At the most, a couple of square kilometers around the hole. But there's no guarantee that Laputa won't crack to bits anyway. We could split from stem to stern long before this part of the island reached the Ridge."

"Maybe. But I think it's worth trying."

"So do I," said Steve. "And I suggest we put everybody on it, right away. Just stripping the insulation off the cable is going to be a huge job."

"All in favor?" Hugh asked.

Everyone's hand went up. After Katerina and Ivan explained the matter to Yevgeni and Kyril, they cheerfully raised their bandaged hands as well.

The seminar was held on the evening of April 27. That same night, Carter, Herm, and the technicians met to plan the details of the project. The next morning, almost everyone but the Dolans, the Vostochni, and one or two others started stripping cable. It was cold work in the tunnel, but no one complained; there was a lot of good-natured kidding, and even some singing. Some stripped, others gathered up the insulation for disposal, and others rewound the cable in hundred-meter lengths. The blizzard went on.

After two solid days of work, over two kilometers of cable had been prepared. Rather than run it through the tunnels and hangar and then out to the drilling rig, the technicians decided to lay insulated cable directly from the reactor building to the hole. This would save several hundred meters, but it meant teams had to work outside in hundred-kilometer winds and near-zero visibility. Ray Crandall and George Hills were frostbitten; after that, no one could work outside for more than twenty minutes every two hours.

At 0235 hours on the morning of April 30, the Grid South end of Laputa struck the Ridge. The shock was not great enough to wake anyone, but those who were awake could feel it. A geranium in the greenhouse was knocked off a table, and Shackleton's portrait fell off the wall in the mess hall. In the tunnels, frost fell beautifully from the ceilings.

Later that day, the diesel generator went on, filling the whole station with a monotonous hammering roar that gave everyone headaches. Tremors continued. Will theorized that the end of the island was disintegrating a little at a time.

Around 1000 hours on May 1, the snake-eye went back down the hole with the first length of cable attached to it; the cable, in turn, carried chunks of styrofoam attached by wire every ten meters. Given the length of the snake-eye's own control cable, it had been decided to deploy several relatively short loops, like the petals of a flower. After the first one, Jeanne had relatively little difficulty.

"Our only real problem is the bloody current," she remarked late that afternoon in the drilling shed. "It's almost impossible to put anything Grid North of us and keep it there. You've got to find a crevasse and wedge the cable in without losing the snake-eye at the same time."

Nevertheless, she managed. Current went on at 2030 hours that evening. The snake-eye showed no dramatic change, though the water temperature did begin to show a very slight rise right at the bottom of the hole; the warmed water was rising into the crevasse. As soon as this was announced at the seminar, Katerina ordered Jeanne to stay out of the drilling shed and to take at least a solid day's rest. She was glad to obey.

The tremors continued to strike the station every

few hours, but no one seemed alarmed. The only problem was the fact that the CANDU required more snow than ever to keep its boilers going at full capacity to produce enough electricity for the cables. Snow mining now went on around the clock, and the conveyor that fed snow to the melter added its clatter to the noise of the generator.

On May 3, Penny went along with Steve, Tim, and Sean McNally on a traverse to the Grid North end of Laputa. The blizzard had finally exhausted itself, and the moon was bright through broken clouds. The Sno-Cat was cold, but it was worth it to be outside breathing clean air.

Penny sat on the floor of the cab next to Steve while Sean and Tim steered through sastrugi and drift. "Isn't this fun?" she said. "Like going on a hayride."

"I remember the last time you and I went for a ride in a Sno-Cat," Steve said shyly. "You went to sleep on my shoulder."

She felt comfortable and happy with him for the first time in weeks.

It took them six hours to cover fifteen kilometers. The Sno-Cat floundered through deep, soft snow most of the way, and finally came to a halt at the crest of a rise. Here they made camp; beyond they could see crevasse fields running in dark lines to a distant mass of pressure that gleamed blue in the moonlight. Snug in a warm tent, they made supper, drank beer, and talked desultorily for a while before falling asleep. Penny found it odd to sleep in a bag by herself, with Steve on one side and Tim on the other.

During the noon twilight next day they took telephoto pictures of the pressure ridges between Laputa and Lilliput. To Penny they looked very much like the Queen Maud mountains: sharp peaks, manteled in drift, stretched from west to east. After she had watched the pressure for a while, though, she saw that the peaks kept changing. Directly ahead of them, a spire of ice rose and snapped off; to the right, a row of jagged-edged hummocks sagged almost flat. A constant snapping and creaking came from the pressure, and Penny could feel the ice shaking beneath her feet.

The moon was fairly high by noon, and by its light they could just make out a misty blueness beyond the pressure: the surge ice, rearing high above Lilliput. Penny got a brief glimpse of it through binoculars before the lenses iced over, and shivered.

"This place scares me," she told the men.

"Me too," said Tim. "I think we've seen as much as we're going to, Steve."

"Right. Let's get going. If we're lucky we'll be home for supper."

They weren't. About halfway back, the Sno-Cat shuddered violently and slewed sideways down a slope into a drift-choked depression. When they got out to start digging snow away from the treads, they could feel the surface shaking.

"Another earthquake?" Sean asked.

"No," said Steve. "I think this end of the island is breaking up." He began digging, his breath glinting in the Sno-Cat's headlights.

In the two hours it took them to get underway again, they felt several more shocks. Many small crevasses now intersected their track, but Sean drove straight across them without difficulty. They got back to Shacktown around midnight and stumbled into the mess hall for some coffee.

"Welcome back!" George Hills greeted them. "What's it like out there?" He was hunched over a table with the Vostochni, teaching them Monopoly. Nearby, Ray Crandall and Herm Northrop were playing cribbage.

"Noisy," Penny said. "And cold."

"Lilliput is breaking up Laputa," Steve said. He yawned. "If we're still here tomorrow, I'll go see how the seismographs are behaving. How's the melting going?"

"Very well, I gather," Herm nodded. "Jeanne says the crevasses are getting wider."

"When are we scheduled to go over the Ridge?" Penny asked.

"A day or two. Will says we'll know when it happens."

George looked up from the game. "Damn stupid, if you ask me, Herm. Here we finally got some clear weather, and nobody's even talkin' about sending Al out. Even if we do get over the Ridge, we'll be in the same fix."

"Yes, George," Herm said neutrally. He looked at his watch. "Well, it's just past twelve hundred; time to head down to the snow mine."

Ivan and the others came over to talk to Steve. "We are worrying about arguments. You have problems here."

"Some," Steve agreed.

"Why is this arguments permitted? This is not good time."

"We do things a little differently here, Ivan."

He shook his head. "Very dangerous. Very dangerous. I am sorry; the guest shall not be critic. But we are worrying."

"So are we," Penny said.

On the morning of May 8, a tremor almost as violent as the icequake hit the station. No one was hurt this time, but boxes were once again strewn all over the tunnels. The shock was followed by lesser tremors for several hours.

Steve spent most of that day in his seismograph tunnels. At the seminar that night, he said that Laputa's Grid South end had probably broken up on the Ridge. Colin Smith agreed: he had determined that Laputa had moved some five kilometers since the tremor that morning.

"That's a hell of a rate of speed," Carter said. "Does it mean we're over the worst of this?"

"I doubt it," Will replied. "The broken-up parts of the island are passing over the Ridge now, and the rest of Laputa is shooting forward as a result. We'll have more tremors. But at least we won't have Lilliput treading on our heels for a while, I hope."

"You're probably right," Steve said. "All the tremors have been coming from the Grid South today."

"How's the immersion heater doing?" Hugh wanted to know.

"Very well," Jeanne said. "But I've given up trying to keep the cables evenly spaced around the station. The current from Grid North is too strong. So now they're all fanned out in front of us, which is probably just as well. I had a little trouble with the snake-eye today—couldn't see what's going on too well because the water is just opaque. I think that's because the melting is releasing a lot of mud from the ice. At least I like to think it is."

Books suddenly catapulted from their shelves, and there was the sound of breaking crockery in the kitchen, followed by Terry's violent swearing. The lights flickered for an instant, and Tom Vernon bolted from his chair to attend to the generator.

"Jesus H. Christ," Gordon burst out. "Hugh, when are you gonna wake up? When are you gonna send Al out?"

"When I bloody well think we need to!" Hugh roared. It had been so long since anyone had heard him speak above a murmur that his bellow startled them more than the tremor had. Hugh stood up and walked deliberately up to Gordon. The Canadian was almost a head taller, but he seemed to shrink under Hugh's glare. "Gordon, you have been a pain in the collective ass. If I hear any more of your nagging and complaining, I will have you confined to your room. I would rather do without your services than pay for them with divisiveness and low morale."

"Well, gee, Hugh—I didn't—you—" Gordon sat down. Hugh turned and went back to his chair.

"Let's get on with the seminar," he said calmly.

Within twenty-four hours Lilliput caught up again with Laputa and began pushing it across the Ridge.

On May 11, after two days of almost constant minor tremors, there was another major shock that made the science huts temporarily uninhabitable; all the ventilation ducts above Tunnel C were disconnected. The seismographs indicated that the Grid North end of the island had crumpled under Lilliput's pressure. Steve and Tim went out in a Sno-Cat and fired some seismic shots which Will monitored; they showed several stress belts running the length of Laputa.

That same day Al got drunk. During a quick check of possible damage after the shock, Roger Wykstra and Max Wilhelm found him in his cubicle, lying face down on his bunk. An empty bottle of Mortlach whisky lay on the floor beside him. Only half-conscious, Al was singing "Happy Birthday" over and over again.

"What's the matter with him?" Roger asked softly.

Max shook his head. But he remembered the conversation he had had with Al on the flight to McMurdo. "Let's go," he said. "He'll be all right when he sleeps it off."

For the next five days Laputa moved slowly and violently over the Ridge. Hugh instituted daily evacuation drills, regardless of the weather, and the Otter was kept fueled and warmed for a possible trip to Taylor Dry Valley. The cables went on pouring heat into the water below them until 1335 hours on the afternoon of May 17, when they were snapped. The ice below Laputa was now in contact with the Ridge.

In the few minutes before she lost the snake-eye, Jeanne saw on the console that Herm had been right. The crevassed ice, weakened by days of heat, crumbled away as the island scraped over the immovable stone. Hugh told the people waiting in the chilly hangar to go back to bed.

The next day, just before noon, a crash like thunder pealed across the island. Howie and Simon went out on skis to investigate and found that Laputa had broken apart less than three kilometers Grid North of the station. The huge fragment left behind was breaking up in slabs that were rapidly filling the gap.

Laputa still moved Grid South, toward the distant Pacific Ocean, but more slowly than before. During the brief noon twilights, those who wanted to could ski from the station to the new edge of the island. There they could look down on a gray-green plain of floes and bergs that extended to the dim horizon in all directions. The chaotic ice beyond the Ridge was lower and thinner than Laputa; in the grip of a deep-running current, the island drifted through the growing super-shelf.

"Now we start to winter over," Steve said.

10

WINTER

Will Farquhar stood near the edge of Laputa and looked Grid East. The night was still; the moon was full, and bright enough to smother the stars. Clear to the horizon, the Shelf glowed silver-blue, a gently rolling plain broken in many places by ice islands rising like desert mesas, with steep sides and flat tops. It was very quiet.

He looked down. Elsewhere, Laputa's cliffs were as much as fifty meters above the new Shelf, but here they had collapsed into a kind of scree slope over which the blizzards of the past few weeks had formed a thick, hard windcrust. The boxes that he and Tim Underwood had pushed down the slope had scarcely scratched it.

Tim came out of the Sno-Cat, his frosted beard glittering in the moonlight. He was lugging a crate of gelignite. "This is the last of it," he said. Will nodded. The two of them dragged the crate to the top of the slope and shoved it over. It slid down with a faint hiss, and came to a stop near the rest of the gear in the shadows of a pressure ridge.

"All set, then?" Will asked.

"Yup." Tim clipped himself to a rope secured to the Sno-Cat, and gingerly let himself down the slope. His newly healed wrist took the strain without a twinge. The gradient was not very steep, but the wind-crust gave little purchase even to crampons; without the rope, he would have slid helplessly down into the pressure ridge.

Will followed a few moments later. Without talking much, the men dragged their gear through the pressure ice and out onto the snow. For an hour they hand-drilled holes in the ice beneath, and then set off seismic shots. Each charge went off with a thump that echoed from the cliffs of Laputa, and sent a silver-blue geyser of ice crystals and smoke into the still air.

When they were finished, they returned to the foot of the slope and Tim began the climb back. Will turned to look across the moonlit Shelf. He thought he had never seen anything as strange or as beautiful in his life.

Seminars were held less often now, and this one attracted only about a dozen people. Even so, Tim looked nervous as he stood up with a couple of sheets of paper in his hand, and Will's encouraging smile seemed to fluster him all the more.

"Uh, we got some good data from the shots yesterday," Tim began. "First, from the ones we did on Laputa, it looks like the island is pretty well intact, with no major stress areas or fractures. Our average thickness is about four hundred and fifty meters, so the Ridge must have taken off a bit more than we thought.

"The Shelf ice seems to be consolidating very fast. It's about eighty meters thick, at least around Laputa. In a few places it's as thin as—" he glanced nervously at his notes—"as, uh, forty meters, and as thick as a hundred and five. There's a lot of new snow on it. We had to drill through damn close to ten meters before we hit proper ice."

"Don't tell us about new snow," George Hills said. "We been whisking it off the roof for weeks."

"And we'll be doing it some more," Colin Smith added. "Looks like another storm coming in tomorrow."

There was an outburst of groans and swearing. To the fascination of Colin and Sean, and to the dismay of everyone else, more snow had fallen in the past month than this latitude of the Antarctic normally got in five years. The reason, Colin believed, was that warm moist air was being drawn toward the pole too rapidly to permit it to drop its precipitation out over the ocean. The Antarctic desert was turning into the equivalent of a raincoast.

Steve raised his hand. "Tim, how solid is the new Shelf? Any big gaps or soft spots?"

"Not that I could find." He turned to the map of Antarctica on the wall of the lounge, and pointed to the Ross Sea. "Uh, we're right about here, just where the old Shelf ended. The new Shelf must run way beyond, maybe all the way to 55 degrees—the Antarctic Convergence. Will says the temperature gradient rises so fast north of there that you couldn't keep the ice welded together. At least not until you had a few years to cool the ocean down. I don't know if I'll go along with him, but he says New Zealand could start seeing winter pack ice around South Island by 1995."

"Serve the bloody Kiwis right," Gordon Ellerslee laughed, but no one joined him.

Carter cleared his throat. "Well, we'll see. Anything else to add, Tim? No? All right, thanks very much. Anything else, anybody?"

"One small thing," Max Wilhelm said. "We're almost due Grid West of Ross Island now, and whenever the wind blows from there we still get a great deal of volcanic ash. It looks as if Erebus is still at it."

"Mm-hm. And on that cheery note, I think we'll adjourn."

"Monopoly? Monopoly?" Kyril asked; Yevgeni nodded eagerly.

"Okay," said Gordon. "I'll take you Communist bastards on and teach you how it's really played."

"You'll be sorree," Howie warned. The Russians had taken to the game at once; they consistently beat everyone else before turning on each other with a merry ruthlessness, as if trying to vindicate Marx and Lenin. Tonight, as Gordon soon learned, was no exception.

Al Neal went down Tunnel D to the hangar next morning. The blizzard had arrived during the night and was gusting up to 220 kph; wind moaned in the ventilators, and the air was full of fine snow that got in somehow and hung in the huts and tunnels like grain dust.

Gordon and Howie were playing cribbage in the machine shop while Tom Vernon methodically took apart one of the Sno-Cats' engines. They greeted Al with casual nods.

"What's new, Papa Al?"

"Nothing much. Just wandered up to look over the plane."

"Goin' somewhere?" Gordon grunted.

"Nope. See you guys." Al went on into the hangar and made his way to the Otter. Laputa had drifted almost 90 degrees counterclockwise since passing over the Ridge, and the hangar doors now faced Grid East; they were solidly drifted over, but each gust still struck them like a battering ram. Al wrinkled his nose at the stink of diesel fuel and JP4. The ice floor of the hangar was soaked with it, the result of dozens of minor spills over the months, and it worried him.

He stepped up the ladder into the cabin and went forward to the flight compartment. Settling into his seat, he turned on the instrument panels. Everything read normal. All the fuel tanks were full, and the engines were being kept warm on current drawn from the reactor. The Otter could fly on a moment's notice.

"But there's nowhere to go," Al said out loud.

Laputa continued to move Grid South at about two kilometers per day; as the surge ice moved across the Ridge, it pushed the newly coalescing Shelf ahead of it. Temperatures rose and fell and rose again as storms swept in from the distant Pacific and collided with katabatic winds bearing dry, bitterly cold air from the polar plateau. Snow fell and consolidated into a hard crust; whisking parties used axes as often as shovels. The dome was repeatedly drifted over, frustrating Carter's efforts to film the very faint auroras that sometimes appeared in clear weather. Gerry Roche's instruments began to detect the fragile beginnings of a new ionosphere, one which vanished again and again under the onslaught of solar flares, but which persistently renewed itself.

"It's like ice on a pond in the winter," he said to Penny one day. "You keep throwing rocks in, the water's too stirred up to freeze. It calms down a little and bingo, ice."

"And we're the minnows down at the bottom."

"Yeah." Gerry smilingly lit the stump of a cigar.

"Oh, please don't!" she snapped. She was intensely conscious of the way things smelled these days: the latrines, the mess hall, the men who troubled less and less to keep themselves clean.

"You don't like it, you can leave," Gerry retorted. "It's not like I had a whole lot of pleasures to choose from."

She stalked out of the geophysics lab. Everybody and everything seemed to grate on her. The kitchen was a stinky, noisy pit where she slaved for a surly, self-pitying Terry and a slatternly Suzy. The mess hall furniture felt so greasy that one night she had washed it all, only to find it just as bad a day later. The lounge was a claustrophobic box cluttered with shabby armchairs and couches, always filled by shabby men. The Kiwis' and Australians' nasal whines made her grit her teeth; the Brits' accents weren't much better; the Canadians' slow drones made them sound like retarded Americans. She was ashamed of herself for it, but the Russians' mutilated hands nauseated her.

Even the greenhouse was no solace. The fluorescent

lights made her head ache, and the plants looked like drab, stunted parodies of what they might have been in a proper climate. Penny sat on the same bench where she had scrawled her impressions of the icequake all those long months ago, and glowered at the floor where she and Steve had taken part in the least graceful copulation in polar history.

On June 20 everyone began preparing for the Midwinter Day party; this meant extra work for the kitchen people, and Penny was exhausted when she got to her cubicle a little before midnight. Steve was asleep already, but he woke when she turned on the light and began noisily undressing.

"Hi, love. Had a long day, eh?"

"Yes, I had a long day, eh. I washed a lot of dishes, eh. I fed a lot of overgrown boys, eh. I'm goddam tired, eh. Why don't you turn over, eh, and go back to sleep, eh?"

"With pleasure."

Good; she'd annoyed him. "Don't bother to be sympathetic—just go back to sleep and I can listen to you snoring all night." She threw her clothes in a corner. "Keep yourself warm tonight; I'm sleeping in the top bunk for a change. At least I won't have you thrashing all over me in your sleep, and groping me in the morning, if there ever is a morning in this goddam shithole." She turned off the light and hoisted herself awkwardly into the bunk. The sleeping bag there was cold, and out of habit she'd taken off her long underwear, but she would be damned before she'd get out and put it back on again.

"I can't stand much more of this, Steve. We've got to get out of here."

"Thank you, Gordon Ellerslee."

"Drop dead. Gordon's not the only one who thinks we ought to do something, *do something!* And you just want to sit and gloat over your goddam seismographs and think about how famous you're gonna be."

There was a long silence. Then she felt the bunks

sway as he got up. The light went on, blinding her. Steve put on his pants and shirt.

"What are you doing now?" she demanded.

"Moving out, Pen." He pulled on his boots and began lacing them; she noticed how cracked and calloused his hands had become from weeks of work in the seismograph tunnel. "I'm sorry. This was all a bad mistake, I guess. I'm sorry." He rolled up his sleeping bag and put it under his arm.

"Not as sorry as I am." Penny turned over and glared at the raw plywood wall until he turned out the light, opened the door, and quietly left.

The party was not a success. The Dolans' special dinner was so good and so plentiful that it made some people resentfully aware of how little they got the rest of the time. Beer and wine were abundant, and two or three of the men were drunk before dessert. When the party got under way in the lounge, Roger Wykstra—with five cans of Swan Beer already in him—knocked over the big bowl of rum punch and nearly got into a fight with Terry about cleaning it up. Various bawdy toasts were drunk to Shacktown's couples, embarrassing and annoying the women. Penny and Steven were absent, prompting cheerfully obscene comments from some, and alarmed whispers from those who already knew that they'd split up.

By 2200 half the station had turned in and the other half were quarreling drunkenly. Carter ended the festivities half an hour later by enlisting Howie as bouncer and dousing the lights and heat.

Katerina and Ivan shared the last of the Bulgarian brandy she had brought with her to Shacktown last November. They lay comfortably bundled up in bed, listening to the Dolans arguing next door.

"Like student days in Odessa," Ivan sighed. "Remember that Polish couple? Spitting at each other, throwing plates, and making love like cats all night."

"Trust an old tomcat like you to remember that. You used to be one of her greatest admirers."

"Another long memory!" He put down his empty glass and nestled under her arm, his eyes closed. His beard tickled her breasts. "This too I remembered at Vostok. I would lie in my bag, listening to the ice breaking all around us, feeling everything shake, and I would dream of you. Of the little scar on your breast; and the freckles on your shoulders, and the mole on your cheek. And now this seems like the dream."

She kissed the top of his head. "To me, you are a wonderful dream also." Terry's voice, thick and bitter, rose over Suzy's sobbing. "Ah, these people—they are much too real. Like spoiled babies someone has left us to look after."

Ivan grunted. "I do not understand them. As individuals they are fine, wonderful people. Al and Will are very brave men—Hugh and Carter, good leaders —all are good people. But, my God, the bickering, the resentment! Never would they be picked for a Soviet station. Yet they survive, while our own people—"

"Hush, hush." He had been having nightmares about the Vostochni who had left for Mirny before the icequake. "They *are* good people. But with nothing to do, they fall apart. If Hugh told them to build a ladder to the moon, they would be happy again."

Ivan was silent for a moment. "No wonder these English swarmed all around the world. Without something to conquer, they go mad. If it goes on like this, when they find us in the spring there will be four Russians and nobody else."

"No doubt a Soviet plot."

His laughter was so loud and delighted that it brought an unexpected end to the squabbling next door.

Two nights after the party, Penny came back to her cubicle to find Ben Whitcumb sitting at her desk.

"What are *you* doing here?"

"Waiting for you. Hi."

"Hi. Look, I'd love to talk, but I'm pooped. Some other time, okay?"

"Penny, this isn't what you think it is. I just want to talk for a while."

"I don't think it's anything at all. And I don't want to talk at all. Good night, and good-bye."

Ben shrugged and stepped toward the door, but as he passed he gripped her shoulders and kissed her. Penny brought the heel of her hand up hard under his jaw, and he staggered back against the doorframe. He caught his breath, grinned uncertainly, and shook his head.

"Well. Well. I can take a hint. Sorry to be a— nuisance." And he sidled down the corridor.

Penny sat down on the edge of her bunk, breathing hard and a little high on adrenalin. Before it wore off, she went out and down the corridor to Don Treadwell's cubicle. She rapped on the door and went in. The Jamaican was doing a watercolor of the greenhouse; he looked up at her, surprised.

"Hi. I want a lock on my door. Got one in stores?"

"I think I might, Penny. Have you lost anythin'?"

"No, and I don't intend to."

She began to realize that she must look a bit distraught, with her uncombed hair and her flushed cheeks. Don gave her a hint of a smile.

"Well, there's no point in lookin' for a lock right now, because we couldn't install it tonight, could we?"

"Why not?"

"Well, think of the noise. People are gettin' ready for bed, you know."

"All right, all right. First thing in the morning, then."

She wandered aimlessly from one hut to the next, proud of having coped with Ben and horrified of what might happen if someone like Gordon or Simon or even placid Howie decided to move in on her. Gordon would—and she—

Neutral, public territory seemed safest. She went into the mess hall. There was Gordon, sitting with Simon and Al; Penny nearly turned and ran, but Al beckoned her over.

"Hi, Pen. Thought you'd had enough of this dump for one day. Keep us company."

"Oh—sure." And she pulled up a chair next to Al, across from the other two. They were examining a map of Antarctica on which various penciled lines had been scrawled.

"Brother Ellerslee's got an idea," Al said.

"Yeah?"

Al tapped a finger on the map. "Cape Hallett."

Penny remembered flying over it on the way to Mc-Murdo, but it had been hidden in clouds. There was— or had been—an American weather station there, and an airstrip for emergency landings. It stood on a corner of the continent overlooking the Southern Ocean at the point where it merged into the Ross Sea, and it was a very lonely place.

"We're about seven hundred kilometers from Hallett now," Gordon said. "About half as far as Vostok was when Al and Will flew there. If Al could reach Hallett, he could either radio to New Zealand, or refuel and fly on out."

"If Hallett is still there," Al said. "And if there's a radio, and conditions are right, and if there's fuel."

"Even if there's none of those things," Gordon answered solemnly, "you could come back, or tough it out there for the rest of the winter. Hallett will be the first place they'll reach in the spring—maybe even sooner."

Al laughed. "So I freeze my buns while you guys sit here nice and snug, worrying yourselves sick about me."

Gordon looked disconcerted; he tugged his nose as if, Penny thought, a good argument were lurking inside it. Gordon was, for him, deferential. She wondered why, when he usually blustered at everyone; and why he should be talking to Al when the two of them for some reason had said nothing to each other for weeks.

Simon spoke up: "There's always a risk, Al. Sure, you're the guy who gets stuck, and you always have been. You know that."

"Mh." Al raised his eyebrows. He looked down at the map between his big, blunt hands, and Penny felt she could read his mind: he was thinking of the long flight across the new Shelf, under a dark sky, with the yellow-green twilight low on the Grid South horizon. Or with a black, shrieking storm that blotted out everything, including himself and the plane.

And then across the ocean, she thought. Aloud, she asked: "Could you make it all the way to New Zealand?"

"No." He pointed to a cluster of islands Grid South of Cape Hallett, far out in the Southern Ocean. "There's a weather station at Cape Smith in the Balleny Islands. That's seven hundred kilometers from Hallett. It's only been there about two, three years, and the Kiwis may have shut it down. But . . . there's an airstrip, and probably a few drums of JP4. It's a gamble—sort of like drawing three cards to an inside straight." Al sat back and looked at the map. His face was unreadable. "Well, I'll think about it."

"Okay," Gordon nodded. "That's fair enough."

July 2 started with a clear, star-filled sky, but the temperature soon rose ominously, and by noon another blizzard had come roaring down from the Southern Ocean. It blew itself out by evening, leaving high drifts over the station. Hugh sent out a whisking party, but they came back almost at once; it was impossible to work in darkness and blowing snow with the temperature at -30° and gusts up to seventy kph.

"It'll be better in the morning," Colin told that night's seminar. "Looks like a day or two of clear weather ahead. I *think*. Good whisking weather." Everybody groaned at him.

"If we got good weather coming," Gordon said, "I got a suggestion."

"Let's hear it," said Hugh.

Gordon presented his idea for a flight to Cape Hallett. He was calm and deliberate; Penny thought he sounded a bit like Steve. When he finished and sat down, there was a moment of silence. Hugh broke it.

"Ordinarily, I would approve or reject a proposal like this one on my own authority. Under present conditions, however, I feel we ought to have at least a consensus. Plus, of course, Al's opinion. Anyone want to speak against the idea?"

Penny looked across the lounge at Steve. He winked enigmatically at her and steepled his fingertips.

Will got up. "I think it's daft. Most of us haven't really seen what the surge has done—but I have, and Steve, and a few others. Al's seen more than anyone. It was bad enough when we had daylight, but now— my God, not in a Twin Otter. A Hercules, perhaps. But not in a small plane like ours. Not until September, anyway, and maybe not even then."

"Very good, Will. Anyone else?" No one spoke. "Anyone want to support Gordon's idea?"

Hands went up all around the room. "Don." Don Treadwell stood up, looking diffident. Penny couldn't recall the last time he'd spoken in a seminar.

"I feel it's dangerous, yes, but we have got no choice. We are on rationin', but the food is still runnin' out. We'll have our last steak some time this month, at this rate, and by August we'll be out of potatoes, flour, rice—we'll be eatin' canned fruit and survival-pack rations. We are goin' to be mighty hungry by spring. If Al goes, maybe we'll get out of here before then."

"If Al goes," Penny said, "I want to go with him."

The look on Steve's face was hard to judge: he was surprised, but something else showed as well—alarm? Concern? Contempt? Relief? It took away most of her pleasure in causing a sensation; how could she have lived with a man for months and still not be able to understand him or predict his reactions?

"I think it should be me," she went on. "Al shouldn't

have to go alone, and Shacktown shouldn't lose anyone essential. That leaves me." No one said anything. Penny saw some of the men exchanging looks. She left unsaid her main reason: that if she stayed, someone was going to get hurt.

"Perhaps we can consider that," said Hugh, "after we've heard from Al."

"I'm willing to go," Al said quietly, "and I'll be glad to have Penny come along."

Hugh stroked his thick red mustache. "Very well. Penny and Al will make a sortie to Cape Hallett in the morning. Now, we'll need a detail to dig out the hangar doors as soon as the wind drops a little. Any volunteers?"

11

SORTIE

"You're sure you want to go through with this?" Hugh asked. He and Al were the only people in the mess hall; it was about 0600 on the morning of July 3. Each man had a cup of instant coffee; the real coffee had run out a week before.

"Give me an alternative," Al said. He sipped his coffee, grimaced, and lit a cigar.

"Wish I could. At least you'll have a chance to get back if Hallett's no use." He looked hesitant, then asked: "What about Penny? That all right?"

"Yeah. She's okay. She doesn't go nuts when she's scared, and she's not dumb."

"So she'll be some help."

Al laughed and coughed on cigar smoke. "If I need help, I'll be *beyond* help. She'll be company, and she'll be out of people's hair."

Hugh studied the portrait of Shackleton on the wall beside them.

"It's our household god I've been thinking a good deal about lately," he said. "Bloody good man he was. I keep thinking how he got everyone across the ice when the *Endurance* broke up—hauling their lifeboats, getting them to Elephant Island, and then sailing across the worst ocean in the world to get help. And not a single death. Every last one of 'em brought out safely."

"Including one who'd had a heart attack," Al smiled.

"I take a lot of consolation from that, yes," Hugh

said. "Of course, Shackleton himself died of one a few years later. Good God, this coffee is rotten. Well, we haven't a lifeboat, so I can't sail off to South Georgia. But do me a favor—don't get killed."

"I won't. Believe me, I won't take chances."

"Good enough." Hugh put out his hand and rested it lightly on Al's wrist. "We'll be praying for you."

Penny woke; someone was rapping lightly at her door.

"Yeah?"

"It's Suzy, love."

"C'mon in. . . . Hi. What time is it?" She looked at her watch: 0717. "I better get up. Is the weather still okay?"

"I guess so. Have you talked with Steve?" Suzy asked suddenly. Penny had been expecting the question.

"No."

"Perhaps you should. He's worried about you."

"As well he should be. Why, did he say something to you?"

"Didn't need to. The poor bastard's been moping around like Ben on a bad day."

Penny was pulling on her boots. "I've seen him, all right. And a million other guys like him. They're so out of touch with their real feelings they don't even know how to feel sorry for themselves. Steve's more worried about losing the Otter than losing Al and me."

Everyone showed up for breakfast, and there was a mood of anxious cheerfulness in the mess hall. Penny and Al sat with Hugh, Will, Jeanne, and Herm, their meal repeatedly interrupted as people came over to wish them luck. Steve and Tim were among them.

"I think you're bonkers," Steve smiled, "but have a good time."

"We'll drop you a postcard," Penny said.

"Do." He nodded and turned away. Penny was so intent on noticing her reaction to him that she didn't react at all.

By 0830 the mess hall was emptying: the mechanics left first, to make last-minute checks of the Otter, and soon most of the others were on their way outside to see the plane off. Penny and Al, escorted by Hugh, walked down Tunnel D.

"I almost wish the weather would turn bad," Hugh said. "We'll be worrying about you."

"Don't bother," said Al. "We'll probably be back for supper."

Penny groaned. "God, if we are, Suzy will make me wash the dishes." The men laughed.

A few minutes later, the Otter stood in the glare of the floodlights outside the hangar. Through the windshield, Penny stared at the drifts that had built up, and which Howie had had to bulldoze away during the night. Outside the pool of light, everything was pitch black; anyone who stepped into the darkness vanished instantly. The green anoraks of the bystanders were vivid, almost fluorescent, and the fog of their breaths glittered around their heads.

Suddenly the floodlights went out. Al paused in the middle of start-up, and slid open his window. "What's the problem?" he called. Several voices answered at once, and Penny could hear boots crunching in the snow. Light still came from inside the hangar, throwing long shadows across the blue-white surface. A minute or two passed; then Penny could hear the voice of Reg Lewis, the electrician.

"Looks like some kind of wiring problem, Al. Might be awhile before we can track it down and fix it. Can you get off okay anyhow?"

"Sure."

"Okay—piss off, then, Yank, and don't come back without a Hercules."

Al waved and shut the window. Start-up went smoothly. With both engines going, he turned on the taxi lights and moved away from the hangar. The runway was anywhere Al chose; in all directions there was the same undulating surface. It was harder than it looked, and as they accelerated they could feel the plane jolt and sway. Penny refused to let herself be scared, but it was hard for her to keep her eyes off Al's face. In the dim yellow light of the instruments, he looked old and intent, almost grim. Not until they were airborne did he relax.

"Well, that wasn't too bad," he remarked as the Otter climbed to two thousand meters. He dimmed the instrument lights and peered out at the sky to the Grid South. "Sky looks good. We should reach Hallett about 1100; there'll be a little light in the sky by then. Let's hope it's a dull flight. Did you bring a book?"

"Forgot. But I've got my notebook. Hey, we're on our way! We're really going!"

Al smiled at her. "Are you glad to be leaving?"

"I'm not sure." She hesitated. "Glad and sad. Like the morning of the icequake, remember? We were all going to evacuate that day."

"I remember. It seems like a long time ago." He doused the instrument lights completely; as their eyes adjusted to the dark, the Shelf slowly emerged below them. It was a vast blue-gray plain, seamed with pressure ridges and mottled by sastrugi fields. Ice islands rose steeply from the Shelf in a few places; some were many kilometers long. The air was very clear.

Penny felt an unexpected contentment, a gladness at seeing something so beautiful and new; yet she realized that even the cold and empty grandeur of the ice was as transient as a field of wildflowers. Some day the sea would free itself again, and its waves would run unhindered till they crashed on the ancient rocks of the Antarctic shore. It would not happen in her lifetime, or even that of mankind, but it would happen. Some day rivers would run again in the glaciers' beds, and trees would take root and grow on old moraines, as they had long ago.

Al turned on the lights again and checked their course. He tried to raise Shacktown, but got only static. Then, as he was about to turn the radio off, he paused.

"Put on your helmet," he said. Penny yanked it on as he plugged it into the radio, and she heard a fuzzy voice in the earphones:

"Mayday, Mayday! Mayday, Mayday!"

"Mayday, this is Otter Five-Three," Al said. "We read you. Identify please. Over."

"My God." The voice sounded shocked. "Otter Five-Three, this is Outer Willy. Where are you? Over."

"Ah, we're over the Shelf, bearing Grid 125 degrees, about three hundred kilometers Grid Southwest of Cape Crozier. What is your location? Over."

"We figure we're about a hundred and fifty kilometers Grid South of Ross Island. Where are you going at this time of night? Over."

"Just stepping out for a beer," Al laughed, "We're en route to Cape Hallett, from New Shackleton Station. Over."

"I'll be damned. You guys got through okay? Over."

"Yup. But we're trying to get help. Hey, I thought Outer Willy was abandoned before Erebus blew up. Over."

"It was. We got here too late to be picked up, and we've been sitting here ever since. There are three of us. Over."

Al had already switched on the radio direction finder. "Any problems? Over."

"Wow. Well, no, but we'd kind of like to be rescued. Over."

The Otter banked left onto a new course.

"If we can land," Al said, "we'll take you along to Hallett. And if there's enough gas there, we'll go on to the Balleny Islands; if there isn't, we'll play poker all winter until somebody shows up. Is that all right? Over."

There was a pause. "Sounds interesting. Listen, you must be pretty close. We'll start sending up flares, once a minute. Let us know if you can't find us. Over."

"I'll find you. Just keep sending. Where were you guys when everything happened? Over."

"Up on Nimrod Glacier, doing geology. We had

some trouble with our helo—by the time I got it fixed, everybody must've been evacuated. We had a few bad days until we got past Erebus. It's been okay since then. What happened with you fellas? Over."

Al described events at Shacktown, speaking almost absentmindedly. He had turned down the instrument lights again, and was scanning the blue darkness ahead. A thin belt of cloud passed under them. Penny began to think they must have overflown the airstrip; she wondered what would happen if the Otter ran low on fuel before they could reach the geologists. Presumably Al would then fly them all back to Shacktown and try again for Hallett. If the weather held. In a way she would be relieved to be back in the familiar stinks and drafts and noises; but it would be horrible as well—especially to have to deal with Steve again.

"—barely got over the Ross Sea Ridge in one piece," Al was saying. "Whoops, there you are!" A brilliant red star burned in the darkness, a little to the right of their course, and Al changed direction. "Send up another one, will you? Over."

"Will do. Earl, he wants another flare. Okay. Uh, we don't have a real landing field now, but we can burn a couple drums of gas just to show where the buildings are. Over."

"Thanks. Can you give me wind speed and direction? Over."

"No wind to speak of. Uh, maybe you better make a couple of passses, just to see what it's like. Last time we looked, there were some sastrugi Grid North of the buildings. And there's a big old Herc half-buried out at the end of the skiway."

"A Herc—right, I remember it." The next flare went up, visibly closer. "Keep those flares coming; we're almost there."

The surface below them was strangely mottled now, like the marbled endpapers of an old book. Penny realized that the dark patches and streaks must be a layer of volcanic ash, buried in some places and exposed in others.

"Can we land on that stuff?" she asked. "On skis?"

"Well, I'd rather not try it."

The third flare was very close, and they could see a rosy blur of reflected light under it. A few moments later, the Otter dropped low over the huts of Outer Willy. There was little to see: three burning fuel drums and rows of snow-buried buildings.

Al circled, searching for a smooth, safe place to put down. The best he could find was over a kilometer Grid East of the buildings. After one trial approach just a few meters above the surface, he landed the Otter without incident.

The air seemed much colder than it had at Shacktown, and made their noses run. —Won't I look lovely? Penny thought, annoyed to be meeting strangers with a lump of frozen mucus on her lip. They walked quickly across the windcrust toward the burning drums, crossing some patches of ash that grated under their mukluks. Off to the left, the horizon was reddening a little.

A white spark appeared not far ahead, and came flickering toward them. A minute or two later, they heard someone call, "Hello!"

"Is that the welcoming committee?" Al called back.

"Sure is." A bulky shape in a blue-and-orange anorak became visible. The man extended a hand. "Hi—I'm Mike Birnbaum. Glad to meet you."

"Al Neal. And this is Penny Constable."

The flashlight glared in Penny's face. "Well, hello. What's a nice girl like you doing in a dump like this?"

"I keep asking myself the same question," Penny laughed. She took Mike's hand and felt oddly shy.

Mike must have felt the same way, because he said little as they went on to the buildings. He led them past the half-buried orange helos and into a Jamesway hut, a big semicylinder of canvas. The hammering of a diesel generator was loud until they got inside.

The Jamesway had been Outer Willy's mess hall and kitchen; most of the tables had been shoved to the far end of the room to make way for cases of canned food brought from elsewhere. Oil stoves burned at both ends of the hut, making it almost too warm; fluorescent lamps threw a bluish light. The ripe smells of oil, food, and sweat reminded Penny of Shacktown.

Two men in dirty trousers and plaid shirts stood by the cold porch. There was a round of handshaking and backslapping, and one of them gave Penny a hairy, unselfconscious kiss.

Mike Birnbaum, Penny now saw, was a short, slender man in his early twenties, with a downy black beard and dark eyes. Bob Price, the man Al had spoken with on the radio, was tall, gaunt, and very blond, with a silver ring in one ear; it gave him a piratical look, but Penny wondered how he kept from freezing his earlobe. Earl Bollinger, the third man, was a round-faced Black, even bigger than Howie O'Rourke, with a meticulously trimmed goatee.

"It's really great to see you," Bob said. "Would you like some lunch?"

They all sat down at a table near a big oil-burning range; Bob served them corned-beef sandwiches on fresh rye bread, fried potatoes, bean salad, and canned peaches. Over coffee, the geologists described how they had been caught by the quake; they'd had to clear a frozen fuel pump before they could get back to McMurdo Sound. They had finally reached Outer Willy a couple of days after Al and Max had tried to land there; seeing Erebus in continuing eruption, the geologists had stayed put. As their ice island had moved past Hut Point Peninsula, ash falls had nearly buried the buildings, but a change in wind direction had saved them from the worst of it. Outer Willy had moved rapidly down McMurdo Sound, and hadn't frozen into the new Shelf until June. The geologists weren't surprised to learn that the earth's magnetic field had reversed, since their own compasses had behaved crazily since last summer. They listened with professional interest to Al's description of the effects and extent of the surge.

"Sounds like you folks have had a lot of fun," Bob

remarked. "Least you've been getting out and seeing things. We've been sitting on our butts for six months, wondering what the hell's been going on."

"Well, here's your big chance to see the world," Al said. "We're planning to check out Cape Hallett. If there's gas, we'll go on to the Balleny Islands or maybe even New Zealand. If not, we'll hole up at Hallett till spring."

Bob lit a cigarette and looked thoughtfully across the hut; then he looked at Penny. She recognized something in that look. He was a calculator, like Steve, a weigher of costs and benefits.

"You mentioned that over the radio," Bob said at last. "I'm not sure we'd need to go if we weren't gonna go any farther. Hallett is right in the path of every storm coming in off the ocean. And it's not a big place—it wouldn't have much of a fuel dump, or a whole lot of supplies. It probably got evacuated, but if it didn't the guys there wouldn't need five extra mouths to feed."

"I know," Al nodded. "It's a very long shot. We've got to try it, but I wouldn't blame you for staying put."

"There's another possibility," Bob went on. "The Hercules."

Al looked at him cautiously, like someone who finds himself dealing with a self-possessed lunatic. "Oh?"

"You might go out and look it over if you have the time. I only know about choppers, but I couldn't find much wrong with it. The batteries are just about dead now, but I checked out the instruments back in March. Just for something to do, really. There was something wrong with the hydraulic system, or else the wiring. But everything else looked good. She was all gassed up and ready to fly; if they hadn't been in such a hurry to get out, they probably could've fixed her up in a day or two." He shrugged, an amateur unsure of his judgment against that of a professional.

"Well, well, well." Al looked at his watch. "Can we get inside it fairly quickly?"

"No sweat. We dug a tunnel. Want to see her?"

In a few minutes they were back outside, walking across snow that glowed pink-violet under a crimson sky. It was just bright enough for them to see where they were going, but all of them stumbled at least once. Penny, walking between Al and Mike, shivered with something more than cold: a frightened excitement, an anxious exhilaration.—Oh God, if it can only fly, if it can only fly. . . .

Drifts had piled up on the port side of the Hercules, but relatively little snow lay banked on the starboard side. Compared to the Otter, it seemed monstrously large, too large to fly. The starboard wing alone was as long as the Otter's full span, and the turboprop engines looked grotesquely big. Bob led them under the wing and along the starboard side toward the tail.

"The passenger doors are drifted over," he explained, "but the rear cargo door is open."

"The inside must be full of snow," Al said.

"Pretty near."

The rear of the fuselage tapered up and away from the snow toward the tail assembly. Drift had spilled around the plane here, and rose well above their heads. Bob shone his flashlight on a bamboo pole, then dug into the snow beside it. He pulled out a sheet of plywood, revealing a narrow black opening in the drift.

"I'll go first," he said, and went in on his hands and knees.

Penny went third, after Al, and was surprised to find the tunnel relatively warm. She crawled for some uncertain distance, watching Al's backside in the light of her flash. Then the tunnel sloped steeply upward, and its floor turned from packed snow to thickly frosted metal. The cold suddenly bit through her mitts and trousers, and she remembered how Al had made them abandon the helo after the crash.

The tunnel ended, and she stood up in freezing darkness. Bob and Al were shining their flashlights around a space that seemed as vast as Shacktown's hangar, even though the interior of the Hercules was half-filled with snow. Earl and Mike came through, and their lights made the space a little less cavernous; but she remembered that each of Shacktown's huts had been carried intact in the cargo compartment of a plane like this one.

Where the drift hadn't reached, the cargo compartment looked like a cave: every surface was crusted with glittering frost. Simple seats—red plastic webbing over steel frames—had been bolted to the walls, facing each other across a wide aisle that could hold personal baggage and other cargo.

"It'd be some job digging this out," Al grunted. "Let's take a look at the flight deck."

They had to struggle through knee-deep snow until they reached a door and forced it open enough to squeeze through. Penny gasped in shock at the dim red light that came from the far side.

The flight-deck windows, though frosted, were translucent enough to let in the noon twilight. Al looked around for a moment before settling into the pilot's chair; he swept the flashlight beam over the instrument panels. Penny felt a pang of disappointment: so many gauges, so many switches and knobs and dials—anything as big and complex as this couldn't be repaired by a few people on an ice island, with the nearest proper facilities thousands of kilometers away.

Al pressed a switch and a faint yellow glow appeared in the gauges.

"Yeah, not much life in the batteries any more," he said almost to himself. "Gee, this is an old Herc!" He turned the flash on a small metal plate and scraped the frost away, revealing the number 56740. "I'll be darned—I've flown this one before. Used to belong to VXE-6 before we sold her to the Kiwis." He tried some more switches, rubbed frost from the instruments, and muttered to himself as she watched the feeble responses they made.

Penny began to feel the cold; so did the others, but Al seemed oblivious. After a very long time he got up and poked around the flight deck, pulling panels away to inspect the wiring behind them. Finally he turned to Bob and asked: "What about the skis? Any damage?"

"No—I don't think so, anyway. They were drifted over with ash when we got here, and they're probably frozen into the snow by now, but I don't think we've got a real problem."

"Well. Let's get out of here."

The Jamesway was like a Turkish bath; they pawed themselves out of the top layers of their clothing while fingers and toes came painfully back to life. Al found a cigar butt and carefully lit it. He took a few puffs.

"I think we can do it," he said. "There's a leak in the hydraulics, all right. The booster system—the rudder and the starboard-wing spoilers—are out of action. But the wiring's okay—if *that* was the problem, we'd be out of luck. And if the skis are damaged we're really out of luck. But I'll bet they're okay."

"What'll it take to fix the booster system?" Bob asked.

"You know anything about Hercs?"

"No."

"Well, I know a fair amount, and there must be some manuals around. We got one or two guys at Shacktown who could help—Simon's worked on the Hercules a few times, and there's a Russian aircraft mechanic who knows his stuff." Al blew a smoke ring. "Might take a couple of weeks. Maybe less."

"What about spare parts, tools, all that stuff?" asked Earl.

"Shouldn't be a problem—they always kept most of the essential equipment here, to save time commuting to Inner Willy. We can make do."

Mike said: "So what's your program?"

"Penny and I go right back to Shacktown. I bring Simon and Kyril here, and maybe a few others, and we go to work. By the middle of the month we should know if the Herc will really fly. If it will, we take it to Shacktown and then fly out to New Zealand. If it won't, we stay put until spring."

"Sounds okay," Bob said. "We can give you some help, too, but bring as many people as you need—there's plenty of room in the other Jamesways, and enough food for everyone. Well, for ten or twelve if they end up staying all winter," he added.

"Christ," Penny groaned. "I'll be back home washing dishes tonight." The men laughed; Al patted her arm. "You're sure Cape Hallett is out?" she asked.

"Gee, you really don't want to wash dishes, do you?" Al smiled. "Yeah, Hallett is out. If you've got to gamble, you might as well play the odds."

The three men walked out with them to the Otter, dragging a sledge loaded with supplies: coffee, canned food, cigarettes, candy. Then they all shook hands again. Mike said, "When you're gone we'll be sure it was all a hallucination."

"I already think *you're* the hallucinations," Penny answered. "Good luck—see you again in a few weeks, I guess."

"*I'll* be back by suppertime," Al said. "Unless the weather breaks."

They all looked up. The horizon was dark again, and the sky was full of stars. There was still no wind.

Al tried to follow his own tracks in taking off, to avoid hitting an unseen hole or sastrugi. As the Otter climbed and circled, three flares went off over the little base; Al blinked his running lights in reply.

"Are we really going to fly our way out of here?" Penny asked, feeling a little giddy.

"I believe we are. I truly believe we are." Al rubbed his hands together, like a stage villain anticipating the success of his schemes. "We're gonna freeze in that Herc for a couple of weeks, but it'll be a lot of fun."

"Whoopee," Penny drawled.

"Aw, where's your spirit of adventure?"

"It's all very well for you—you'll be having fun with your grease-monkey friends in a nice cool airplane while I'm slaving in that hot kitchen."

After a while she said: "The real piss-off is being back with Steve."

"How so?"

"I don't like failures. He's not a failure, and I'm not a failure, but we sure failed together." She waved at the cigar smoke filling the compartment. "And I kind of expected that, because he's a lot like my ex-husband. But that lasted four years, and this lasted four months."

"Being on the ice will do it," Al said. "Whatever you are when you come here, this place will intensify it. Steve came here as an ambitious guy with a reputation to make. You came here as an outside observer. And I think you were kind of on the run from something."

"What did you come as?" she asked quickly, feeling the subject was getting dangerous.

"I was on the run too." He looked at her, his expression almost unreadable in the dim light. "Guys Steve's age, if they're any good, are hungry. And they think about that hunger, and how they can feed it. It makes 'em kind of calculating sometimes, but it also makes 'em—oh, exposed. Like anybody who wants something really bad. I don't know what made you guys decide to split up, but I wouldn't be surprised if it had to do with his being involved in the quake."

"Hey, Al, you and I were involved too, remember?"

"Not the way Steve was—intellectually involved, emotionally involved. You and me, we just got knocked down. *He's* the Frankenstein who invented the monster. And then it surprised him, and he's had to try to understand it, get it all—get it all into his head, into words and numbers."

She suspected Al was right; she had known a lot of men, and a few women, with that urge to reduce the world to a pattern of symbols. She had the urge herself. But to understand Steve was not to forgive him.

Conversation lapsed. For a long time there was only the rumble of the engines, the vibration of the plane, and the darkness. Al tried several times to raise either Shacktown or Outer Willy, with no luck. At 1500, after they'd been in the air almost an hour, he shook his head in annoyance.

"I'm still not getting TACAN. And we must be almost on top of Shacktown."

Penny put on her helmet and plugged it in, but only static came through the headphones. Al took them down to five hundred meters, but there were no special landmarks—only the Shelf and a scattering of ice islands.

"I see a light!" Penny said. She pointed a few degrees to the right of their course. "See it?"

Al doused the instrument lights. "Yup. That must be the place."

They flew toward the light for several minutes, but it seemed to grow no closer. The high cliffs of an ice island rose under them, scarcely visible in the darkness.

Now the light did grow: it pulsed and flared, a yellow-orange flower. They were over it, circling down, and their beacon was Shacktown itself, burning in the ice.

12

FIRE

Reg Lewis had gone right to work to find the cause of the floodlights' failure, but it hadn't been an easy job. A hundred cables ran down Tunnel D into the hangar; some were exposed while others disappeared into the hangar walls. The floodlight cables were in the walls, and also supplied current to several other outlets. Reg methodically worked his way around the dark hangar from the machine shop, and it wasn't until almost 1000 hours that he began to smell smoke. He yanked off a glove and held it against a wall panel without quite touching; then another. The fifth panel was noticeably warm. So were the sixth and seventh. The eighth was hot.

"Fire!" he shouted, and began running toward the nearest drum of fire extinguisher. It was a fine red powder that could be sprayed or even shoveled— ordinary fire retardants were liquid and therefore useless in the cold. He wrestled the drum closer to the hot panel, aware of footsteps thudding toward him from the machine shop.

"Where?" It was Gordon Ellerslee, with George Hills right behind him.

"Behind the bloody wall. That bloody old aluminum wiring they put in two years ago." He ripped the shovel out of the drum and jammed its blade between two panels, then pried one panel loose. Smoke puffed out, black and acrid.

"Better be quick!" Gordon said. Reg heaved on the

177

shovel and the panel screamed away from the studs. The smoldering wood ignited; Reg stumbled back and plunged the shovel into the top of the drum. As he threw the retardant over the fire, sparks scattered over the duckboards and oil-soaked ice beneath their feet.

Suddenly they were standing in a pool of blue and orange flames, a pool that spread erratically along the hangar wall and across the floor. The three men threw handfuls of retardant around themselves.

"Aw, hell," Reg said. "We better get out of here."

"No shit," Gordon snapped.

They stumbled through the flames, coughing. The hangar looked strange in the bluish firelight, and they almost lost their bearings. The forty seconds it took to reach the machine shop seemed much longer.

George Hills, in first, slapped the FIRE button on the wall by the door to Tunnel D. A shrill clanging began at once. Gordon snatched up the phone and punched Hugh's number. No answer. He tried the lounge.

"Fire in the hangar!" he bellowed as soon as someone picked up the phone. "It's bad. We need everybody." Then he dropped the phone and lunged toward the switches controlling the hangar doors.

"Gord—don't," George said. "You'll just feed the fire."

"We gotta get the fucking vehicles out. The fucking fire will burn right through the roof anyways. Jesus—the fuel bladders."

Two big fuel bladders, one for diesel Arctic and the other for JP4, were buried in the ice just beyond the burning wall. The diesel was probably safe—it was farther away from the fire, and not easily ignited—but the JP4 bladder could go off like a bomb.

Men began to pour into the machine shop, and up the ramp directly into the hangar. The big doors banged open, and the fire reached farther back in the hangar, sweeping delicately around the snowmobiles, Sno-Cats, and the D4 bulldozer. Oily black smoke retreated, thickening, before the cold air from outside.

Hugh was suddenly in the machine shop, his anorak open and his head bare. "Get on those vehicles and get 'em outside," he said calmly. "Howie, take the D4. Then come back for the Nodwell. Steve, the snowmobile by the rear wall. Will, the other one. Simon, take Sno-Cat 1. Gordon, Sno-Cat 2." He stopped the three Russians. "Get the sledges down from the wall on this side, and get as many crates onto them as you can. Take them outside, dump them—"

"Dump?" asked Ivan.

"Turn over. In the snow. Then come back with the sledges and take more crates."

"Okay."

The fire was eating rapidly into the far wall, and part of the floor was now a pond of burning oil and gas, floating on a few centimeters of meltwater. Steve's snowmobile snarled through the fire and outside into the dark. The Sno-Cats and the other snowmobile followed, skidding in the water. Terry and Suzy, along with Don Treadwell, joined the men spraying and shoveling fire retardant along the edge of the burning pond.

Howie O'Rourke loped back in and headed straight for the huge green Nodwell tractor, which looked like a house on caterpillar treads. The pond had already spread around it. Howie bent and wrenched a three-meter length of duckboards right out of the ice, and slid it into the flames. It began to burn, but it gave him a chance to sprint across to the tractor. He climbed over the tread and into the cab. The Nodwell's engine, unstarted in weeks, refused. Howie leaned out of the cab.

"Get the cable, somebody—we gotta winch this stupid beast outa here."

Max Wilhelm dragged the cable in, and Howie came back across the duckboards. He pulled them to within a meter of the front of the Nodwell, carried the cable out, and hooked it up. Then he waved a signal to Hugh, up in the machine shop, and the cable went taut.

Very slowly, the big tractor began to grind across

the floor. No one but Howie paid it any attention; most were trying to get to the burning wall and keep the fire away from the JP4 bladder. The hangar was filling with ice crystals as well as smoke: as the fire melted the floor, steam escaped through the flames into air that was -45°C. The crystals fell back into the fire, or swirled in the turbulent air, glittering like sparks. It took over ten minutes to haul the Nodwell outside into the darkness. By that time, Howie had gone to join the others along the wall.

They worked clumsily but systematically, coughing in the smoke as they shoveled retardant. Tears poured down their faces and froze when they stepped back from the flames. The overhead lights went out; emergency lamps tripped on, but had little effect in the smoke. The men fought the fire by its own light.

Without warning, a jet of fire rose almost to the ceiling. Howie knew at once what had happened: the fuel line from the JP4 bladder had burned through, and fumes from the bladder, drawn out by rising air, had ignited.

"Everybody out!" he screamed. "Out, out!"

Those near the back of the hangar raced for the ramp to Tunnel D; Howie and the others turned and went outside. The vehicles gave a little shelter from a rising breeze, but it was horribly cold.

"Okay," Howie rasped, "when the bladder goes, we gotta sneak back in and keep the fire outa the tunnel."

"How?" Gordon panted. An instant later the snow lit up, a lambent red-orange, and the men saw each other clearly. They crouched behind the Sno-Cats as the bladder exploded in a geyser of fire and steam. The wall of the hangar, already weakened, caved in. The roof sagged and cracked; flames shot up through it into the smoking dark.

"Hugh's still in the machine shop," Steve yelled over the roar. "Let's get in there."

"Wait a minute," Howie yelled back. "He'll be down in the tunnel. Go in there now and you're dead." He looked grimly at the fire, and swatted at a fragment of glowing ash that settled on his sleeve. Despite the flames, it was hard to see the interior of the hangar, but the floor was still burning, sending still more black smoke into the air.

"Let's bulldoze it," Steve said. "Get the D4 and D8 moving, and bury the fire on the floor."

"Good." Howie grabbed Simon Partington and hustled him over to the D4. As its engine started, Howie went on to the D8, which had been outside for days. The night before, he'd had to blowtorch its pony engine to thaw it enough to start the diesel so he could clear the snow from the hangar doors. The pony engine was frozen again, but Howie stolidly dug the blowtorch out of the cab and went to work. Ben Whitcumb lurched up beside him.

"I got the flamethrower," Ben said. "It ought to work faster."

"You know how to use it?"

"Yes." Ben didn't bother to put on the flamethrower's backpack; he leaned it against his leg and put the nozzle close to the engine. A long yellow flame gushed out, and Ben hastily twisted the nozzle until the flame was hot and blue. It took over five minutes, but the pony engine caught the first time Howie tried it, and the diesel bellowed into life a moment later.

Simon meanwhile had driven the D4 back to the hangar, with the bulldozer's blade pushing a mound of snow ahead of it. A cloud of ice crystals formed around the D4 as it entered the hangar; the snow was melting, vaporizing, and refreezing. But most of it stayed solid, and Simon was able to lay a two-meter strip along the edge of the burning pool. He backed out, scraped out more snow, and went in again.

Howie, with the D8's huge blade, rapidly made up for lost time. The smoke was less of a problem, since the fire had burned through the rear wall and more of the roof. After four runs, however, Howie had to stop: most of the floor fire had been smothered, but the burning fuel bladder was so hot that getting close to it was impossible, and chunks of the roof were falling around the bulldozers in showers of sparks.

Steve clambered up into the cab. "What about the diesel bladder?"

"It oughta be okay. There's thirty meters of ice between it and the JP4."

"I hope you're right. Let's see what needs doing in the tunnel."

Howie, Simon, Steve, and three or four others went into the hangar at a clumsy trot, coughing in the smoke. Behind the machine shop, the fire had spread along the rear wall and down the ramp toward Tunnel D. The men went through the machine shop and down the stairs to the tunnel, where they found almost twenty people fighting the fire. Smoke hung like a black fog under the tunnel lights.

From the top of the stairs, Steve watched the fire spreading down the ramp, through the high stacks of crates along the walls. In the dry cold, every scrap of wood, fabric and plastic seemed to ignite instantly. The flames blazed through a pink cloud of retardant, slowed but not stopped. He went down the stairs and found Hugh in the crowd.

"It'll burn right down both sides of the tunnel, and along the duckboards," Steve said. "The hangar's a dead loss. But if we can clear out some of these crates —like a firebreak—"

"Good. Ray, George, Ivan! Come on back. And you chaps too." Hugh soon had a team working on each side of the tunnel, moving crates away from the approaching fire.

"Anyone hurt?" Steve asked Hugh.

"No, thank God." Hugh coughed. "Smoke's a nuisance. Anything left of the hangar?"

"The far side is completely gutted. We kept it away from the machine shop, but if any more of the roof comes down, that could be wrecked too."

"Bloody hell. And tons of snow on the roof." He looked quickly up at the roof of the tunnel. Long icicles were forming from it, and above the ramp the frost was entirely gone. Where the crates had been removed, the tunnel walls glistened unnaturally. "We may lose part of the roof here as well," Hugh said.

"That ought to put out the fire, anyway," Steve answered.

Despite all their efforts, the fire spread through the crates right up to the firebreak. Hugh ordered everyone down the tunnel. The icicles had vanished; twenty meters of roof plate, four whole sections, were bare and dry above the fire. The walls were hidden in smoke and steam; burning crates crashed to the floor of the tunnel. The stink of roasting meat drifted through the smoke, and canned goods exploded with muffled bangs.

"About time we had a cook-out," Gordon laughed, and everyone else laughed too. No one seemed dejected; the mood, as far as Steve could tell, was a mixture of annoyance and excitement.

"All right," Hugh shouted. "Everyone into the huts. I think the roof is about to go."

It went before anyone could move. The right-hand wall gave way, and an instant later the roof plates sagged and fell. The lights went out all the way to the junction with Tunnel E; out of the murk came a hissing cloud of smoke, steam, and powdery snow, driven by cold outside air. It filled the tunnels like a gray smog, but dissipated almost as quickly as it had come.

Someone went into Tunnel C and came back with some flashlights. Steve, Hugh, and Carter took them and walked cautiously into the darkened end of Tunnel D. An irregular mound of snow choked it, rising in places to three or four meters above the floor. Beyond it was the orange glare of the still-burning hangar. Above it was a ragged rectangle of blackness, out of which snow still sifted in tiny cascades. The men could hear the distant hoarse roar of the burning JP4, but other than that there was little sound.

Hugh shivered. "Damned cold. Well, that'll teach us not to play with matches."

They became aware of a faint buzzing overhead. Steve looked up, expecting to see a sparking wire.

There was nothing. The buzzing turned to a deep drone, and then they saw the Otter's running lights as it crossed the black rectangle of sky.

With the temperature in the tunnels close to -40°C, the huts were far colder than usual. Everyone at that night's seminar was warmly dressed, and a few even wrapped themselves in blankets. But Hugh had ordered full rations for supper, and no one seemed unhappy.

Al and Penny reported on their trip to Outer Willy and the possibility of repairing the Hercules. When they had finished, Hugh asked for comments.

"We've got to go," Steve said at once. "As soon as possible."

"Easier said than done," Will remarked. "It'd take the Otter at least two trips to ferry everyone there; probably four or five if we took some supplies and our scientific data. I don't think the weather would co-operate that long."

"Anyway, we don't have enough gas for four or five trips," Al said. "Almost all the JP4 is gone, except for three or four drums and what's left in the plane. What we could do is, take the mechanics back to Outer Willy, fix the Herc, and fly it here to pick up everybody else. But that would take two, three weeks, maybe more—assuming the Herc will fly at all. And Shacktown wouldn't be a very comfortable place to wait."

"That's an understatement," said Colin Smith. "The next blizzard will fill the tunnels with drift, and maybe even bring down more of the roof. We'd be better off in igloos on the surface."

Hugh leaned over and spoke quietly with Don Treadwell for a few seconds. Then he said: "We have another choice. One group flies to Outer Willy to fix the Hercules. The other traverses the Shelf."

"That's goddam dangerous," Gordon said. Hugh nodded.

"It's three hundred kilometers by air, and a good deal more on the surface, I'm sure of that. But our vehicles are intact, and Don tells me we ought to be able to carry enough food to keep everyone on normal polar rations for three weeks."

"That's assuming that we don't have to rely on whatever they got at Outer Willy," Don added. "If we have to winter over there, and they don't have much food, then we all go on short rations again."

"Does my idea meet with your approval?" Hugh asked. "All in favor—" Everyone's hand went up. "Any opposed? None. Very good. I suggest that the mechanics and the women—and the Russians—all fly. The rest of us will do the traverse."

Arguments broke out at once over who should fly and who should traverse. Hugh refused to fly, but Katerina overruled him. When he gave in on that, she pressed her advantage and announced that she would be more useful with the traverse party. Jeanne and Suzy didn't want to be separated from their men, and some of the mechanics argued that they would be more useful servicing the vehicles they knew than trying to help Al with the Hercules. Penny, somehow dreading relegation to the Outer Willy kitchen more than the hazards of the Shelf, insisted on being in the traverse party.

Hugh irritably put an end to the bickering. "I am abiding by the tsarina's ukase," he growled, "but I must insist on deciding who's to fly and who's to walk. And I'll be grateful if you would all go along and spare us any more fuss." He jotted down some names and read them off: "The Otter party will consist of Al, Kyril, Ivan, and Yevgeni; Jeanne and Suzy; Reg and Simon; and myself. The rest of you will be on the traverse, with Carter in charge. Colin, what's the weather like?"

"Wind's picking up from Grid North. I think we're in for another blizzard tomorrow."

"Right. I'd like the Otter refueled and flown out of here at once. Take the bare minimum of baggage, but you'd better carry along some food and medicine as well. We don't want to be total sponges on the Ameri-

cans," he added dryly. "Any tools or spare parts that
you think you'll need should go along as well." He
stared around the room. "Well, don't just gawp at me
—get along!"

It took just over an hour to prepare for the flight.
At 1945 hours, the Otter took off in the light of the
haloed moon. Steve, Carter, Gordon, and three or four
others went into the ruins of the hangar, which was
still smoldering, and salvaged some big tarpaulins that
had been stowed on the roof of the machine shop.
They dragged the tarps outside, pounded the folds out
of them, and stretched them over the gap in the roof.
The tarps would not survive a serious storm; if the
wind didn't rip them loose, snow would bear them
down into the tunnel. But in the meantime the tunnels
and huts could warm up a bit, and salvaging supplies
for the traverse would be easier.

Under the tarpaulins, Tunnel D was dark, and stank
of burnt debris. The men groped cautiously over the
icy duckboards until they reached the undamaged part
of the tunnel. Carter touched Steve and Gordon: "We
ought to talk a minute. Hugh's office will do."

"Sure," Steve said.

"The rest of you lads go have a beer," Carter said;
the men, scarcely seeming to have heard him, plodded
on down to Tunnel A without a word.

In Hugh's office, Carter dropped into his accustomed
seat; Steve and Gordon took two other chairs, leaving
Hugh's empty. "Pretty busy day," Carter grunted.
"Tomorrow will be worse. Look, don't do a damn
thing more tonight. But tomorrow morning I'd like
you two to start organizing the evacuation. Steve, that
means sorting out all the scientific material—computer
tapes, whatever—and deciding what to take."

"What about instrumentation?" Steve asked. "We
could do some work on the traverse."

"Sure, as long as it's simple, light stuff. Gord—you
have a tougher job, in a way. Get your technicians
together and figure out every possible thing that could

go wrong with those bloody vehicles. Then decide what you'd need to fix it once you're out on the Shelf."

"How much time you giving us?" Gordon asked.

"Two days. Maybe more, if Colin's blizzard is a long one, but don't count on it."

"Okay. Listen, we'll have to build some wanigans that'll fit on the sledges. Otherwise we'll never be able to shelter everybody."

Carter nodded wearily. "Of course, very good. Take whatever steps you need to build them. And I'll look after the nontechnical support—just Terry and Don now, I guess. Let's meet tomorrow afternoon—just after lunch, say—and compare notes. With luck, we'll be ready to go by the evening of the fifth."

Steve and Gordon went straight to their cubicles, too tired even to walk straight. When Steve opened his door, he saw Tim sprawled face-down on the bottom bunk, asleep in his soot-blackened clothes. Steve sat down and tugged vaguely at his boot-laces for a minute before waking enough to do the job properly. He got out of his anorak, and found himself shivering. The big electric baseboard heater was turned up to maximum, but the cubicle was almost freezing. At least the upper bunk would be a bit warmer. He found a spare blanket and put it over Tim, then heaved himself into the upper bunk.

"What time?" Tim mumbled.

"Almost 2100. Go back to sleep." Steve zipped himself into his bag and leaned out to turn off the light.

"Why don't you go see Penny?" Tim asked.

"The idea occurred to me. But I'm just too goddam tired."

"Well, you better do something t'morrow, man." Tim's voice was a thick monotone. "Sure don' wanna cross the ice with you mopin' around lookin' sorry for yourself."

Too restless to sleep, Penny went for a walk to the greenhouse. The lights burned as brightly as ever, but it was uncomfortably cold; many of the plants had already died. She picked some seed pods from the sweet peas and tucked them into her shirt pocket; then, a little scandalized at her sentimentality, she went to bed.

The bunk was cold, and stayed cold. She wondered what it would be like out on the Shelf, sleeping in the Nodwell or one of the wanigans, with the wind crashing against the walls; and she imagined them all freezing in some endless blizzard. They might write letters home, like Scott, but no one would come to seek those last documents.

Everyone was up early the next morning, and Penny and Terry worked frantically to get them all fed. Then the others dispersed, and the mess hall was chilly and silent.

"Right, forget the dishes," Terry said. "We got to start sorting through the shelves and see what goes and what stays."

It was hard work, lugging out crates of food from the stores room and into a corner of the mess hall. Terry and Carter argued about what would be needed, with Terry usually getting his way. Even so, the amount of food they would take did not seem very large.

"Carter and his fussing about 'acceptable loads,'" Terry growled. "Worries about fuel for the damn tractors and forgets fuel for the damn people. Well, as long as everyone gets plenty of carbohydrates and protein, we'll manage. Right, now—let's lay on some lunch."

It was a cheerful meal, with conversations sputtering at every table and men moving about to see how other groups were doing. When Herm Northrop came in, Penny handed him a bowl of clam chowder and three big sandwiches.

"When do you shut down?" she asked.

"Last thing. We're only running at five percent capacity now." He smiled a little uncertainly. "I'm not sure I'm sad or relieved to be leaving the core here."

"It'll be safe till spring, won't it?"

"Oh, no doubt. Still—it's a little like leaving a sleeping baby alone in the house."

There was no seminar that night. A tense quiet filled the station, broken by the occasional snarl of a power saw or the scuffling footsteps of men hauling loads up the newly repaired ramp. The wind picked up, and by midnight the tunnels were full of blowing snow. The tarpaulins banged and flapped. Carter went out to the men working on the vehicles, and ordered them inside.

The wanigans—and two extra sledges—were finished by noon on the 5th. After lunch, the sledges were loaded and covered with tarps. The wanigans, little more than A-frame plywood boxes lined with fiberglass insulation, were equipped with stoves and battery-powered lamps. After looking inside one, Penny was guiltily relieved to be assigned to a proper bunk in the back of the Nodwell.

Most people took a nap that afternoon, but Steve and Tim spent the time analyzing the last of the seismographic data, and Colin made weather observations from the dome. The wind had died down again, but an overcast had turned the moon to a white blur; there would be snow by morning, but not enough to force a delay.

Supper was quiet. As people finished, they drifted out by ones and twos to check for forgotten items, or to haul duffel bags and instrument cases out to the vehicles.

All of Penny's gear was already aboard the Nodwell; she went back to her cubicle to dress, and went out for a last walk in the tunnels. The duckboards were already drifted ankle-deep in snow that rose like fine mud in a disturbed pond as she walked through it. After a minute or two she realized that the tunnels, the huts were empty. The only sign of life was the symphonic roar of the vehicles echoing against the high walls. She turned at the end of Tunnel D and began walking toward the ramp and the outside.

The lights went out without warning. She gasped and stumbled, then caught her balance. The darkness seemed total, and the noise from outside disoriented her, made her feel she was in a far narrower space. Groping, she took a few steps, then a few more.— What if they leave me?

A light flashed on in the darkness ahead of her, and she heard men's voices.

"Hello?" she called.

The light swung round and dazzled her.

"Aha," said Herm Northrop. "Sneaking in after curfew, eh?"

"What on earth are you doing here?" Carter asked. "I thought everyone was outside by now."

Their dark figures came close. Carter patted her shoulder, and guided her toward the little circle of light that Herm's flash made on the drifted floor. She followed it out into the cold.

13

~~~~~~~~~~~~~~~

TRAVERSE

The air stank of diesel fumes, burned wood, and
scorched metal. Penny was glad to get into the rear of
the Nodwell. It was rather like a trailer, with a sink,
a chemical toilet, and several canvas bunks rolled up
against the walls. Apart from a narrow, divided windshield in the driver's cab, the only window was a small
porthole set in the rear door. No one seemed interested
in looking outside; the five people in the passenger
compartment were trying to shout to each other over
the noise of the engines. Katerina was sitting on one
of the bunks, and made room for Penny. Herm, Don
Treadwell, and Ray Crandall sat amiably crowded on
the bunk opposite; Sean McNally, their driver, was up
in the cab.

The vehicles' noise changed pitch, and the Nodwell
lurched slowly forward. The convoy was heading Grid
Northeast, toward the scree slope where Will and Tim
had descended to the Shelf. The two snowmobiles went
first, ridden by Gordon and Roger. Next went Sno-
Cat 1, with Will driving. Its wanigan, riding on a
sledge, carried Steve, Carter, and Ben. Tim drove
Sno-Cat 2; his passengers were Terry, Max, and Colin.
The D8 was Howie's, with Gerry and Bruce as passengers. Tom Vernon drove the D4 with only George
Hills as a regular passenger; Gordon and Roger would
use the D4 wanigan for sleeping and foul-weather shelter. The Nodwell came last.

No one in the Nodwell said anything about leaving the station; conversations centered on the weather and the likely condition of the surface once they got down onto the Shelf. Penny found herself feeling a little depressed about going, and guessed the others were too.

Compared to the Sno-Cats, Penny found the Nodwell relatively smooth-riding, but slow and noisy. There was frost on the walls and floor, though at head level it was warm. To heat the whole cabin above freezing was impossible: it would mean risking wet feet every time someone came in from outside, and the snow that would inevitably blow inside would melt and soak into everything. Every time the tractor went over a bump, there was a grating noise from the roof of the cabin, where a portable crevasse bridge was lashed down.

Before long, Sean invited Penny and Don to join him in the cab. Through the double-glazed windshield, they watched the running lights of the other vehicles. The Nodwell's headlights glared on glittering windcrust, upon which even the D8's treads had left little mark. "Good sign," Sean said. "It's no fun bogging down in something as big as this beast."

The tractor moved at little better than walking speed, and the rest of the convoy gradually pulled ahead. Occasionally, as they heaved over the crest of a ridge, they could glimpse lights ahead; otherwise they might have been utterly alone. Apart from occasional sastrugi and the convoy's faint tracks, there wasn't much to see.

It took almost another hour to reach the edge of the island, where the rest of the convoy had halted. It was just past midnight. Carter Benson came in through the rear door and gratefully accepted a hot cup of tea.

"We've already sent people down the hill to look for soft spots," he said, speaking mostly to Sean. "We're lucky—the slope faces the wind, and it's packed down like cement. Howie's taking the D8 down first. He should be able to push through the patch of pressure ice at the bottom. Then we'll let the sledges down. The rest of the vehicles will follow. You'll be last."

"Think it'll hold us?" Sean asked.

"Yes, but it'll probably be the most exciting part of the whole traverse."

They worked for the next few hours in a glowing ice fog formed by the vehicles' exhaust. The D8 made it down without incident; the first sledge, however, bogged down and had to be manhauled most of the way to the Shelf. The rest of the sledges were winched down by the D8.

It was past 0600 the next morning, July 6, before the entire convoy stood on the Shelf. Penny found herself stuck yet again with kitchen duty, though only for the Nodwell crew. Sean, Don, and Herm went outside to make sure everything was secured on the sledges, and to refuel.

"My God, it's cold out there!" Don gasped when they got back inside. His short black beard was heavily frosted, and his dark face was gray. "The wind is picking up, too."

All three of them unrolled their canvas bunks and wrestled themselves into sleeping bags.

"Aren't we pulling out soon?" Penny asked.

"Not until eleven hundred," Herm said. "Carter says everyone should get some sleep."

"Easier said than done," Sean shivered, "when your balls are frozen solid."

"Well, can't you even start the engine and warm this place up?" Penny asked plaintively.

"Uh-uh. Carter says we gotta save fuel. And it's not so cold that the engine might seize up."

"Hell." Cold was already seeping through the fiberglass in the walls. The primus stove gave a little light and less heat—which was lost in any case, since Katerina insisted on turning it off to prevent carbon monoxide buildup.

Penny thought she would be unable to sleep, but suddenly woke to find the engine roaring again and the Nodwell swaying as it began to move. Now, she thought, the journey's really begun.

Gordon and Roger roved ahead of the convoy, looking for the easiest route. Their snowmobiles were fairly new Bombardiers, with semi-enclosed saddles, good radios, and powerful headlights. Even so, they found it hard going; a wind was rising from Grid South, chilling them, and the headlights weren't much use against the drift. At least they had good radio contact with the convoy, and it was reassuring to eaves-drop on the vehicle drivers' chatter.

Their course had been roughly Grid Southeast since leaving the scree slope, and Laputa's cliffs were now only a distant grayness off to the right. The horizon was a dim band of greens and pinks, against which another ice island stood out in black profile. The shelf was smoother than Gordon had expected, with only occasional hills and hollows, and the windcrust was firm.

It was nearly noon, and they were about to stop for lunch when they suddenly came upon a pressure ridge looming out of the drift. Gordon stopped, swore, and picked up his microphone. A hundred meters to his left, Roger's headlight showed that he had also halted.

"How does it look over there, Roger?"

"Pretty bad. Must be four, five meters high, and really rough."

"Same here. Well, I'm gonna climb over it and see what the other side is like."

This side of the ridge was in the lee of the wind, but the ice was jagged and bare. Gordon had to pick his way slowly, a flashlight clumsily held in one mitt, and it took him almost ten minutes to reach the top. The wind was like a punch in the face. Squinting, he tried to see how far the ridge extended. It seemed to run Grid South for at least a couple of kilometers. But it wasn't very wide—maybe ten meters—and the Shelf beyond looked clear and smooth.

He slid back down, glad to be out of the wind, and got back on the radio.

"Carter, this is Gordon. We've hit a pressure ridge."

"Can we get over it or around it?"

"I don't think so. But we oughta be able to blast a hole through it."

"Okay. Sit tight. We should reach you in an hour or so."

Gordon saw a light twinkle briefly in the distance: one of the vehicles, coming up over a rise. It made him feel good just to see it.

The convoy, however, took almost three hours to reach the ridge. The wind was a full gale now, carrying enough snow to half-blind the drivers. Gordon and Roger had pitched a tent under the ridge, and listened to the bellowing of the wind while they ate a tepid stew for lunch. The wind was so loud that the sound of the D8's engine was drowned out until the big bulldozer was almost on top of them.

The men crawled out of their tent and stumbled toward the convoy. Carter, who'd been riding in the cab of Sno-Cat 1, got out and led them to the wanigan behind it.

"Hell of a wind," he said as Gordon and Roger huddled around the heater with Will and Ben. "But it shouldn't take too long to plant some charges and start clearing a way."

"Good. Well, come along, Ben. I'll teach you the fine art of blowing holes in ice."

"Where's Steve?" Roger asked.

"He's been driving the Sno-Cat for the last hour," Will said. "We've been spelling each other—just too bloody cold to stay in the cab more than an hour at a time. Speak of the devil," he added as Steve came in.

"Hi, you guys," Steve said. His beard and eyebrows were thick with frost. "Thank God you found this ridge. I'm not sorry to stop."

"Neither were we," Gordon said. "Jeez, and this is just the first goddam day."

"We haven't done too badly," Steve said, pouring tea into a mug. "Almost twelve kilometers since we left the slope. Not bad in this weather."

"At this rate we'll reach Outer Willy in about a

month," Will muttered as he tightened the drawstrings on his anorak and stood up.

The wind increased all afternoon. When the charges were detonated, no one in the vehicles could hear them; there was just a trembling in the ice while the wind went on screaming. Howie in the D8, and George in the D4, began to bulldoze a path through the fractured ice of the ridge. The work went slowly, and more charges had to be set off that evening before the path could be finished. By then a blizzard was raging, but Carter ordered the convoy through at once; he was afraid the path might drift over if they waited.

On the far side of the ridge they were exposed to the full force of the storm. Carter held a quick meeting by radio with the vehicle drivers, who reluctantly agreed to push on until midnight. The snowmobiles were lashed to a sledge, and their drivers happily moved into the D4's wanigan. By 2000 hours the convoy was moving again, with Sno-Cat 2 in the lead and the others following at close intervals.

In the next two hours they covered less than a kilometer. Tim, driving Sno-Cat 2, could see only a few meters ahead; he had to send Colin out in front, roped to the nose of the Sno-Cat, to guide him. After fifteen minutes Colin was too numb to continue, and Max Wilhelm took his place; then Terry. It was soon impossible to hold to a straight line, and Tim had to rely on an uncertain compass to bring them back on course after each detour. The surface was softer than it had been on the other side of the ridge, and the Sno-Cat labored in low gear. Tim tried to keep out of the hollows, where they were likely to bog down, but the rises weren't much better.

At 2200 he called Carter. "This is ridiculous," he shouted hoarsely into the microphone. "We've got to stop, Carter. I'm gonna burn out my transmission at this rate."

"Okay, Tim. We'll start up again at 0600. Everybody—keep your engines running tonight."

No one got much sleep. The wind and the hammering of the diesels were incessant, and each vehicle had to be refueled to keep the engines going. It was almost a relief to get up for breakfast at 0500, and Penny even volunteered to help refuel the Nodwell before they got underway. The wind took her breath away, and she could scarcely move against it; wrestling the drum of diesel fuel off the sledge was torture, even with the help from Herm and Don. By the time they got back inside, the oily stink of the cabin was like the perfume of tropical flowers to her.

The blizzard had weakened a little, and it was possible to see as much as twenty meters ahead. Tim led off again, and had actually got up to a speed of three kilometers per hour when Sean McNally reported that the Nodwell had lost its sledge. By the time the tow rope was secured, the blizzard was blowing with full force again, and everything came to a frustrated halt.

For the rest of that day, July 7, the engines idled but nothing moved except the snow and the wind. Carter sat in his wanigan and computed fuel consumption. Others played cards, slept, read, and waited for mealtimes. Late that afternoon, Katerina examined everyone in the Nodwell. The men all showed a slight rise in blood pressure, and everyone had headaches. She suspected carbon monoxide might be leaking into the cabin, and ordered the back door opened every twenty minutes.

"Oh, come on, Katerina," Ray protested. "It's just the damn noise and inactivity. Why should we freeze as well?"

"Do not argue!" Katerina snapped. Then she rubbed her face and sighed. "I am sorry. We are all irritable. I wish we were moving, too."

The storm ended at midnight; half an hour later the convoy set out again. The sky was clearing rapidly, and a haloed moon shone through the clouds. Will, in Sno-Cat 1, led them for eight uneventful kilometers, and when they stopped for breakfast everyone was tired but cheerful. Refueling was relatively easy with

no wind to fight, and they were on their way again by
0500. Almost at once they encountered the edges of a
sastrugi field, but managed to keep going for over an
hour before the sastrugi became too high and steep to
negotiate.

Carter stood in the cab of Sno-Cat 1 with Will,
looking at the sastrugi glittering in the headlights. He
shook his head and got on the radio to the D4.

"Tom, tell Gordon and Roger to get off their duffs
and make a run to Grid South. If the sastrugi keep
on going after four kilometers, they can come back
and try in the other direction."

An hour later they were back: the sastrugi extended
as far as they had ventured to Grid South. The reconnaissance toward Grid North, however, soon turned up
a gap in the field.

"It'll be rough," Gordon warned. "But we oughta
be able to make it."

It was very rough. The vehicles heaved and lurched
and skidded for hours over a surface little better than
a tank trap. Around 1500, Sno-Cat 2 lost its right
tread. Tom and Howie managed to repair it, but it
took them three hours in a rising wind that carried
drift as fine and sharp as ground glass. They had to
work with their mitts off, and the cold bit easily
through their wool gloves. Katerina treated them for
frostbitten fingers and noses, but they seemed otherwise all right.

"We're not stopping for dinner," Carter announced
as the convoy started up again. "I want us out of
these sastrugi before the real storm hits."

It didn't happen. By 1930 hours the vehicles were
bogged down in another blizzard with sastrugi all
around them. There they sat for the rest of the night,
and the next day, and a second night. On the morning
of July 9 the blizzard ended and the temperature
dropped from -20° to -45°C in less than an hour.

The convoy was heavily drifted over. To save fuel,
engines had been turned off during the first night of
the blizzard, and all were now frozen solid. Most of

the day was spent in digging the vehicles out and getting the engines started. Ben Whitcumb was outside for hours, the flamethrower strapped to his back as he went from one vehicle to the next; snow vaporized in the orange tongue of the flamethrower, and froze on his clothes in a thickening crust of ice. When all the engines were going, he went back to his wanigan. It took him several hours to warm up again.

The convoy finally moved out a little after 1600. The sastrugi were still there, hidden under the drifts, and the Nodwell bucked and swayed violently. After three long hours, Sean handed the controls over to Penny and went aft for a mug of tea. At first she was terrified, but the driving soon became almost enjoyable. There was a knack to getting over sastrugi without losing either momentum or a tread—and a knack to recognizing when to steer right around a really bad stretch. Fortunately, the Nodwell was near the end of the convoy, and could follow the packed-down trail left by the bulldozers.

"Sean, how's your consumption?" Carter asked over the radio. Penny reached for the mike.

"Not so good, Carter. We've used half a tank in the last three hours."

"That Penny?"

"Hi."

"Hi yourself. Are you driving?"

"Sure. Look, Ma, no hands."

The loudspeaker crackled with eavesdroppers' comments, most of them unimaginative variations on the theme of the woman driver. Then Steve came on.

"You're doing damn well, Penny. Just don't push that thing too hard."

"And watch your fuel gauge," Carter added.

"Okay." She hung up the microphone, feeling very pleased with herself.

The convoy finally got through the sastrugi field, but by then it was 0500 the next morning, July 10. They had traveled a total of about fifty kilometers since leaving Laputa, but only about thirty had been made in actual progress toward Outer Willy. Carter promised them that they would make better time as their sledges' burden of fuel drums grew lighter, but Penny suspected that the weather and surface would continue to slow them down.

She was right. All that day, the convoy floundered through snow as fine and dry as talcum powder; even the weight of the D8 scarcely packed it down, and it seemed bottomless. A steady breeze from Grid West threw drift across their course and cut visibility to less than half a kilometer. By 1800, after nearly twenty-four hours of continuous travel, the convoy had covered about sixteen kilometers.

The Nodwell stopped between the two Sno-Cats. Penny, Herm, and Don went outside to pump fuel into all three vehicles. It was exhausting work, struggling with the drums and manually pumping the fuel out of them. When the job was finished, Steve invited Penny over for supper.

The wanigan was like a miniature A-frame, four meters long and two meters wide and high. The interior was small and cramped: thick batts of fiberglass insulation were stapled to the walls, and more lay under the plywood floor. A tiny loft was packed with food boxes, tools, and batteries that powered a small lamp, a heater, and the radio. There was no headroom.

Ben Whitcumb was squatting at the rear of the wanigan, making stew on the primus stove. Will and Carter sat nearby; there was just room enough for Penny and Steve.

"Well, look who's slumming," Will laughed. "Come to see how the other half lives, have you?"

Carter passed her a bowl of stew and a spoon. "How's the Nodwell holding up, Pen?"

"Pretty well. Mm—good and hot! You're a good cook, Ben. But it sure burns a lot of fuel."

The wanigan shuddered as if something had rammed it. From outside came the crunching sound of metal scraping over ice. The lamp over Ben's head swung hard against the wall; the floor vibrated for several seconds.

Carter leaned over and switched on the radio. "This is Carter. Anyone hurt? Anyone in trouble? Sean? Tim? Howie? Tom?" A fuzzy chorus replied: everyone was all right, but no one knew what had happened.

Steve crawled over Penny's legs and opened the door. The others followed him outside.

The vehicles' headlights glared through ice fog. Someone walked in front of the other Sno-Cat, and his shadow loomed up against the fog like a misshapen giant. The snow underfoot was fine and gritty, almost like sand, but Penny could still sense a trembling in it, far below the surface. Out in the darkness beyond the convoy's oasis of light, an irregular metallic banging arose: the sound of breaking ice.

"What is it?" Penny shouted over the engines.

"I think it was an earthquake," Steve shouted back.

"We're in the middle of the goddam ocean!"

"Tsunami. The quake was probably back on the mainland, but it could've started a wave under the ice. I'm surprised there haven't been more quakes—the whole continent must be rebounding with so much ice off it." Steve turned to Carter. "I think we should reconnoitre the whole area—see if there's been any crevassing that might get in our way."

Inspecting the vehicles and sledges took almost an hour. There were more shocks, none as violent as the first, but each one made Penny want to scream and run. At last Carter sent her back to the Nodwell, where Katerina gave her cup after cup of hot water. It took her a long time to stop shivering.

Carter came on the radio around 2200. "Well, we've been through a real icequake, it seems, and no harm done. Some of the lads have made a quick trip round-about, and there don't *seem* to be any crevasses nearby. Even so, from now on we're going to probe the surface before we move across it. I suggest we all get some sleep and be ready to move out at 0600. I'll need at least five volunteers for the probe team."

The snowmobiles stayed on their sledge; now men went out on skis, roped together and carrying long aluminum poles. From the cab of the Nodwell, the men were gleaming green shapes that cast long shadows ahead of them as they advanced to the limits of the headlights' beams. Then, having tested the snow, they would signal the convoy to move up while the process was repeated.

By noon of July 11 they had covered six kilometers, without incident but very slowly. Now, as the sky flamed red above them, they reached a crevasse field. The probers ventured cautiously into it, relying on the windcrust to hold them up, and then came back to the convoy to confer with Carter. At 1300 he discussed strategy with the drivers.

"The field isn't too wide, thank God. The snow bridges seem good and thick, but the quake probably weakened them. How about sending the D8 in first?"

"Okay," Howie nodded. "Whoever comes after me, stay on one side or the other of my trail. If I drop a snow bridge, they can cross where it's still holding up."

The D8 growled ahead of the convoy and stopped beside a bamboo pole marking the far side of the first crevasse. The probe team followed it, and found that the snow bridge had settled by almost a meter. Tom Vernon, in the D4, crossed about a hundred meters to the right; Sno-Cat 2, about a hundred meters to the left.

Will got Sno-Cat 1 across, but the bridge gave way while the sledge was still on it. A gap appeared, almost two meters wide and fifty meters long; it crossed the tracks left by the bulldozers. Will edged forward until the sledge was past the crevasse, while Steve, Carter, and Ben watched from the edge. Then Carter went back inside to talk to Sean on the radio.

"The whole snow bridge looks ready to fall," Carter said. "You'd better get the crevasse bridge out, and use it to cross over."

Sean, Herm, Don, and Ray went outside and awkwardly slid the bridge off the roof of the Nodwell. Penny and Katerina watched them drag it to a part of the crevasse still concealed by snow.

"How is *that* going to hold up this monster?" Penny muttered. Katerina said nothing.

Just visible in the headlights, Sean waved. Carter's voice crackled over the radio: "Any time you're ready, Pen."

She put the Nodwell in gear and slowly advanced. The ends of the bridge overlapped the crevasse by only two meters on either side; it was easy to imagine the surface giving way and dropping them into the darkness.

Sean stood on the bridge, guiding Penny onto it. He walked backward as the Nodwell ground slowly onto the narrow aluminum strip. Halfway across, the tractor shuddered as the snow gave way and the bridge sagged; Sean caught his balance, paused, and then beckoned Penny forward again. They were across.

"I'll be back in a minute," Penny said to Katerina. She scrambled out of the cab as the men crowded through the rear door, cheering and slapping her shoulders.

"Excuse me, you guys." She sidled around to the chemical toilet. "I've really got to pee."

They were in the crevasse field for three more days. It would have been less, but a blizzard kept the convoy immobile for a day and a half. On the afternoon of July 14 they finally reached a hard, flat surface, and began to make up for lost time. Carter kept the convoy going until 0300 hours on the morning of the 15th; by then they had traveled over a hundred kilometers from Laputa.

Most of the party slept for twelve straight hours. Howie and Tom Vernon made some repairs to the D8, clearing the fuel line of the pony engine used to start the big bulldozer's diesel. Early on the 16th, the convoy moved on.

For Penny, time began to blur. Sometimes the sky

glowed red, and gave a pinkish tint to the snow; more often there was only darkness and the glare of drift in the headlights. Sometimes there was the roar of engines, sometimes the moaning of the wind, and sometimes an absence of sound that was more startling than ordinary silence.

They drove when they could, for an hour or for ten, and slept in catnaps or around the clock. The Shelf was rarely smooth enough for a long run; though there were few bad crevasses, the sastrugi fields seemed endless, and some low-lying stretches were treacherously soft.

No one talked much, except about food. They ate stew and meat bars and canned vegetables while debating the menu for their first meal in New Zealand. It would be a gargantuan feast: rare roast beef, fresh lamb, chicken, and ham. There would be new potatoes drenched in melted butter, fresh peas, and asparagus (never mind that it was winter in New Zealand), and exquisitely crisp salads. There would be fresh bread and rolls dripping with butter and honey, and great hills of fresh fruit. They would eat and drink and smoke, take long hot baths in deep tubs, and sleep in warm beds between fresh sheets until they felt like getting up to eat some more. After an hour or so of such conversation, they would crawl into their damp, sour-smelling sleeping bags and shiver themselves to sleep.

On July 17 the convoy stopped for maintenance and repairs. Steve and Will took advantage of the pause to fire some seismic shots; when they came into the wanigan for lunch, Carter and Ben gaped at them.

"You two look sunburned," Carter said.

Steve touched his cheeks and nose, but they were numb with cold. He found a small mirror and looked at himself. Carter was right: Steve's face was dark red, and hard little blisters had already formed on his nose. Will was burned too.

"We must be getting some diffracted ultraviolet," Steve said. "Can you get Gerry on the radio?"

He asked Gerry to monitor ultraviolet intensity; a few minutes later, Gerry called back to say he'd gotten a reading almost as high as those recorded in the summer weeks after the icequake. "We better be careful," Gerry added. "How do your eyes feel?"

"They itch," Steve replied.

"Yeah. You must've burned 'em a little."

"Christ," Steve murmured after Gerry signed off. "If the ultraviolet is bad here, what's it like where the sun is shining?"

"Worse," said Will.

Later that day one of the D8's sledges was abandoned, and the loads on the others were redistributed. So much fuel had been burned that Carter began to doubt whether the whole convoy would make it to Outer Willy. There was so little gasoline left that he decided to save it for the pony engines, and the snowmobiles were left behind as well. Gordon and Roger were not sorry.

For some days, temperatures had stayed between -60° and -40°; on the 19th the sky clouded over and the temperature rose in an hour from -45° to -15°. By 1500 hours, a blizzard stalled the convoy near a pressure ridge, and there they stayed.

On the second day of the blizzard, Carter made a routine radio check with the other vehicles. There was no answer from Sno-Cat 2. After trying to raise them for five minutes, Carter gave up and called Sean in the Nodwell, which was parked next to the Sno-Cat.

"I hate to ask it of you," he told Sean, "but could you just pop across and see what the problem is?"

"No problem," Sean grunted. "I was just about to walk the dog anyway."

The Nodwell, like all the other vehicles, was almost completely drifted over. Sean, with help from Herm and Ray, managed to force open the rear door and dig his way out of the drift. With a safety line tied to his waist, he groped his way to the dark mound of the Sno-Cat, and then to the wanigan behind it. He dug away part of the drift over the door, and pounded on the plywood. There was no response. He shouted, but the wind drowned him out.

Growing frightened, Sean began shoveling at the drift, throwing the powdery snow back into the wind. The cold clamped hard on his arms and legs, and began working inward to his chest and belly. The only light came from the cab of the Nodwell, where part of one window was clear. It was just a few meters away, but made only a ghostly yellow blur in the screaming night.

At last he was able to yank the door open. A lamp was on, but nothing moved. By the time Sean wrestled his way in, snow filled the wanigan with billions of glittering-cold sparks. A primus stove burned against the rear wall; the four men lay unmoving in their sleeping bags. When he saw their flushed, almost purplish complexions, Sean heaved the door open again and wedged it in place. The wanigan was full of carbon monoxide.

After a minute Tim began to stir, then Max and Colin. Terry Dolan took longest to come to. Sean turned off the primus, shut the door, and got on the radio.

"Carter, this is Sean. They nearly caught it— monoxide. But I think they'll be all right. Katerina, can you hear me?"

"Yes. I will be there as soon as I am dressed."

The four men were very sick for the next couple of days, but by the time the blizzard finally blew itself out they were fully recovered. Carter ordered regular ventilation checks to be made thereafter, and there were no more incidents. Sean's nose, however, was grotesquely swollen with frostbite, and he had bad dreams for the next few nights.

After a week's hibernation, everyone was impatient to get moving, but it took a full day to dig out the vehicles and warm their engines. At 1700 hours on July 27, they set out and made good progress until the next morning, when they had to bulldoze through another pressure ridge.

The sun was close below the horizon now; the sky reddened as early as 1000 hours and didn't darken until 1500. But Gerry's ultraviolet readings grew more ominous. What little UV diffracted to their latitude was as much as three times normal daylight intensity. In the outside world, Gerry estimated, ultraviolet must be seven to eight times normal.

"That ain't the worst of it," he said to Carter over the radio. "When you lose the ozone layer, you start cooling right down to the surface. Not much—maybe half a degree Celsius, overall. But that gets you halfway to an ice age all by itself, without the surge."

"So much for the greenhouse theory," Steve put in. "They've been saying for years that we're putting so much carbon dioxide into the atmosphere that the earth would be warmer by the turn of the century than it's been in eight thousand years. Even if that were true, the only way to overcome the present cooling would be to burn every drop of oil, and every stick of wood, as fast as possible."

"I hate gloaters," Carter snorted.

The D4 burned out a bearing on July 30, and was abandoned. Its wanigan was attached to the Nodwell, and the men in it—Tom Vernon, George Hills, Gordon Ellerslee, and Roger Wykstra—became regular visitors in the tractor.

By August 1, when another quake hit, the strain was getting to all of them. No one had expected the traverse to take this long; the tons of fuel were almost all gone, and so was the food. Carter estimated the convoy to be no more than thirty kilometers from Outer Willy, but there was scarcely enough diesel fuel even for that distance.

Will, Tim, and Steve made a scouting trip on skis after the quake, to see if any crevasses lay across the convoy's path. While they were gone, everyone slept or talked or played games.

The wind was rising. It thumped the walls, moaned, threw snow hissing against the windows. In the cabin, with only a small battery lamp to illuminate it, the shadows were deep and cold. Penny tried to warm her hands between her thighs. How had she ever enjoyed being snowbound?

She dreamed, half-awake, that she was outside trying to find Steve in the darkness. She was naked; her bare feet sank deep in the snow, and she knew she would freeze in just a few more moments. She called him, but the wind muffled her, choked her; she was coughing blood the way she had on the walk back from the helo.—Steve, Steve, I'm bleeding! She waited for the grip of his hands on her shoulders, but it never came.

Somewhere far away there were voices, then a blast of cold air and a slamming door. Penny woke to see three bulky shapes standing in the cabin, their faces muffled. One of them squatted awkwardly beside her bunk. He pulled off his ice-crusted wool mask and brushed frost from his beard.

"Hi, Pen," Steve said quietly. "Could we have a cup of tea? We brought our own snow in."

"I love you," Penny said. He looked surprised. A little hesitantly, he took off one of his bearpaw mitts, the leather glove beneath it, and then the wool shell. He reached out and touched her cheek.

"Your face is warm," he smiled.

"Your hand is freezing. I still love you."

"I love you too. How about some tea?"

While the kettle clanked and pinged on the primus, Steve got on the radio to Carter. "We just got in; we're in the Nodwell."

"How's the surface up ahead?"

"Good. A few sastrugi fields, but nothing bad. No crevasses. But listen, Carter—we're closer than we thought. There's an ice island only about ten kilometers away. I'm pretty sure it's Outer Willy."

14

ICEWAY

Ten minutes after the convoy got underway that evening, Sno-Cat 1 lost its right rear track. Carter ordered it and its sledge abandoned, and moved into the wanigan behind Sno-Cat 2. The others scattered to various parts of the convoy; Steve and Will crowded into the Nodwell.

There was nothing to see through the windshield but the D4's sledge a few meters ahead, and an occasional bamboo pole left by the ski party to mark the route. The windcrust glittered in the headlights; the sky had a faint reddish tint from dust particles high enough to reflect the light of the sun.

Penny and Steve sat together on her bunk, talking and laughing with the others. The cabin still smelled of the lamb curry they'd had for dinner, and Don had miraculously produced six bottles of Swan Beer.

They reached the ice island just after midnight on the morning of August 3. It rose only about ten meters above the Shelf, and its sides were mostly gentle slopes. The temperature was rising; another storm would be upon them soon. Carter ordered the ski party out to reconnoitre a safe path up the slopes.

"If you can't find a good route by 0300, come straight back," he told them. "I'm not going to lose anybody when we're this close."

"If this *isn't* Outer Willy," Howie broke in, "don't come back at all."

Penny went outside with Steve and Will; Tim skied up from the D8's wanigan.

"You guys ready?" he asked.

"All set," Will nodded. He looked up at the sky: the reddish glow had vanished in a thickening overcast. "We'd better make it fast."

"Break a leg," Penny said.

Steve patted her arm, and grinned through his wool mask. "Don't worry."

It wasn't easy for two people in thick anoraks to embrace, but they managed. Then the three men were off, vanishing into the ice fog around the convoy.

They were back in less than two hours, with the storm at their heels. After talking briefly with Carter, they returned to their vehicles. When Steve and Will came into the Nodwell, Carter's voice was already on the radio:

"—they've marked out a route, but if we wait for the storm to blow over, the poles could be buried. And we don't have enough fuel left to let the engines idle for two or three days. So we're going up the hill right away. Howie, you'll go first. Then Tim, then Sean, and Tom will follow up. Any problems? Any questions? —Right, let's go."

The convoy traveled less than a kilometer along the Grid West side of the island before reaching a hard, gradual slope. The fluorescent-orange pennants on the marker poles were snapping violently in the wind, and blowing snow crackled against windshields, loud enough to be heard even over the engines. Howie was an experienced trailbreaker by now; he found the easiest surfaces, and bulldozed right through any unavoidable obstacles without even pausing. But as they neared the top of the slope, the wind increased and snow thickened, blowing horizontally across the top of the island.

Penny had taken a turn at the wheel of the Nodwell, and swore as the tractor bellowed up off the slope onto the flat surface at the top. The snow was so thick and swift that it created a miniature whiteout in her headlights. Outside that wedge of seething white, there was nothing but blackness and noise.

Visibility was now almost zero. The interior of the Nodwell was full of snowflakes. Conversations died. Everyone huddled in sleeping bags, trying to keep warm. Despite the hot air forced in between the double panes of the windshield, frost kept forming on the glass; every few minutes Steve had to scrape it off. Finally he picked up the microphone and called Carter.

"I think we'd better call a halt. We can't see a thing, not even Tim's sledges. We could drive right past Outer Willy and never see it."

"You're right, Steve. Okay, everybody, we'll make camp—"

"Nonsense," said an unfamiliar voice. "Just use your RDF, for God's sake. You can't be more than a couple of kilometers away."

Steve guffawed. "Hugh! You old bugger—why didn't you call before?"

"It wasn't for lack of trying. We've been picking you up for the last two days, off and on. *And* trying to raise you."

"Well," said Carter. "Well, by God, put another onion in the soup and we'll be there before you know it."

Sno-Cat 2 had the best RDF equipment in the convoy, so it replaced the D8 as lead vehicle. The radios were full of crackling and babbling as everyone tried to talk with the people at Outer Willy. Katerina and Will alternately grilled Jeanne and fretted over her; Terry and Suzy exchanged shy, caustic greetings; one of the Russians, probably Yevgeni, kept yelling, "Monopoly! Monopoly! Gordon, ve play Monopoly!"

At 0658 hours on August 3, the convoy halted alongside a row of drifted-over Jamesway huts. One of them had a light burning above its doorway, just visible through the blowing snow. Carter sent people inside a few at a time, and made sure all the vehicles were empty before he himself cut off the Sno-Cat's engine and plunged out into the wind. Twenty steps took him to the door; he went into the cold porch and slammed the door shut behind him. The floor of the cold porch was a trampled mass of snow and discarded anoraks. The interior of the Jamesway sounded like a wild party.

Carter took off his anorak and added it to the pile on the floor. Then he turned and slammed his fist exultantly against the outer door, jubilantly uncaring that bits of skin stuck frozen to it.

"Did it. *Did it!*"

The celebration lasted all day. Terry took over the cooking from Suzy, and fixed a second breakfast that started with steaks and eggs and ended, several courses later, with pancakes and waffles in strawberry jam. The aroma of fresh-ground coffee overcame even the stink of the more than thirty unwashed bodies; evilly exquisite cigarette smoke thickened the air. The American geologists were shyly genial hosts, and proudly escorted everyone around: the Jamesway was now linked by snow tunnels to three adjoining ones, all snug and warm, that had been used as dormitories for the original station personnel. There was even a separate women's latrine and shower.

"We got enough water in the snow melter for everyone to take a shower if they want," Earl said with an embarrassed smile.

Penny and Katerina looked at each other. "Shall we?" asked Penny.

"Of course."

Somehow it was stranger to stand naked in a stream of hot water than to rot in an anorak. Penny looked down at her body as if it belonged to someone else: it was thinner than she remembered, and harder; her skin was pale and even the freckles seemed to have faded. Her groin and armpits were chafed and reddened, cracked to bleeding in places, and the skin on her hands and face was dry and rough. But the sensation of wrapping a towel around wet, clean hair was worth all the discomfort. Draped in a blanket, she hurried into the cubicle she'd been given and found Steve just dropping off her duffel bag.

"I thought you'd probably want a change of clothes," he said, "so I went out and got your gear."

She pushed the door shut with her hip and let her blanket drop.

Katerina and Ivan sat together in the mess hall after she came back, fresh and smiling, from her shower. They wanted to hold hands, but it was *nekulturny* to do so in front of their celibate companions. She studied Ivan, Yevgeni, and Kyril as they talked; all seemed well, though Kyril's face and hands showed signs of recent frostbite.

"And how is the airplane?" asked Katerina.

Kyril gave her a black-and-white smile. "What a machine! It is almost ready. The booster hydraulic system was leaking, and there were some minor things as well. We've been checking it out for the past week. All the engines are working well. But the plane will have to be dug out, and that will be hard. Especially after these blizzards."

"But we really can fly it to New Zealand?"

"We'd better hope so," said Ivan. "There's not enough food here to keep us all until spring."

"And when could we go?"

"Ask Al." Ivan beckoned to Al Neal, who had been talking animatedly to Hugh and Carter. Al came over; he looked thinner, and his beard and ponytail were longer. When he smiled, Katerina saw that his front teeth were only blackened stumps.

"Your teeth—" she said.

"Believe it or not, they froze and cracked about three weeks ago. Darn annoying, but I'll get 'em fixed in New Zealand. How are you, Kate?"

"Very well, thank you. How good it is to see you! And the plane is ready to fly?"

"Almost. When the wind dies down, Kyril and I will run some last-minute checks while everybody else digs the plane out. By the time that's done, we ought to be ready."

Katerina's examination of Jeanne was slow and thorough. When it was over she called Will into the cubicle. Jeanne and Katerina sat on the bunk; Will leaned against the plywood wall.

"It looks good, but not as good as I would like. You are young and strong, but this is no place to be pregnant. You are underweight for seven months, and the baby has already dropped."

"Not sorry about *that*. At least I can breathe again."

"Yes, but you may very likely deliver prematurely. Anywhere else, it could be prevented or delayed. But here I can do nothing except to keep you rested until we fly."

"That's no problem either," Jeanne grinned. "I'm too bloody pooped to do anything." She winked at Will. "You're sleeping in the top bunk, mate."

"Judging from the looks of you, there'd be no room in the bottom one," Will said. "Don't worry, Katerina —I'll see she gets plenty of rest."

When Katerina left, Will moved shyly over to sit beside Jeanne. It was good to put his arms around her again, to smell her hair.

"God, I was so worried about you," she murmured. "We all thought you'd be here in no time, but then it was two weeks, and I was sure you were all dead."

"And I was sure you'd crashed the Otter." He lightly touched her belly, feeling the baby's kicks and tapping gently back at it.

"I feel like a bloody cow."

"More like a cheetah with a good breakfast."

Jeanne began to cry. "Will, I'm scared again."

Late in the evening of August 3, Hugh and Carter sat down with Al and Bob Price in the mess hall. The huts were quiet at last. All four men looked exhausted. Al had cracked lips, with scabs that kept breaking, and his hands were mottled pink and gray. Bob was in better shape, but his clothes hung loosely on him.

Hugh's red mustache was turning off-white, and his eyes seemed a little unfocused; Carter, now that the traverse was over, felt dizzy with fatigue and relief.

"The main problem is fuel," Al said. "We gotta run the generator around the clock—not just for this place, but for the Herc. With all the available heaters going, we can at least keep the hydraulics from seizing up. And we have to keep the plane's batteries charged. But we only have a little more fuel available. Unless we want to freeze, we gotta get out of here by the 7th or 8th."

"Can we do that?" asked Hugh.

Al nodded. "If the weather co-operates. Kyril and I are gonna need another day, maybe, to check everything out. If the wind drops, it'll take a day to dig out—"

"Yes?" said Hugh.

"But I'm worried about the skis. They're really frozen in, and it'll be some job to get 'em loose."

"We'll manage," Carter said. "So it's just the weather."

Al turned and smiled blackly at him. "Yeah, just the weather." He guffawed, and the others joined in.

"What if something goes wrong?" Carter asked. "Suppose the weather stays bad for a week or more?"

"We start running out of everything," Bob said. "Food, fuel, water—there's just not enough to keep thirty-three people going for very long. Four or five could winter over all right, but not everybody."

"Well, if we *are* stuck," Hugh said, "we'll eat the pessimists first."

All the next day, the wind blew. Al and Kyril worked inside the Hercules, sometimes drafting two or three others to help for a while. When Penny went outside for a few minutes at noon, she saw the plane glowing crimson under a flaming sky. Lights burned in the big flight-deck windows. She was about to get in out of the wind and drift when one of the Herc's starboard engines boomed into life. The propellor blades merged into a shimmering red disc, and the noise drowned out the wind. Then another engine caught, and the third and fourth. The plane's nose turned golden as a limb of the sun rose—by diffraction—above the Grid South horizon. A moment later it was gone again, but the big engines kept up their thunder.

Penny went back inside and hugged the first person she saw; it was Howie. "We're really going to go," she shouted. "We're—you should see what it looks like out there, with those engines going and the lights on and—"

"Aw, calm down," Gordon said. "Think you'd never seen an airplane before."

That night, yet another blizzard hit. It was one of the worst of the winter, with winds that never dropped below 100 kph. A marathon Monopoly tournament started after supper, and went on all night and all the next day. Al, Kyril, and their helpers played as energetically as everyone else. The air in the mess hall was thick with smoke and profanity, but no one seemed perturbed by the weather.

Around suppertime on August 5, the Jameaways shook briefly: another quake. It caused little comment and no concern. It was as if everyone had grown jaded with danger; people preferred to gossip, insult each other, and plan their homecomings.

An hour later, Bruce Robinson yelled "Shuddup!" He had been sitting at the radio, headphones on and a growing stack of empty beer cans under his chair. Conversation stopped dead. For a minute or two Bruce scrawled rapidly, then took off his headphones and stood up.

"Got something from Australia," he told the people in the mess hall. "They have an unconfirmed report that President Wood has resigned and handed over executive power to the Joint Chiefs of Staff. A military government has been formed in Britain. And a typhoon has wrecked Darwin. Which never was much to begin with," he added.

"Know what I'm gonna do when we get home?" Gordon asked. "Going to move into a hotel in Calgary and drink myself stupid until fall. Then I'm gonna go get a job in some place like Saudi Arabia. Between the booze and the heat, I figure I'll thaw out by this time next year."

"If you melt the permafrost between your ears, you'll have mud for brains," Ben remarked. Gordon ignored him—which, for Gordon, was equivalent to retreat.

"For some of us," Max Wilhelm said, "it'll be easy to decide what to do. We'll just get back to New Zealand, go home, and go back to work."

There was an uncomfortable silence. After all the months of speculation, they realized they would soon be in a world very different from the one they had left last year. At length, Yevgeni said: "All scientists, all technicians, they will need. Every place will be good place for us."

"Probably for all the wrong reasons," Colin added.

Early the next morning, Will tapped lightly on the Varenkovs' door. Ivan opened it. "Jeanne says she's lost the mucus plug."

"What is—? Oh." He turned and called to his wife in Russian. Katerina appeared in the doorway, buttoning her shirt.

"When?"

"Sometime during the night."

"I will come to see her very soon."

She quickly examined Jeanne. "Well, it will not be long now. Everything looks all right, but it will be early. Have you been doing your breathing exercises?"

"Yes."

"Good. I will be back later."

She went into the next Jamesway and found George Hills. He woke slowly and heavily.

"George, I need you to build for me an incubator."

"A what?"

Patiently, she sketched her requirements on the ply-wood wall: a solid, double-walled box that could hold plenty of insulation. A small heating coil in the base would be plugged in to the hut's electrical system. "Or into the system of the airplane. Can you do this?"

"Oh, I guess. Have to talk to Al. But I think so."

"Very good. I will need it by noon."

By breakfast time, everyone knew Jeanne might have her baby very soon. The atmosphere in the mess hall was subdued; the blizzard was still going strong. Hugh held a meeting that morning, as much to give people something to do as to plan the details of the evacuation. After lunch, most of the men met in small-er groups to plan loading, snow clearing, and the flight itself. A few people irritably did the inevitable chores: refueling the generator, filling the snow melter, cooking and cleaning up. Penny found herself working with the Dolans again, but now that the flight was so close she didn't mind. —Every time I wash a dish for the rest of my life, I'll think of the ice.

So the day passed.

Between 0500 and 0600 hours on August 7, the blizzard ended.

A dead calm hung over the Shelf, and the stars glittered in a clear sky. Al Neal stood outside the Jamesways and looked around. The snow was thick and soft, at least on top; a few centimeters down it seemed hard-packed. In the distance, the Hercules rose like a long hill, heavily drifted over. The Otter stood not far from it, with only its tail and one wing show-ing above the snow.

The cold made Al's teeth hurt badly. He went back inside, where the American geologists were having breakfast with Penny and Suzy.

"It really looks good out there," Al said. "But I don't know how long it'll last. Let's get everybody up."

"Only quietly," Penny urged. "Jeanne didn't sleep well. Katerina thinks the baby might—" She clapped a hand over her mouth. "Oh, Al, we can't go today. We can't."

"Not with a baby due any minute," Suzy agreed.

Al looked distressed. "Kids, it's now or never. We could lose this weather by noon, for all we know."

"You better talk to Katerina," Penny said. "*Then* wake up the others."

He tugged his white beard. "Damn it, *you* talk to her. I've got better things to do." And he strode angrily into the tunnel to the next hut.

"Wow, is he angry!" Suzy whispered. "I never heard him swear before."

"Me neither," Penny said. "Look, I'll start getting breakfast ready. You go get Katerina." Then she added: "Gee—the kid might even get born in a proper hospital."

"You don't have to sound so disappointed," Bob said.

By 0645 the mess hall was crowded with men who bolted their hotcakes and sausages and hurried outside. Hugh, Carter, and Bob went from table to table, assigning people to different jobs. The temperature was down to -40°C, and it wasn't until well after 0700 that blowtorches and the flamethrower had warmed the bulldozers' engines enough to let them be started. After that, the huts shook whenever the D4 or D8 passed nearby.

Katerina ignored the vibration in the floor as she sat beside Jeanne's bed, watching the sweep hand of her wristwatch.

"Only ten seconds," she said when Jeanne gasped and nodded. "And the contractions are still twenty minutes apart. It will be several hours, maybe a day, before the delivery."

"God, I really timed it well, didn't I?"

"Yes. Suppose it had come while we were still on the traverse. How would these men have done?"

"Ugh. I don't want to think about it. Katerina, am I going to be all right? Really?"

Katerina's deep laugh boomed out. "You will be very good."

Penny and the Dolans hastily prepared food for the journey: sandwiches, soup, cold cuts, and big urns of coffee. Around 1030 they lugged it all outside in cardboard boxes. The sky and the snow were the same predawn pink. The bulldozers were working around the sides of the Hercules, clearing away the drifts. As they approached the plane, Penny saw a dozen men digging and chopping at the snow around the nose landing gear. One of them was Steve; he paused as Penny and the Dolans came by.

"How's it going?" Penny asked.

"Not fast. The snow and ash are mixed together like cement." He grinned at her and went back to work.

As she followed the Dolans in through the crew door on the port side, Penny could see the problem: the plane was low-slung, and the whole underside of the fuselage was buried in compacted drift. Tom Vernon, driving the D4, was clearing most of it away, but he couldn't get too close or the fuselage might be damaged; it had to be cleared away with shovels, axes, and even hands.

The interior of the Hercules was almost as cold as the outside. They stowed their boxes in the galley, just ahead of the crew door, and Penny took a quick look around. With the lights on and the snow cleared away, the plane looked very different from the last time she'd seen it. The flight deck was littered with tools, tattered maintenance manuals, and the remains of meals; the cargo compartment looked even more cavernous than before, now that it was cleared and lighted. The aft cargo door was open, and men were hauling in boxes and duffel bags while others lashed them down in the broad aisle between the rows of seats. Near the cargo door, Katerina supervised Ben and Simon as they rigged a stretcher along the wall. The white glare of the overhead lights, reflecting on the frosted walls, reminded Penny of Shacktown, and she felt a pang of homesickness.

"Come on, Pen," Terry said. "Let's get the hell back inside and warm up. These buggers'll want elevenses pretty soon."

When everyone was in the mess hall for coffee and sandwiches, Hugh stood up.

"We are about ready to go," he said quietly. "Al tells me the aircraft is in good shape for the flight. But I want everyone to understand that this will be a very dangerous trip. It's almost five thousand kilometers to Christchurch. We have no idea what the weather will be like en route. If anything goes wrong, and we go into the sea, we will have virtually no chance of survival. And there is always the chance of something going wrong, even in the best of circumstances. If anyone chooses to stay here, they should be fairly comfortable until spring. There will surely be flights to the ice then, and anyone here could count on being picked up."

No one spoke.

"Very good," Hugh went on. "Then good luck to us all. We'll be in Christchurch by suppertime, I trust."

While most of the people went aboard, a small crew resumed cutting the Hercules' landing gear free of the snow. Once a ski was cleared, the crew forced tar paper under it to keep it from refreezing to the snow. Ben Whitcumb then went along the sides of the plane with the flamethrower, melting the last few lumps of ice from the fuselage. By noon the job was done. Will and Howie carried Jeanne out on a stretcher and made her as comfortable as possible.

"I feel like such a twit, with everyone else doing something," she said to Will.

"Don't be silly," he said. "Still, it's a pity the baby couldn't have been born in Antarctica."

"Oh, Will, I'm sorry." She started to cry.

"Och, there, there," he consoled her. "I'm only joking, love." He patted her hand and she calmed herself. Then he strapped himself into the seat at the foot of her stretcher; Katerina was sitting by her head.

Carter came aft, checking to make sure everyone was aboard and strapped in. "It'll be a rough takeoff," he said quietly to Will. "And this beast climbs like a rocket. Keep an eye on her."

"I will."

A few seconds later the engines started. The noises reminded Penny of the beginning of the surge, and she realized that it had been exactly six months since the icequake. She found herself gripping Steve's hand more tightly than necessary; he smiled at her, and squeezed back. The plane began to vibrate, and the pitch of the engines rose, but nothing happened.

The engines stopped. People began to mutter and laugh, their breaths frosty in the chill air. Al appeared in the doorway to the flight deck.

"We're still frozen in," he announced. "I need some people to get outside and see what the problem is. Ben, where's your flamethrower?"

"I left it outside." Ben was on his feet. Steve and Howie unstrapped themselves and followed him forward.

There was a long, tense wait. Penny could faintly hear scrapes and bangs under the fuselage. Across the aisle, Katerina took out a cigarette and then put it back in her pocket. Ivan touched her hand. Jeanne gasped and began breathing in a controlled rhythm, her face to the wall.

The scraping and banging ended. Penny got up and went to the latrine at the rear of the cargo compartment. When she came out a minute later, there was a confused babble of shouts from the front, and a crowd was milling around the door to the flight deck. Steve's face, blackened and savage, appeared in the doorway.

"Katerina!"

She unstrapped herself, grabbed her medical bag from between her feet, and ran to the door. The crowd pulled away, but not quickly enough for Steve. He shoved Gordon and Simon roughly out of Katerina's way.

"Somebody get a stretcher!" he shouted.

There was one stowed under Jeanne's stretcher; Ivan pulled it out and hobbled forward with it.

Hugh got everyone seated. "We've had an accident," he said. "A bad one. Ben . . . Ben Whitcumb is dead." He took a deep breath. "The damned fuel tank on his flamethrower exploded. He—he was very badly burned—went into shock—and died."

"God rest his soul," George Hills said, crossing himself.

A few minutes later, Steve and Howie carried the stretcher into the cargo compartment. Ben's body had been wrapped in an orange nylon tent. They lashed it to the icy metal floor. The stink of gasoline and burned flesh filled the compartment.

"All right," said Hugh. "Everyone strap in."

The engines started again. Steve slumped back into his seat, and the scorched smell was thick on his clothes. He leaned toward Penny, his voice faint over the growing roar of the engines.

"He was just unstrapping the tank. I don't know why it happened; maybe he didn't shut the valve completely. But it just—blew up in his face. His clothes caught fire—"

She gagged, and shook her head; she didn't want to hear any more.

"—we rolled him in the snow, but his clothes were soaked with gas. He kept—and then he just convulsed, and died."

The Hercules bumped, and heaved, and began to move. Steve leaned back and closed his eyes. His beard was singed half-off, and his eyebrows were gone. The front of his green anorak was full of black-edged holes. Penny took his hand very gently, and held it as the plane gained speed and lifted abruptly from the ice. —It isn't fair, it just isn't goddam fair! She felt tears run coldly down her face.

There were not many portholes in the cargo compartment; the nearest one was across the aisle and several meters forward. Through it, Penny could see a tilted surface of pink and black. Then, as they climbed still higher, the porthole blazed with the blinding yellow light of the risen sun.

15

〰〰〰〰

NORTH

For the first three hundred kilometers, the weather held clear. Seven kilometers below, the Shelf stretched endlessly in all directions, its irregular surface red and black under the low rays of the sun. They were well to the north—true north—of Cape Adare, and out over the Southern Ocean, but the Shelf seemed as solid as it had been on the traverse.

Al paid little attention to the view. It was good to be flying a Herc again, but without a copilot or navigator he was working very hard. Kyril, as flight engineer, monitored the plane's systems, but if anything went wrong Al would have to fix it—if it could be fixed.

Hugh sat in the copilot's chair, silent and grim. When Al finally put the Herc on autopilot and paused to light a cigar, Hugh said:

"I really thought we were going to get home without a single death. I really did."

Al nodded. He wore glasses against the glare of the sun, and his face was unreadable. After a while he said, "I felt pretty bad when I couldn't get those guys off Observatory Hill. But—" He spread his hands. "You don't quit, but you don't expect to win."

"I did. I still do."

Al leaned over and tapped one of the dials on the copilot's instrument panel. "That's the pressure in the booster hydraulic system. If that needle drops, you can expect to go on winning for maybe three minutes.

That's how long it'll take us to hit the water. Or ice, as the case may be." Then he grimaced. "Sorry, Hugh. That sounded pretty cynical."

Hugh nodded.

Clouds thickened beneath them, and reared up ahead. Unable to trust his compass systems, Al shot the sun and lifted the plane another two thousand meters. They would pass safely over the storm, but at the cost of increased fuel consumption. He plotted the howgozit and talked briefly with Kyril over the intercom system. Kyril said everything was "Okay-khorosho." Al buzzed Gerry Roche in the cargo compartment, who told him Jeanne was definitely in labor, but doing all right.

"How soon is she gonna have the baby?"

"I dunno, Al. Just a minute, eh? . . . Katerina says she's dilated about eight centimeters, whatever the hell that means. And, uh, I don't think she likes people asking questions."

The plane thumped into a region of turbulence, and the flight grew increasingly rough. Al forgot about Jeanne; his attention was focused on maintaining the plane's stability, and on the hydraulic-system gauges.

Gerry's voice buzzed in Al's headphone: "Hey, Al, any idea how soon we get off this bumpy road? Jeannie, she's kind of upset."

"That makes two of us, but don't tell her I said so. Maybe twenty minutes, maybe less. How's everybody else?"

"Okay. Say, what's our ETA at Chee-Chee?"

"Sometime around 1600 hours."

The turbulence worsened. Clouds boiled up toward them in slow geysers of black and white; the sun, low on the horizon, burned redly through the far edges of the storm. Al lifted the Hercules two hundred meters, knowing that the increased altitude would increase fuel consumption to the danger point. They might have to change course for Dunedin after all, but he didn't want to: the airfield there was likely to be closed down by the storm. He got up and shot the sun through the sextant mounted in the roof of the flight deck, and wished he could pick up Christchurch.

Jeanne was past transition, and pushing hard. Will knelt beside her, counting slowly to time each push while she breathed in quick, infrequent gasps. Her face was congested and mottled with the fine red lines of broken blood vessels.

"Very good, very good," Katerina said. "The baby is crowning. Very good, again, push, push. . . ."

Suddenly the baby's head emerged. Katerina's hands gently turned it, and Will saw its face. Dark red beneath a cap of wet, dark hair, the face was impassive and serene, its eyes closed. Katerina drew mucus out of its nose and mouth.

"Now push again."

"What does it look like?" Jeanne panted. "I can't see it. What does it look like?"

"Beautiful," Will said. "Push!"

It was out, its body purplish-gray and steaming in the cold air.

"A girl," Katerina said.

Jeanne's face blazed with delight and surprise. "A girl! A girl! Oh my God, there she is! Hullo, baby. She's so tiny." Katerina placed the baby on Jeanne's belly while she tied and cut the umbilicus. "Oh, she's so hot."

The baby yelped for a few seconds as Katerina dried her and wrapped her in a soft towel. Once in her mother's arms, she fell sound asleep. "What a funny little thing," Jeanne said. "She looks just like my grandmother." She beamed up at Will and Penny and Suzy, who had been standing beside her to screen her off from the other passengers. "Isn't she lovely?"

The plane jolted and vibrated through the anticlimax of the afterbirth and Katerina's deft, careful stitching. "Now you can rest," she said.

"Oh, I'm too excited to rest." But a moment later she was asleep. Katerina took the baby and placed her gently in the incubator beside Jeanne's stretcher.

The baby woke, blinked her dark, unfocused eyes, and went to sleep again.

The storm was enormous even by the standards of the Southern Ocean, and crosswinds were fierce. Not until 1600 did Al finally pick up the Christchurch beacon; he found he was almost 10 degrees east of his proper heading, and adjusted accordingly.

"The needle just dropped," Hugh said.

"I know." Al could feel the rudder freeze, and reached instantly for the bypass switch. "Grab that handle and start pumping," he ordered. Then he called to Kyril: "We have a malfunction. We are on manual for the booster hydraulic system."

"Okay," Kyril replied cheerfully.

By the time the rudder responded again, they were 20 degrees west of their proper course. While Hugh pumped, Al cautiously swung the plane back.

"Are we going to make it?"

"Ask me again in half an hour."

The crosswinds were weakening, and the beacon was increasingly clear. He wouldn't have to ask much of the booster system until they made their landing approach; if it then collapsed completely, they could easily fly into the ground, or overshoot the runway. They could try to ditch in Lyttleton harbor if necessary, but Al had never ditched a Hercules and didn't want to.

The clouds stretched to the horizon, giving no indication of what lay below them. But the plane must be rapidly approaching the South Island coast. Maybe they were close enough for line-of-sight radio contact.

"This is RNZAF Hercules 56740 to Harewood Tower. Hercules 56740 to Harewood Tower. Do you read me? Over."

After a brief pause, a surprised voice crackled in Al's headphones. "Harewood Tower here. Hercules 56740, where are you? Over."

"Harewood, I estimate my position at about 220

kilometers south-southwest of you, approaching on 355 degrees. Request landing instructions. Over."

"Ah, Hercules 56740, you must be the UFO we've been tracking here for the last few minutes. Your true distance is 195 kilometers. Can you confirm as Hercules five, six, seven, four, oh? Over."

"Harewood, yes, this is 56740, property of the Royal New Zealand Air Force. Somebody left it in the Antarctic with the key in the ignition. We thought we'd bring it home before somebody swiped it. Over." To Hugh he said: "Keep pumping."

"Hercules, who in bloody hell *are* you? Over."

Al roared with laughter. "The name is Al Neal. I'm the pilot for the Commonwealth Antarctic Research Programme, and my passengers are the personnel of New Shackleton Station. Plus a few hitch-hikers, including a brand-new baby girl. Over."

"What's the name, Hercules? Over."

"I don't know if the mother's chosen one yet. Over."

"No, no, *your* name! Over."

"Al Neal. Listen, Harewood, we are having some mechanical problems. Our hydraulic system is breaking down, and I'll only have one shot at landing. We've got skis, so I'll have to come down on grass. Our ETA is—" He recalculated—"about 1625. What's the weather like down there? Over."

"Uh, uh—Hercules, ceiling is three hundred meters, visibility about four kilometers. It's raining hard, and there are winds from the southeast gusting to 50 kph. You can land just to the east of Runway 20. Repeat, just to the east of Runway Two-Oh. It's good and wet, so you should have no problems. Keep the runway lights to your left. Over."

"Thank you, Harewood. Beginning descent."

The Hercules edged down into the clouds. In seconds they were flying in opaque grayness, with rain hammering at the windshield. Al kept an eye on the hydraulic pressure: it was low, but it would do. The controls responded heavily, sluggishly, but properly.

He switched on the P.A. system in the cargo compartment.

"We're approaching Christchurch. Everybody strap in. The weather's not so good down there, but we should be on the ground in about fifteen minutes." He switched off. "Keep pumping."

The rain intensified until the windshield wipers could scarcely keep up. The gloom lightened, and then they were through, three hundred meters above the sea and just a few kilometers from the dark loom of land.

"Hercules 56740, this is Harewood Ground Control," a new voice announced. "Raise your angle of approach by three degrees, please. Another degree—very good. Now four degrees east. Good. . . . Two degrees west. Good. You're right in the slot, Hercules."

The plane swept low over Lyttleton harbor. Al stared: the oil-storage tanks along the south shore were like little circular islands well out in the water, and the docks west and north of them were gone. Streets ran down into the water and drowned. There were few lights despite the twilight gloom, and he saw no cars in the dark streets.

Gradually he lowered the flaps and ailerons, reducing speed as quickly as he dared. The runway lights stood out brightly, but Christchurch itself, off to the north and east, was oddly dark. Suburban rooftops and gardens slid by under the plane. Al extended the landing gear; at least the utility hydraulic system was working well. Runway 20 was dead ahead, a dim, straight line extended into the murk. He steered a little to the right, lining up with the long strip of dead yellow grass along the runway, and brought the Hercules down as gently as he could.

The grass was half-flooded; the skis touched water and began to hydroplane. Al cut speed, trying to get the plane's weight onto the grass before it could skid out of control. It wasn't enough. The Hercules began to swing to the right; the nose ski struck something and sheared away with a detonation that shattered the windshield. The ruined landing gear ripped into the soil, and the plane pivoted through 180 degrees before it came to a shuddering halt.

Al caught his breath and threw the P.A. switch: "Okay, everybody out by the nearest exit. Right away!" Through the crazed glass of the windshield, he saw flashing red-and-blue lights approach down the runway. Kyril was shouting something in Russian, and confused voices echoed from the cargo compartment. Al checked the fire detection system: there was no fire, at least not yet.

He unstrapped himself and helped Hugh get to his feet. Kyril was already heading for the exit. "Follow him," Al said, and went into the cargo compartment.

Someone had already got the aft cargo door down, and most of the passengers were already on their way out. He saw Will and Steve carrying Jeanne's stretcher down the ramp; Katerina and Penny were right behind with the rough wooden incubator. Others were struggling to unlash the crates of scientific records, and ignored Al's commands to get out at once.

Gordon Ellerslee appeared at Al's side. "C'mon, Al, gimme a hand with Ben."

"Sure."

They wrestled the stretcher to the crew door. Al jumped a meter to the ground, and carefully hauled the stretcher out into the pounding rain. The air was dank and cold, colder somehow than Antarctica had ever been. The light was failing fast.

Two fire trucks and three ambulances braked a few meters away, on the edge of the tarmac. The men who emerged from them wore dark-green rain ponchos over combat uniforms.

"This fellow need help?" one of them asked Al.

"He's dead. But there's a newborn baby and her mother somewhere over near the rear cargo door."

The man turned and gestured violently to the driver of one of the ambulances; it drove off at once toward the people milling about near the tail of the Hercules. The man turned back to Al. "Well, we'll put this poor fellow in the ambulance. Better get in yourselves, before you're soaked. We'll have you all indoors in a jiffy."

"Thanks."

"Oh, wait a sec—is there fire on board?"

"No, at least not yet."

"Right. See you later."

Al and Gordon carried Ben's body into the ambulance and sat awkwardly on the jumpseats beside it. The driver smiled at them through the window behind his seat. Kyril clambered in next, and a moment later Hugh looked in.

"Everyone all right?"

"Okay-khorosho," Al nodded.

"Good." He looked expressionlessly at the stretcher. "Thanks for getting him out. I've got to find whoever's in charge here, and get in touch with the local CARP office." He pushed rainsoaked hair off his forehead. "God, and I thought *snow* was a nuisance."

They sat dripping in the ambulance, not saying much. A few minutes later the Dolans and Herm Northrop were escorted in by the man Al had first spoken to.

"We've got the rest of you in the other vehicles," the man said as he climbed in. He offered Al his hand. "Ewan McDermott."

"Al Neal." He introduced the others and then asked, "What's the military doing here?"

"We keep asking the same question. Christchurch is pretty quiet; it's Wellington and Auckland that need us. A riot a night up there."

"What in hell about?" Terry asked.

"Food, mostly." McDermott looked surprised. "Or don't you know what's been happening? D'you know New Zealand's under martial law?"

"No," said Herm.

"Too true. That's why I'm in this monkey suit—in real life I'm a physician. Between the weather, and the ultraviolet, and the energy shortage, it's been pretty nasty. Not so bad as you fellows must have had it, of course, but—" He looked at Kyril, who gave him a toothless grin. "Are you *all* from New Shackleton?"

"Most of us," Al said. "Kyril here, and a couple of others, are from Vostok, and there are three Americans from Outer Willy."

"From where?"

Al patiently explained. The doctor shook his head.

"Well, I'm afraid you've come from the frying pan into the fire," he said.

"More like the freezer into the fridge," said Herm.

There was a brief pause at the terminal building. Hugh and the officer in charge of Harewood had a hurried conversation before one ambulance was sent off to a nearby hospital with Jeanne, the baby, Will, and Katerina. Dr. McDermott told Al that everyone ought to go in hospital, at least for a checkup, but there were just no beds available; they would have to be put up at a local hotel and examined next day.

Hugh stayed at Harewood while everyone else was put on to a bus, escorted by a couple of noncoms carrying sidearms. The bus wheezed slowly away from the terminal building; there was no other traffic, and the parking lot in front of the building was empty.

"Gee, it looks dark and deserted," Penny said. "It was a lot livelier last Christmas."

"Not much need to come out to Harewood," a noncom said. 'No regular flights anymore, at least not for civilians." He looked at his watch. "And it's nearly 1700—that's when curfew starts."

"Curfew?" Penny echoed.

"Till 0700. Makes life a lot easier. Nothin' to do after dark, anyway." He looked at her incuriously, clearly preoccupied with greater concerns than explaining the facts of life to naive outsiders.

The bus stopped three times at military checkpoints before arriving downtown at the Hotel Avon. Across the deserted street was a park on the banks of the Avon River; the willows beside the water were obviously dead. Penny could see a statue in the park, looming dimly in the growing darkness. The noncoms escorted everyone out of the bus.

The hotel's plate-glass doors were crisscrossed with heavy tape, and only a couple of lights burned in the lobby. Once the passengers had been shepherded inside, the noncoms left without a word. A gaunt, sallow young man in a dirty brown turtleneck sweater came out from behind the reception desk.

"You're the explorers, right? Well, Colonel Chase himself told us you were coming, but we didn't get much notice. Anyway, uh, welcome back, and I hope you enjoy your stay with us." He gave them an uncertain smile.

The restaurant, just off the lobby, was dim and obviously neglected. Two teenage girls were hastily setting a few of the tables and gawking over their shoulders as the newcomers came in and hung up · their anoraks.

Penny sat down at one of the tables and looked warily around the room. "Not very festive, is it?" she muttered to Steve.

"Feels colder than the cab of the Sno-Cat." Then he grinned and squeezed her hand. "Here I've been moaning for months about how awful it must be on the outside—but I always expected we'd get parades, TV interviews, a big fuss—"

"You really are a total egomaniac. Oh God, Steve, we're really back."

"We're really back. Oh, thank you." One of the girls was serving bottles of Kiwi Beer.

"You're welcome. But I'm afraid there's only one to a customer."

Howie O'Rourke, at the next table, looked dumbfounded. "Only one? You're kidding!"

She wasn't. The meal itself was a frozen TV dinner, with slices of lamb in a gelatinous gravy, scalloped potatoes, and mushy peas. There were no second helpings. "Thank God for small favors," Herm grinned sourly. The coffee was terrible, and there was only saccharin to put in it. Howie was recruiting for a raid on the kitchen when Hugh came into the room, accompanied by a badly sunburned colonel.

Someone started clapping, and then they were all on their feet, cheering, pounding on tables, and whistling. Hugh, who had begun to speak to Carter, looked up; his surprise turned to embarrassed pleasure. When the uproar ended, he said:

"Thank you. I—can't tell you how happy I am to see us all here. Before—before I say anything else, let's remember Ben Whitcumb. We might never have got here without him."

The room was silent; in the kitchen dishes clattered and a girl sang as she worked.

Hugh looked up again. "And I must thank all of you. It's proud that Shackleton would have been of you. . . ." He hesitated and smiled shyly. "I could go on, but I'd sound like an ass. Would you mind if I shut up and let this fellow have a word with you? He's an old friend, Colonel Tommy Chase."

They thumped and applauded as Hugh sat down. Colonel Chase was a tall, heavy-set man in his forties, with a pink and peeling scalp and a pale strip around his eyes.

"Hugh—everyone—I wish we were able to give you the welcome you deserve, with bells ringing and reporters pestering you. But you've returned at a very bad time, as I'm sure you expected.

"New Zealand has been under martial law since May. I have the doubtful honor to be the military governor of Canterbury District, including Christchurch. Our job is to maintain order and to ensure that everyone gets a fair share of the remaining food and energy. Even returning Antarctic heroes. I won't burden you with the details of our problems—you'll learn them soon enough—but I should tell you that we've lost virtually all our agriculture. Our harbors were wrecked in the tidal waves last summer, and sea level has risen almost two meters since then. We've been able to import very little oil, and the price is about ten times what it was a year ago. Our overseas markets have vanished. We're almost as cut off from the world as you were down on the ice.

"Nevertheless, we're better off than many other parts of the world these days. Those of you who aren't New Zealanders may choose to stay. In fact, you may have to—there's not much travel to the outside."

Penny looked at Steve; his face was impasssive.

"Most of you are members of CARP," the colonel went on. "Or were. The Programme no longer exists. Neither does the Commonwealth, in any meaningful sense. So if you do choose to return to Britain, or Australia, or Canada, or wherever, it'll be at the expense of the New Zealand Provisional Government. And at its convenience. In the meantime, you'll be expected to aid our efforts in every way possible. God knows there's enough work to be done."

Terry Dolan was on his feet. "You mean to say you're too bloody cheap to send us home to Australia?"

"Too bloody poor," Colonel Chase barked. "Aircraft and fuel are scarce, and no one flies unless it's absolutely essential. I'm not sure I'd want to be in Australia in any case."

"Why the hell not?"

"They've lost their agriculture, just as we have, and they've more mouths to feed. There's a coalition government in Canberra, but no one seems to obey it. We understand the cities are being evacuated, but there's not much left in the countryside."

"What about Britain?" asked Colin.

"We don't really know. They've got a military government like ours, and they face the same problems we do, but on a greater scale. All of Europe seems to be in the same boat—too many people, and not enough food or energy, and the weather getting worse all the time.

"As for Canada and the U.S., they're very near collapse. The Canadians have lost their entire wheat crop. I think the Americans managed to save part of theirs, but they're fighting a civil war that's totally disrupted their economy. The federal government is being run by the Joint Chiefs of Staff, but not very well."

He paused. "We still have newspapers, of a sort. I'll see that you get copies of them. . . . Anyone here from Christchurch?"

"I'm from Dunedin," Simon Partington said.

"You'll be allowed a phone call in the morning. The phone system is open from 0900 to 1400 hours daily. I'm sure your family and friends will be overjoyed to know you're safely home. Those of you from North Island can give us the names and addresses of your people, and we'll have them notified by telegram.

"I haven't much more to say. For the time being, you're our guests here. Wellington will have to decide what's to be done with you. Again, I'm sorry to offer you such poor hospitality, and such depressing news. If it's any consolation, your safe return is the best news *we've* had all year. God bless you all."

He sat down in a nervous, rustling silence. Hugh stood up again.

"We've been given rooms on the second floor. I suggest we choose our quarters and plan on an early evening—Tommy tells me the lights go off at 2100 hours. At least there'll be plenty of hot water, and I for one intend to soak in a tub for an hour or two."

The sallow young man showed Penny and Steve into a second-floor room facing the river; apart from the dust on the furniture and a stale, unopened smell, the room might have been in Omaha or Honolulu.

"Too big," Steve smiled when the young man left. "You could get lost in a room this size." He'd grabbed an armful of magazines and newspapers in the lobby; dumping them on the bed, he began to undress. "Let's take a shower."

Under the hot, needle-sharp spray, Penny found herself looking at Steve's body as if for the first time: it was hard, pale, and very thin. His hands and feet, scarred with frostbite, looked like those of an old man, and his face looked older too. His nose, sunburned almost purple, jutted like a beak from the lined, taut skin over his cheekbones; his lips were puffy and cracked. Her own body looked strange as well, the belly flatter than it had been in years, breasts beginning to sag, skin pale and dry and speckled with sores. It hadn't mattered on the ice, but now her unattractiveness embarrassed her. With guilty relief, she stepped out of the shower and wrapped herself in a big towel.

Like a dull old married couple, they got into bed and started reading. Penny picked up a July issue of the Christchurch *Times*: it was just four tabloid pages, without photographs or advertisements.

"Didn't Al say someone told him there was rioting in Auckland and Wellington?" she asked when she'd finished.

"Mmph."

"Not a word about it in here. Just stuff about military regulations and how to save food and energy."

Steve was engrossed in a magazine, but showed her the cover.

"TIME *Monthly*. Monthly?"

"Look at the price," Steve said. "Ten New Zealand dollars." It was printed on pulp, even the cover, which showed a black-and-white photo of President Wood looking grim. "The only article in the science section is something about a 'loyalty shakeout' of what they call 'renegade scientists.' "

They read more or less at random, gradually sifting out the events of the last seven months from masses of propaganda.

The disappearance of the earth's magnetic field, back in January, had crippled the world: radio communications broke down, and both the ozone layer and the ionosphere disintegrated under the continuous bombardment of solar flares. International trade dwindled to a trickle. The industrial nations were convulsed by strikes, riots, even insurrections, all made worse by food shortages. It was some compensation, though, that military electronics systems were as deranged as civil-

ian ones. Missiles died in their silos; the computers
that ruled the armies went mad; bombers and fighters
became dangerously unreliable. With each country absorbed in its own problems, none could risk war.

Then the icequake struck. Steve had been right—
the tsunamis rose across the Southern Ocean, across
the Pacific, and focused their energies in the Aleutians
and the Bering Strait between Alaska and Siberia. The
north polar ice, only a few meters thick, shattered as
the waves crashed repeatedly into the Arctic Ocean.

Not many Pacific coastlines escaped. From Lyttleton
to Vladivostok to Los Angeles to Santiago, the tsunamis
left little but wreckage and oil slicks (a million-ton
supertanker, leaving the Alaskan oil port of Valdez
fully laden, was carried ten kilometers inland before it
broke up). No one knew how many died in the first
two days after the tsunamis struck, but estimates
ranged as high as three million.

San Francisco had been especially hard hit. At the
beginning of February, deranged computers had failed
to produce over fifty thousand unemployment cheques
for the Bay Area. Riots had broken out, and by
February 7 much of San Francisco, Oakland, and Rich-
mond was in flames. The tsunamis struck, carrying
away the Golden Gate Bridge and flooding the rapid-
transit tunnels under the bay. Thousands of people
living on the low-lying lands around the bay were
drowned or driven from their homes.

The rest of the U.S. west coast suffered as well. The
Trident nuclear submarine base at Bangor, Washington, was destroyed; so were the naval facilities at San
Diego and the missile pads at Vandenburg Air Force
Base. A moderately severe earthquake a week later in
the San Fernando Valley north of Los Angeles com-
pounded the disaster.

The world's attention turned, briefly, to the Antarctic; the New Zealand papers, at least, were full of human-interest stories about the evacuation of McMurdo
and the presumed loss of New Shackleton and the other
stations. One Wellington paper ran a photograph of

Hugh, and described with macabre relish how the station must have been buried under its falling roof. There was a mention of the RNZAF Hercules that had vanished on its mission to relieve New Shackleton; Penny remembered Max's photos of the wrecked airplane on the Shelf.

Before the end of February, the rise in eustatic sea level was noticeable all over the world. It was only about eighteen centimeters at that point, but it was enough—with the help of hurricanes and storm tides—to knock out over half of the world's major ports. London was partially evacuated; so were large areas of Belgium and the Netherlands. The oil ports of the Persian Gulf were flooded. Hundreds of airfields, built on low ground near the sea, became tidal marshes. As relatively warm water poured into the Arctic Ocean, its ice cap dwindled to a few bergs.

March brought violent weather to both hemispheres. Unseasonably early frost struck southern Africa, South America, Australia, and New Zealand. In the northern hemisphere, the jet stream swung wildly out of its usual path, carrying warm air into the Arctic and blizzards into the American Midwest and South. All over the planet, crops withered and livestock perished as ultraviolet pierced the endless clouds. Blind and starving, great herds of cattle frenziedly invaded crop lands; in some parts of the American Southwest, napalm had to be used to stop them. With transport systems in ruins, livestock couldn't even be slaughtered to feed the hungry cities; by June, beef was up to $150 a kilo in the U.S.—while the dollar itself had lost three-quarters of its value in six months.

Frustratingly, details were scarcest in the most recent newspapers. North America, as Colonel Chase had said, was locked in a suicidal civil war. After the failure of Washington and Ottawa to cope with disaster, "local councils" had taken over large parts of the U.S. and Canada. Confrontations had led to gun fights, then to guerilla skirmishes, and at last—with the desertion of whole battalions to the rebel side—

to full-scale military campaigns. Battles were fought for control of oil fields and refineries in Texas and Alberta, for coal mines in British Columbia and Kentucky, even for suburban supermarkets. One New Zealand paper, in June, reported a rumor that tactical nuclear weapons had been used to halt a rebel offensive against Chicago.

Still less was known, or at least reported, about the Communist countries. The Soviet Union was believed to be evacuating its Black Sea coast and Arctic ports. The Chinese had abandoned Shanghai to the sea, and were refusing to accept any more refugees from Hong Kong and Macao. North and South Korea were either at war or co-operating in relief operations. Indochina was silent. Eastern Europe was, perhaps, breaking free of Soviet domination, but no one knew for sure.

Cut off from their northern markets, the industrial nations of the southern hemisphere failed rapidly. South Africa's whites were surrendering most of the country and withdrawing to a coastal strip from Cape Town to Durban: "Blankestan," the Africans jeeringly called it. South America was a continent in anarchy. The disintegration of Indonesia seemed, at any rate, to have spared Australia the threat of an invasion. Chase had been right: New Zealand was better off than most of the world, though only relatively.

" 'An estimated six hundred million people have perished as a result of the disasters of the past year,' " Penny read from the Wellington *News*. She looked up and met Steve's eyes. "I don't believe it."

"It's only a guess. They could be doubling the real figure—or halving it." He looked almost like a parody of the man who'd made love to her in the greenhouse: the world was again conforming to his vision of it, but now he took no pleasure—not even *Schadenfreude*—in the fact.

They heard a pounding on a door down the hall, and the voice of the sallow young man: "Power goes off in ten minutes. Power off in ten minutes."

Steve doused the lights. The windows still glowed

with the rain-softened light of street lamps. Penny went to a window and looked down at the empty park: the statue was just visible, a white blur in the darkness. She felt Steve come up behind her and put his arms around her.

"That's Scott down there in the park."

"I know."

Someday Scott would see the sun again, in a thirtieth-century summer as the ice groaned and broke around him, and Wilson, and Bowers. Someday. For some reason, she remembered the seeds she'd brought from the greenhouse. Somewhere she must find another sheltered place for them, plant them and hope that they would grow.

It felt good to be together in bed, listening to the shouts and laughter of friends down the hall.

"What'll we do, Steve?"

"Go where we'll do the most good, I guess."

"Where—the States, or Canada?"

"I don't think so. They don't seem to need science writers or seismologists just now."

"That's not all we're good for, is it? And they're our countries."

"They don't seem to be countries at all. We could choose factions, but even if our side won, it wouldn't bring back the country we left."

"There you go, being cold-blooded and rational again."

He turned on his side and put his arm around her. *"We're* different too, you know. We're new. If this really is a new Ice Age starting, we're the first people who've had to live in it. If we owe loyalty to anyone, it's to the people who come after us. The more we learn, the better prepared they'll be."

"So what do we do—stay here?"

"For now, anyway. They'll be able to use what we've learned, and put us back to work learning more. This time next year, we could even be back in the Antarctic."

The eagerness in his voice would have enraged her once, or made her laugh. But she understood him at last, and knew what he was seeing beyond the rain-streaked windows.

The power went off, killing the street lamps below. The rain fell harder than ever, drumming on the windows and hissing on the empty street, the dead river. Penny remembered the darkness of the crevasse where Will had dangled, and her arrogant, crazy boast that the ice could never kill them. She saw the surge beginning on Beardmore Glacier; she saw the Shelf, glowing blue under the moon and stars. As she put her arms around Steve and felt the reassuring warmth of him, she felt a hunger that was his as well: a yearning for the cold, for the wind, for the high dark sky and the blinding sun, and the ice.

ABOUT THE AUTHOR

CRAWFORD KILIAN was born in New York City in 1941 and grew up in Los Angeles and Mexico City. After stints at Columbia University, in the U.S. Army, and at Lawrence Radiation Laboratory in Berkeley, California, he moved to Vancouver, British Columbia, in 1967. There, he completed a Master's degree in Canadian Literature at Simon Fraser University and began a teaching career. Along the way, he wrote several radio plays for the CBC, including an adaptation of James De Mille's *A Strange Manuscript Found in a Copper Cylinder*—a Utopian satire set at the South Pole, which helped spark his interest in the Antarctic. He has published two children's books, *Wonders, Inc.* and *The Last Vikings;* a widely praised history, *Go Do Some Great Thing: The Black Pioneers of British Columbia;* and a science-fiction novel, *Empire of Time*. He is at work on a second science-fiction novel, *Eyas,* and a sequel to *Icequake.*

Since 1968, Kilian has taught English at Capilano College in North Vancouver, and is the coordinator of the college's Communications Department. He lives in North Vancouver with his wife, Alice, and two daughters, Anna and Margaret.

A Special Preview of
the OUTrageous opening pages
of the most unusual novel
of the year

OUT

by
Pierre Rey

Get ready for a stunning suspense thriller combining
the drama of THE GODFATHER and THE CRASH
OF '79 with the wild humor of THE GANG THAT
COULDN'T SHOOT STRAIGHT.

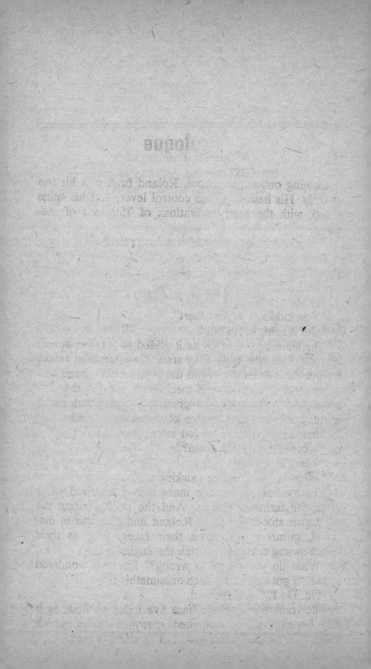

Prologue

Coming out of the curve, Roland braked a bit too sharply. His hands, on the control lever, and his spine shook with the heavy vibrations of 750 tons of machinery.

"Staying with us tonight?" Luciano asked.

Roland gradually lowered the throttle to reduce the thrust of the locomotive.

"I'd like to, but . . ."

"Is she pretty?"

"You kidding? My mother!"

"Cut it some more . . ."

The train hissed softly as it glided to a lower speed. For the first time since they started, the parallel tracks before them did not meet in the distance. His hand still gripping the lever, Roland mechanically noted the concrete platforms growing progressively denser with handcarts, packages, and groups of travelers in ranks that tightened as the train moved into the station.

"What's wrong with them?"

"Who?"

"What the hell're they gawking at?"

The locomotive was no more than a hundred yards from the terminal buffers. And the people along the platforms stood gaping at Roland and Luciano in disbelief, grimaces frozen on their faces, even as their heads swung around to watch the engine go by.

"What do you s'pose is wrong?" Luciano wondered aloud. "I got egg on my face or something?"

"No. Do I?" said Roland.

The train was doing a bare five miles an hour as it slid beneath the glass-paned marquee under which groups of people stood guard over their luggage.

"Train number one-two-seven, express from Geneva, now arriving. Please stand back!" yelled a man's voice, bouncing out of ten loudspeakers that fed back over one another.

Roland saw a plump woman drop her handbag without bothering to bend down and pick it up; then she pointed a finger at him as she covered the bottom of her face with her other hand in an expression of fright.

"Shit!" Roland swore uncomfortably. "What the hell's wrong?"

Wherever he turned, there were the same looks of surprise. As the train went by, everything fell silent. Platform activity usually generated its own typical din: metallic noises, bumps, rumbles, shouts, but now there was nothing except that sullen movement of withdrawal and those gaping eyes.

"Hit it!"

Roland jammed the brake, and the engine grazed the tip of the buffers. Luciano cut the power. Still no one on the platform moved. Two station employees, heads together, were whispering. Then one of them darted toward the stationmaster's office, and the other climbed up the locomotive ladder and came into the cab. He was obviously embarrassed, glancing first at Luciano, then at Roland, not saying a word.

He cleared his throat. "Where did you pick that up?"

"Pick *what* up?" said Roland.

"What do you mean—*what?*"

"Look," Luciano barked, "we're no geniuses! Why not cut the riddles?"

"Follow me."

The crowd remained as if frozen. All that could be heard was the panting of an antique steam locomotive on a siding. Luciano and Roland hefted themselves down to the asphalt, but only when they were in front of their engine did they understand what was going on.

On the cowcatcher, as if delicately placed there by a ghoulish decorator, was a man's leg—neatly sheared off at the groin. One could just make out a rust-colored bloodstain that came through the dark material of the trousers at the point where the bones had probably been severed. The absurd thought that this was a high-class leg flashed through Roland's mind: the black shoe was made of fine leather, and there was a matching silk sock.

On looking closer, he could see that blood was trickling down the sock, onto the shoe, and ending in a dark brown puddle on the engine's steel cowcatcher.

At that moment, neither Roland nor any of the other witnesses could have any idea that this puddle was going to spread with breathtaking speed over several continents. And turn into a bloodbath.

1

Morty O'Brion never dared assert himself with his wife. Judith terrified him. The corners of her mouth twisted with a sarcastic bitterness that no makeup could disguise. When she raised her voice, Morty felt like melting away; when she gave him the silent treatment, it was even worse, for it meant she was either repressing her contempt for him or having the kind of migraine headache he would have to handle with kid gloves.

It had been years since Morty had tried to carry on any real conversation wih her. Since they had been sleeping in separate rooms, their communication had dwindled to short exchanges, summed up by the words *headache, ridiculous, gimme,* and *how much.* When they were first married, Morty had hoped Judith would take an interest in his work, become proud of his success, but all she ever did was nag him about his failures, taking his triumphs for granted, and they had quickly retreated into a kind of deaf-and-dumb hostility, each remaining alone with her or his own thoughts. Judith didn't bother to complain anymore, except by making faces, and Morty was careful never to mention his professional achievements, for he felt she would take delight in destroying his pleasure with a cruel word or a scornful grimace.

Four years before, as a hotshot financial lawyer, he had wanted to crow to her when he was retained to straighten out some of the Syndicate's business deals. But a sixth sense had warned him not to. Even though it was a potential gold mine, this new connection was not going to mean any change in her life—not for the moment, anyway. Judith's closets were already overflowing with furs, her drawers crammed with jewels, all intended in some way to make up for the lack of communication between them.

Judith lit another cigarette and snuffed the match out in the bottom of the coffeecup on her virtually untouched breakfast tray. Morty went about closing his overnighter.

"You going somewhere?" she asked.

"Yes."

"But you just got back from Europe. Oh, what a headache I have!"

"Take some of your pills."

"Where are you going this time?"

He looked up, surprised. She never pried that way, ordinarily acting as if his goings and comings were beneath her notice. He almost answered, What the fuck do you care? but he simply mumbled, "Nassau."

She poured the rest of her coffee into her half-finished glass of grapefruit juice, then dropped her barely smoked cigarette in after it.

"You're lucky."

Taken aback, he glanced quickly at her eyes, relieved to see that they reflected nothing but her usual sullen boredom.

He challenged her. "Be ready in five minutes and I'll take you along."

"Don't be ridiculous. I've got a headache."

If only she knew. She had not realized how he had grown. To her, he was still the penniless young lawyer who almost had to beg to be taken on as a clerk. And she had thought she could keep him under her thumb by castrating him. Even if he told her about it, how would she be able to comprehend what he was about to pull off?

He coughed "Okay, then . . ." He started to bend toward her, as if to kiss her good-bye, but he stopped. "Well, I'd better be going . . ."

Perhaps he should have been bothered by heartrending feelings of finality, as are all the heroes of books when they're putting an end to twenty years of double harness. But Morty O'Brion was as calm as if he were planning to be back home that evening for dinner. The fact that they had no children suddenly made him deliriously happy. Leaving her like this, all things considered, he was simply dropping off one part of himself, a sticky piece of his life that he was embarrassed to think about because he had waited too long to work up the courage to run out on it.

Forty-eight hours from now, he would be far away, in a dream place of which no one in the world even suspected the existence. And he, Mortimer O'Brion, would be the richest man on earth, richer than any other human had ever been, rich beyond the imaginings of the wildest minds.

He was almost at the door when Judith called out, "Morty! On your way out, ask Margaret to bring me some cold water and my pills."

He nodded. How appropriate, he thought, that the last word he heard from her should be *pills*. He turned his back, so she couldn't see his smile.

The small plane was completing its third loop. Once again it swooped down over the main street of Chiavenna, buzzed the ocher rooftops with its powerful vibration, then righted itself just to the left of the church steeple. Looking up, the people in the small town saw a flock of little pieces of paper dancing on the wind, pirouetting gracefully with the hesitating movements of autumn leaves, to land finally on the street, on the tops of cars, on balconies, or on the brightly colored canvas awnings atop the carts of the market merchants.

It was noon, and the market was a once-a-week affair. The street was full of people, and the gentle April breeze off Lake Como outlined the lithe shapes of the younger women who had been the first to take their light dresses out of winter storage.

Two or three boys picked up what they thought to be some kind of advertising leaflet, turned it over between their fingers, then looked at one another in disbelief. One twelve-year-old broke the silence. Tripping over his feet with excitement, he dashed toward his father's bakery, pressing to his chest a handful of folded money. He shouted to his parents, who had rushed out when they heard the noise of the motor.

"It's money! Father! Mother! It's raining money from heaven!"

Suddenly everyone came to life. People were dashing into the merry-go-round of cars occupying the roadway, bending down to get their share of the miraculous catch amid a cacophony of shrieking brakes, cursing drivers, and families yelling instructions to their most agile members. Threats, protests, and shouts of encouragement were suddenly drowned out by the deafening noise of the returning plane. And while a few of the old women chanted "Miracle! Miracle!" as they crossed themselves, more manna came floating down.

Children, held up by sturdier elder siblings, tried to keep their footing on tree branches where early blossoms were flowering into banknotes: real Swiss currency, fine, good bills from the Schweizerische Nationalbank, delicately mauve in shade and worth anywhere from ten to fifty francs. The rush became more violent and people started to fight.

Renata righted her plane and burst out laughing. Seen from above, the view looked something like a chicken coop in which all the birds, suddenly gone mad, had started pecking at imaginary feed.

"You're disgusting!" Kurt yelled at her, raising his voice to be heard over the motor and the wind.

To his utter terror, she let go of the joy stick and

slammed shut the Plexiglas cockpit cover. The plane did a flip-flop, which only made Renata laugh harder as she glanced sideways and muttered, "Serves you right for daring me!"

Beneath them they could see a succession of bright green valleys spotted here and there with the darker green of pine trees.

"Hang on! We're diving," Renata called to him.

"Renata!" Kurt shouted back.

The Piper seemed to fall like a stone on the herd of cows Renata had been aiming for, nearly grazing their backs as they spread across the landscape. For a bare second Kurt was able to see the cowherd motion toward the plane and shake his fist at them.

Trying to sound as reasonable as possible, Kurt said, "Just what are you trying to prove to me?"

Leapfrogging over tiny light clouds that were dissipating in the wind, Renata looked serious. "Simply that you're wrong all the way down the line and not honest enough to give a name to your real wishes. Did you see them run and fight when I dropped that money on them? You claimed that it was degrading, that I was insulting the hardworking population! Well, who was right?"

Feeling slightly nauseated, Kurt slunk into his seat as if he had not heard her. If he stood up to her, he was afraid he might drive her to the kind of daring in which a flight in her Piper turned into a roller-coaster nightmare.

"Well, can't you answer?"

To teach him a lesson, she zoomed into a climb that knocked the wind out of him and pinned him back against his seat. After that she treated him to another straight dive, two or three barrel rolls in which earth and sky seemed to be pushing each other around, and a long upside-down glide. "If, as you claim, money were shit," she said, "then people wouldn't get down on all fours to grab after it!"

He gritted his teeth. If she didn't maneuver a crash

in the next few minutes, he had a chance of being alive when they got back to Zurich, where at the end of the week, on Sunday, April 26, they were to be married.

The military trucks left Geneva, Nyon, Morges, Lausanne, Fribourg, Bern, Lucerne, Zug, and Zurich to drop off their troop contingents. Each man was ordered to explore a three-hundred-meter section of tracks, fine-combing the underbrush for a width of ten meters on either side of the right-of-way. For once agreeing on something, the Swiss police and the army had felt that a human corpse, even lacking a right leg, might constitute a jarring note in the happy Swiss countryside. The police were in charge, but the army was supplying the men. The order was to keep searching until the body had been found. As night fell, the engineers' noncoms gave instructions to turn on the searchlights.

As for the leg that had been found on the cowcatcher of the Geneva-Zurich Express locomotive, it had already provided the investigators with a few good leads. The shoe was from Biasca, a well-known New York bootmaker. The Zurich police had immediately gotten on the phone to their American couterparts, who were investigating too, and with a little luck they would quickly know whose shoe it was. In the pants pocket, apart from a roll of American bills amounting to over five thousand dollars, the Swiss officials had found a ticket to Geneva stamped in Zurich. What really threw them was that the leg had appeared in Zurich when it should have been arriving in Geneva at the same time as the other leg, the head, and the rest of the body of its rightful owner.

Seated snugly between Vittorio Pizzu and Moshe Yudelman, Italo ("Babe") Volpone looked sharply at the twelve men around the conference table. That he was sitting in his brother's chair gave him a feeling of quiet authority betrayed only by the constant darting of his eyeballs, two shards of black coal hiding behind half-closed lids. He was concerned about his voice, which had to remain calm and collected, for he knew it was most effective when it was aggressive or threatening.

He tried once again to get into the skin of the character he was supposed to be playing, ordering his hands not to play with his pen, his eyes to keep still.

For reassurance he slipped two fingers into his jacket pocket, next to his heart, to get a welcome feel of the deck of playing cards he always kept there. At times they were his instruments for gambling—he had always lived off gambling, lived only for gambling—and at other times they were the masters of his destiny, tellers of good and bad fortune. When he traveled, he also carried a miniature roulette wheel. When he rolled its ball time after time to work out endless fascinating systems of probabilities and chances, neither day nor night nor time itself existed, and he entered a kingdom in which figures alone were kings. His record had been three days and four nights in a private gaming room at Las Vegas. At regular intervals waiters had set food and drink before him, which he consumed without realizing it, and when he got up from the table and tried to stretch his weary muscles, he collapsed into the deep sleep of the blessed and had to be carried to his room. He hadn't come to until fourteen hours later.

Now, without moving his fingers from the lucky deck, Italo said, "Your representative, O'Brion, has just reached Zurich. Everything is okay. Here's the cable I just got from Don Genco."

He took from his pocket the crumpled piece of paper that he had reread a hundred times before carrying out his brother's instructions to send out invitations and announce the news.

Ettore Gabelotti glanced at it and silently passed it along to Simeone Ferro, who handed it to Joseph Dotto. While Carmine Crimello, Vittorio Pizzu, Angelo Barba, Vincent Bruttore, Thomas Merta, Aldo Amalfi, Carlo Badaletto, and Frankie Sabatini each read it in turn, Italo Volpone was thinking that this was a historic occasion: the peaceful meeting of the two most powerful Syndicate "families"—the Gabelottis and the Volpones

—after twenty years of cold wars and murderous feuds. Volpone's eyes slipped from one man to the next, noting the uncontrollable shock of satisfaction that, ever so briefly, cracked the artificial deadpans they sported in public. Having gone all around the table, the cable finally came back to Italo.

"So what else is new?" asked Carlo Badaletto.

Badaletto hated Italo Volpone and never missed a chance to defy him. Five years before, when Italo had come back from London, Badaletto had been a member of the Volpone clan. By way of welcome, he had said, *"Come va, speranzaritu?"* and it had gotten him a double fracture of the jaw as well as the loss of his incisors, one of which, after Italo butted him violently, remained stuck in Volpone's forehead.

Speranzaritu was the scornful Sicilian word for local boys who had had to skip abroad. But if Italo had been forced to spend two years' exile in London, the capo of every family on the East and West coasts knew it was on the express orders of his brother, the don, Zu Genco Volpone, from whom a mere wink was a decree that his younger brother was in no position to challenge.

"Nothing else," Italo snarled at Badaletto.

Babe Volpone would have liked to evoke in Carlo Badaletto the same feeling of inferiority that everyone experienced in his brother's presence, without Genco doing anything to make it so. To be sure, people were afraid of Italo, but Genco had something more: people respected him. His seeming gentleness, his open smile, and his natural gift as a mediator were the perfect front for his grasping, pitiless nature. On the contrary, Italo could not for long contain the rage constantly boiling within him. His murderous impulses drove him to satisfy his desires immediately in every area: private, emotional, or economic. Had it not been for his brother's position, Italo's tendency to resort to brute force would have condemned him to the vegetative life of a punk or a hit man. The capi of the Syndicate didn't trust Italo's lack of self-control or his delight in primitive solutions. Times had changed since the days of Al

Capone. Although rough hits might be no less numerous, they were carried out more subtly by nameless characters who were paid off by intermediaries so that the hit men never knew why or for whom they were performing their contracts.

Nowadays each capo had to have the facade of an eminently respectable businessman, so that he could carry on his work without being bothered by the IRS, the police, or the competition. Family investments had the look and the seamless structure of multinational corporations with endless ramifications, and they were directed by an army of lawyers who knew how to put the illegal proceeds of the various rackets into businesses that were beyond reproach. For example, it was not unusual for some of the profits from the narcotics trade to end up, after a mysterious series of twists and turns, financing a hospital for handicapped children, christened by the highest authorities with great pomp and circumstance in the presence of all the local officials, and receiving the deep gratitude of the people.

Zu Genco Volpone's brain trust was made up of the cream of graduates of the best schools of international law, as if buying the top men somehow made up for the fact that, until the age of eighteen, he himself had hardly been able to read.

Moshe Yudelman was the first to speak up. "The first phase of the operation is over," he said. "Within three months all our funds will have been laundered."

Straight out of the Lower East Side, with a brief detour through the Bronx, Yudelman, who had supported himself through school by swiping vegetables from pushcarts and beating the bums on his block at pinball games, could outthink the most cunning head of any international central bank. Born with a God-given gift for figures as some are with eyes of blue, he knew without having to learn, he understood without having to think. He always found the way. This nose for finance was further strengthened by his talent for sharp practice. No contract, however adroitly drawn, could hold him at bay more than five minutes. He could immediately find a chink, the tiny detail, the missing comma that might be used with absolute legality to break off an agreement without anyone even suspecting that bad faith or dishonesty was involved. Better than any computer, his head contained the exact list of holdings, privileges, and profits of all the rival families of the Commissione, that top-level organization consisting of the eleven capi who ran the worldwide business, in which Zu Genco Volpone was not the least important.

When Moshe Yudelman joined Gneco's family, Genco had had to put up a fight with his associates to bring Moshe in as consigliere. The proud Sicilians who made up the top group found it hard to accept a Jew among them. With their ferocious attachment to Old World traditions, they had a gut distrust of anything foreign, lumping together the Irish, Negroes, Jews, Chinese, and Protestants. At the beginning, Yudelman had tried to keep a low profile, giving advice only when it was asked for, never taking sides, never saying anything against anyone. He was there, period; like a piece of furniture that gradually became familiar, that you knew would always be on hand when you needed it. He was too smart not to see that some of the clan's unwritten laws were outmoded, but too shrewd to voice the least criticism. The underground world in which he lived was the only one that could ever assuage his lust for power, his yearning to be the strength behind the throne. His amazing accounting and managerial talents had done the rest.

Although the families frequently killed off each other's members over meaningless questions of prestige, Yudelman had succeeded not only in staying alive, but in occupying a place from which none, not even the members of the Commissione, dared try to unseat him. He owed everything to Genco, who had picked him up when he was poor and defenseless, but it was through Yudelman that Don Zu Volpone had been able to reinforce his own prestige and authority. Thereafter, his role as consigliere to one family had been extended to all parts of the activities of the Syndicate, for it had made Moshe a kind of elder statesman, an arbitrator in matters of the greatest delicacy. These responsibilities hadn't kept him from building up his own fortune, day by day increased through careful investments, split-second decisions, the unbeatable flair of the great predator for any weakening prey on the stock exchange, in gambling, slot machines, bars, taverns, real estate, vending machines, bootleg booze, numbers, championship prizefights, blackmail, loansharking, or pimping.

It was on his say-so that Genco had agreed to make an alliance—who knew for how long?—with the man he considered his number one rival: Ettore Gabelotti. Moshe sneaked a sidewise glance at him now. An old Roman face, heavy pouches under his eyes, Ettore weighed over 275 pounds. He kept up a kindly paternal front that was periodically contradicted by terrible rages that often ended in unquestionable condemnations to death.

It had taken inordinate diplomacy for Moshe to get Gabelotti to admit that, over and above whatever separated them, his interests were the same as Genco's when it came to laundering liquid money. To convince him that their money ought to be pooled had been no easy matter, for the two men held against each other the many corpses that each had sown in the other's camp over now-forgotten disagreements. But the accord had been reached, and today it was about to give birth to the greatest financial operation ever undertaken by the Syndicate.

Gabelotti, who had not said a word, must have felt Yudelman watching him. He looked toward him sharply, then covered up with a smile. Moshe smiled back and looked away.

"Lemme see the cable again!" Ettore asked.

From fingers to fingers, it flew from one end of the table to the other. Gabelotti grabbed it and laughed uproariously as he called to the younger Volpone, "Say, Babe, your brother sure didn't waste any dough on Western Union!"

Everybody joined in the raucous laughter. Italo, on

the defensive, began to laugh along with the others once he realized that Ettore's words contained no hidden sarcastic criticism.

The cable, beyond the indication of its point of origination—Zurich, Schaffhauserstrasse Post Office—and the address, had just one single word, three letters: OUT. But those three letters represented the code name for the joint operation under which those present at the meeting were bringing home clean and free the net returns from all their criminal activities for the calendar year 1978.

And these net returns came to the sum of exactly two billion dollars.

This is only a hint of what's in store for you as the ingenious plan to launder $2 billion in dirty mob money through Swiss banks is put into operation. Along the way you'll meet many more of the cast of unusual characters. They all get embroiled in this plot which builds to a climax that is OUTrageous.

Read the complete Bantam Book, available now wherever paperbacks are sold.

THE LATEST BOOKS
IN THE BANTAM
BESTSELLING TRADITION

RELAX!
SIT DOWN
and Catch Up On Your Reading!

DON'T MISS
THESE CURRENT
Bantam Bestsellers

☐ 11708	**JAWS 2** Hank Searls	$2.25
☐ 12400	**THE BOOK OF LISTS** Wallechinsky & Wallace	$2.75
☐ 11001	**DR. ATKINS DIET REVOLUTION**	$2.25
☐ 12997	**THE FAR PAVILIONS** M. M. Kaye	$2.95
☐ 12683	**EVEN COWGIRLS GET THE BLUES** Tom Robbins	$2.75
☐ 10077	**TRINITY** Leon Uris	$2.75
☐ 13286	**ALL CREATURES GREAT AND SMALL** James Herriot	$2.75
☐ 13287	**ALL THINGS BRIGHT AND BEAUTIFUL** James Herriot	$2.75
☐ 11770	**ONCE IS NOT ENOUGH** Jacqueline Susann	$2.25
☐ 13430	**DELTA OF VENUS** Anais Nin	$2.75
☐ 12386	**NEBRASKA!** Dana Fuller Ross	$2.50
☐ 13065	**THE IRON MARSHAL** Louis L'Amour	$1.75
☐ 13721	**PASSAGES** Gail Sheehy	$3.50
☐ 12370	**THE GUINNESS BOOK OF WORLD RECORDS 17th Ed.** The McWhirters	$2.50
☐ 13374	**LIFE AFTER LIFE** Raymond Moody, Jr.	$2.50
☐ 11917	**LINDA GOODMAN'S SUN SIGNS**	$2.50
☐ 12923	**ZEN AND THE ART OF MOTORCYCLE MAINTENANCE** Robert Pirsig	$2.75
☐ 10888	**RAISE THE TITANIC!** Clive Cussler	$2.25
☐ 12797	**STRYKER** Chuck Scarborough	$2.50